Pursuit of the Frog Prince

Rachel Gripp

By Rachel Gripp

Copyright © 2012 By Rachel Gripp

Book Cover Designer: Austin Tsosie

ISBN-10: 0985939605
ISBN-13: 9780985939601

dedication:

Pursuit of the Frog Prince

"You held me in your arms and said you'd never leave me, but death took you away and left me alone with memories and ashes."

R.L. Carnel

This book is dedicated to the memory of my husband, Leonard P. Gripp, who worked on this novel with me until he passed away in 2011, and to our sons, Richard and Leonard, whose continued support encouraged its completion.

TABLE OF CONTENTS

Chapter 1
Dinner Party

Peggy Roberts sat on her living room sofa feeling smug. The party came off without a snag, and now she was on an all time high, like some drug addict floating with nirvana from a recent fix. It could not have been more perfect if a caterer planned the affair. Everything flowed flawlessly for the anniversary meal.

Early on, she made two decisions: one concerned the anniversary party and the other, much more secret, concerned her plans for later… with Jeff, Peggy's handsome, six-foot Adonis who shared her dreams, her plans and her bed. She had an unexpected anniversary present for him, something that would surprise him after five years of marriage. Would he laugh or would he be pleased that she thought of him that way? How else could she think of the man she loved so much?

Peggy smiled, thinking how silly she felt going into Victoria's Secret for sexy sleepwear. *Thank God the store was empty,* she thought. Two salesclerks, standing by the main desk, helped her select a skimpy, black lace thong with a matching camisole, the shortest she had ever seen. If her navel held a blue sapphire, it would have looked like a third middle eye, the kind that matched her other two. For some reason, the women insisted on seeing her model the two-piece outfit, in the dressing room, of course, and laughed when Peggy asked if the thong was really supposed to ride up the crack of her butt because it was beginning to chafe.

"Honey, we don't worry about that piece of triangular fluff," the tall, brunette goddess told her. "He'll either rip it off or throw it on the floor."

The blonde, older queen immediately interrupted her partner. "If I had her body, I'd just display it over a chair. Go nude with a long string of beads sweeping the boobs," she winked. "Prove to him that blondes really *do* have more fun."

"Let us know if he attacks you," the brunette gave a low growl, "next time you're in."

Peggy laughed as she left the store. *"Next time she's in."* That was her first visit and probably her last. She wondered what she was thinking. Did she really want to sleep in something that rubbed her the wrong way? Was she was being ridiculous trying to be something she was not?

As she thought about the lacy set in the bathroom closet, romance filled her brain. When she melted into Jeff's arms later that night, Peggy wanted him to tear the garment to shreds, much like an anxious groom ready to taste the sweetness of his new bride. But, would Jeff do it, or would he think she was being ridiculous wearing something so sexy? Peggy never wore anything like that during their entire marriage. She was strictly flannel and cotton. The feel of smooth, shiny satin never thrilled her either. The material never absorbed night sweats. Neither did silk, for that matter. Maybe she should forget the whole damn thing. A voice somewhere inside her head yelled, *"Coward."* But Peggy was too happy to be swayed and, as she viewed the dining room from the living room sofa, her mind floated back to the party that had taken place earlier.

Long before the dinner even materialized, when she was in the planning stage, Peggy decided to use her finest tableware to make their anniversary memorable. As much as she wanted to impress her guests, Peggy needed to please her husband more. Make him proud of her. Get him prepped for a later performance...her big seduction scene.

Peggy opted for a modified Russian table service, Jeff's favorite. It had the flavor of quiet elegance, with the candlelight and flowers adding much of the necessary panache. She extended the rectangular dining room table an additional three feet by using both wide leaves. The blue linen tablecloth and napkins matched the swag draperies of the large formal dining room, with its mirrored, mahogany china closet and equally mirrored server that was piled high with an assortment of Royal Doulton bone china, Waterford crystal and sterling silver serving pieces. These were removed from the china closet days earlier.

As planned, only the filled water glasses and silverware would frame the appetizer place settings at the start of the meal.

A shallow spray of mixed flowers centered the table, while a single candle sat at each end and flickered with a romantic glow, highlighting the eight gold chargers that held appetizer plates of Raclite Shrimp Remoulade.

Peggy turned the dimmer switch to low and called her guests to the dining room table from the living room where they sat drinking cocktails. From appetizer to the Bananas Foster dessert, everything was perfect. The Gorgonzola Beef Wellington got raves, the guests left half-inebriated, which was always a good sign of a successful party, and the heavenly scent of mixed roses and freesia everywhere gave the house its needed flair for the celebratory occasion. She had to congratulate herself. The table looked beautiful; the service, impeccable; and the food, simply marvelous.

Her friends and family always said she had the talent of a gourmet cook, but that was no surprise. Peggy knew that already. She more than proved that tonight. Besides, she loved to cook. To be more exact, Peggy loved to experiment with food combinations.

But, she had her share of culinary failures over the years. A smile crossed her face; veal fricassee, her prime number one failure on record. Canned dog food had looked more appetizing than the slimy effort she fed the garbage disposal after that experiment.

As her fingers outlined the pastel pink and blue flowers of the silk tapestry sofa, her thoughts continued to stray from the formal blue room where she sat. She was busy savoring the evening's conversation, particularly, the toast given by Janice Sommers, her gift shop partner and next door neighbor.

"To Jeff and Peggy, happy fifth," the refined woman raised her champagne flute, "and a special thanks to Peggy for a wonderful meal."

Before anyone else could join in, Janice gazed lovingly at her thirty-three year old partner and continued. "She's not only beautiful, but a true friend. She deserves to have it all...a gorgeous house, a thriving business, and a husband who adores her," she said, pausing momentarily. "And we hope we can help celebrate your sixth, next year."

After that heartfelt tribute, the only sound heard in the room was the clinking of crystal. Hearing those accolades, everyone would think Peggy Roberts had everything going for her. That she was the lucky one...that hers was the brightest star in all the heavens.

But, now, as Peggy Roberts sat alone, the grim reality began to set in again, as it had in the past. She did not have it all. She wanted more. Women her age already had children, even those with long distinguished careers. And although having a family was often discussed, other priorities always seemed to take precedence.

So, there she sat at her stage in life, successful in business, happy in a loving marriage... and totally childless. Peggy felt so hollow inside. She wanted to cry, but the tears wouldn't come. *It will happen. I know it will. We will have a family...maybe I'll be pregnant next year.* Peggy refused to feel sorry for herself. On that positive note, she continued to reflect on the evening's festivities.

She and Jeff had planned the evening well...just a small dinner gathering of eight, including family and friends. In addition to Janice and her husband, Fred, the list included Peggy's younger sister, Megan, her husband, Brad Croft, and Jeff's co-worker at Pace Securities, John Beck, with his wife, Alice.

The thought of John Beck and Pace Securities reminded her of an earlier time. It was four years to be exact when she and Jeff moved from Pittsburgh to the tony Buffalo suburb of Amherst, a town of over 100,000 residents, lying just northeast of the city. When the transfer first came up, they traced the entire region north of Erie on a map from the triple A. A large oval area, known to the locals as the Snowbelt, extended north of the Pennsylvania line right through Buffalo, New York, their area of relocation.

Peggy didn't want to think of Buffalo's snowy winters at that moment. She wanted to enjoy the beautiful evening with family and friends, while reliving the excitement of her wedding as a June bride, the most memorable day of her life. That was the day her life really began: when she discovered her real reason for existence. It was the knowledge that Jeff, her handsome husband, would always be at her side. No longer would she be alone. Her life would now be complete.

The jarring sound of kitchen noises interrupted her reverie and Peggy sauntered behind her husband and placed her arms around his chest. She watched him fill two flutes with the party's remaining champagne and nod his head toward the family room couch.

"Lost in thought, are we?" Jeff asked, pressing her hand with a crystal flute as they both sat down. "If you're thinking about the party, the dinner was a huge success."

"I was thinking about us and our move here. Now that you've been promoted, I wonder what John Beck really thinks. He's been at Pace a lot longer than you."

"That may be true, but John realizes he has a real friend in me. He brings in a lot of business and I let him do his own thing," he said, as he swallowed a sip of champagne. "As a matter of fact, he's leaving town tomorrow for an overnight with some new clients. I'd really hate to lose him to another broker, particularly over my promotion. Besides having a good reputation, the man is very thorough."

"I wish I could say the same about Alice," Peggy replied. "She complained all night about John. He's not helping her around the house anymore. The entire conversation consisted of his slacking off and her shift change. I wanted to talk about their mail coming here, but that didn't happen. Alice took the letters, but never mentioned contacting the post office. She seemed so distracted."

"But did you specifically mention their mail coming here to our house?" There was something in the way his dark eyes flashed and the edge of his voice that bothered her. *Why is he so agitated?* She wondered. *Why does he seem to be angry with me? I didn't do anything wrong.*

"But, Jeff, I tried," Peggy insisted. "I really tried to get her to understand, but I was too taken with her new dye job. The darker hair makes her look so different. Even her clothes now," Peggy said, nodding, "they're more..." She stopped.

"Revealing?" Jeff got up to refill his glass. "Maybe John likes it that way."

"As far as I'm concerned, it's too much of a public offering. But, I have to admit, she looks like a different woman these days. Too different for my taste."

"You look pretty dazzling yourself," he said, his eyes meeting hers with a knowing look. "I always liked the way that dress takes on different colors."

As if on cue, Peggy rose from the sofa and curtsied. "Thank you, kind sir. I wore it just for you." She twirled around and around, suddenly feeling beautiful. The long dress of beaded pearls, sequins and calf-high slits was her favorite outfit. It was also her most expensive one.

She took her empty glass from the coffee table and, placing it on the kitchen sink, turned to face her handsome seated husband. "I can't believe how much champagne we got from everyone. They must think we drink a lot." She eyed the filled trash basket, and then pointed to the bottle that Jeff was holding.

"I like that one best. I don't know if I like the champagne or the pretty bottle it comes in."

"You would. It's Perrier Jouet. Fred and Janice brought it."

Jeff eyed the beautiful woman he married five years earlier. He got up from the couch, stretched his arms and yawned. "It's ten o'clock and I'm tired. I've got a long day tomorrow. Some big guns are coming in, so you know what that means. You'll be eating dinner alone again. Sorry, honey."

"It doesn't matter. I'm so proud of you," she said, as she smoothed a wisp of dark hair along the side of his head and fingered the furrow over his dark brown eyes. "I know you're doing this for us." Peggy gave her husband a sly wink and sashayed away from him.

"I'll be up in a minute," she called. "Just remember, anniversary man, we're still going to celebrate," she said, thinking of her surprise for him, and then rushed to rinse out the crystal flutes.

Peggy could hear Jeff's laughter fade as he climbed the stairs to the master bedroom. A huge smile crossed her face. *Laugh, you silly man,* she thought. She would knock his socks off minutes from now and show him how blondes *did* have more fun. She would enjoy doing that.

As Peggy dried her hands, she took the Jouet bottle from the filled trash bag to keep as a souvenir, and then checked the driveway from the living room window. Jeff had forgotten to set out the garbage can for Monday morning's pickup. He seemed to be doing that a lot lately.

"Oh. Hell. I'll do it myself," she mumbled. "It's the least I can do."

Holding a portion of her long, beaded dress in one hand and the trash bag in the other, Peggy walked gingerly around the dark side of the house, fearful of falling on the cracked concrete slab housing the container. As she tossed the bag into the large, green garbage can, a figure quickly emerged from the shadows and covered her mouth, dragging her into oblivion.

Chapter 2
The Search

Jeff hadn't realized how tired he really was. It had been a long day, much longer than he expected. While Peggy dealt with the house and menu, his job was to supply the drinks. That had always been his responsibility when they entertained, and it worked out well. He knew from years of experience to leave his wife alone with her ideas for a dinner party. She had a knack for making everything go smoothly. The woman was a planner. She made lists.

However, he did recall a few conversational lapses during Peggy's carefully prepared and succulent meal. Maybe the pauses came from being together too often. After a while, what does one talk about when the same group meets at different parties? Everyone at their table had already been preconditioned to speak about subjects that could be discussed and to avoid those that could not. So, it was not unusual to spend an entire evening talking about some needed home appliance or summer travel, while eating dry prime rib and drinking non-descript wine. Of course, Peggy's meal transcended that category. But then again, their meals and drinks were always a cut above the rest of the group. They knew how to entertain. They were more sophisticated. Still, Jeff found the evening dull. Maybe that was the reason he was so tired. The table conversation was so uninspiring. Tomorrow had to be better. He needed some real excitement to get his juices flowing...something he sorely missed tonight.

He thought about Peggy and wondered what was taking her so long. He knew how much she hated clutter, and he pictured his wife puttering around the kitchen in her long, shimmering dress with a dish rag in hand.

As he opened his closet, Jeff hung his slack pants and sport jacket meticulously on a neatly-lined bar of clothing, making certain his casual wear was hung on the correct rack, in the correct space and with the correct colors. Jeff's business suits were hung on a bar directly opposite his casual wear and they, too, were neatly grouped and color-coded.

The inside corner of the walk-in closet held four drawers that contained a variety of shirts, socks and underwear. A suspended, but overly-crowded tie bar took up a nearby rack. He paused and, after fingering a few business suits, made a superficial judgment of the next morning's apparel before closing the closet door.

He dropped his boxer shorts on the floor near the bed, a routine he always followed in case of an emergency, and slipped under the covers to wait.

"When is she coming up to bed?" he asked himself, aloud. He wondered how long he would have to wait before Peggy joined him with her anniversary promise.

His awareness of time faded gradually as the sounds of sleep grew louder and louder.

***

Somewhere around two in the morning, Jeff found himself alone and staring at the clock. Jeff realized then that he had left the small lamp on for Peggy. *Where is she,* he wondered. He fumbled around the floor for his shorts, before walking into the front hall that blazed with lights. From the staircase, Jeff could see the illuminating lamps on the floor below.

Jeff knew Peggy's limited capacity for drinking champagne and stepped quietly down the steps, expecting to find his wife asleep on the couch. But, he was surprised to find the living area empty. He began to search the entire house, room by room, calling her name as he went.

He checked the small table near the entry way in the front hall. His wife's purse and car keys lay near the ledger she always carried with her to the gift shop. Jeff walked through the laundry room into the garage and spotted Peggy's silver Malibu. He opened the car door instinctively and found nothing. He laid a hand against the car hood. It felt cold and unused.

For some unknown reason, he felt a compulsion to walk around the back and side of the house. Finding nothing out of the ordinary, Jeff proceeded to the end of the driveway. He checked the street for signs of activity, but found only darkened houses and dimly lit street lights. Everything seemed eerily still.

A feeling of dread swept through him. His wife of five years was nowhere to be found.

He returned to the house and thought of possible situations that could account for his wife's absence. Had something occurred that evening giving Peggy cause to leave without a word? *No.* He answered his own question. That was not even a consideration.

Had Megan phoned concerning some problem? Peggy's sister was always in a state of crisis, usually financial, sometimes emotional, but always in need. Most couples had problems with kids. Their albatross was Megan, the younger sister who moved to Amherst with them and used their money for college tuition. But, the year before graduating, Megan married Brad Croft, who came from a family of philanthropy and wealth and, who owned a large house in the Village of Williamsville, a quaint, small and old, politically independent hamlet of Amherst. For Megan, that was still not enough. She needed the right wardrobe, the right places to be seen and the right people to be seen with. All of which cost money and Peggy's sisterly support. Peggy was always slipping her money, although Megan's husband was more than generous with funds.

On more than one occasion, Jeff raised hell with Peggy about her sister. She was always short of money, yet there was no reciprocity, not even one business referral from her or any of her friends. Megan knew they could use the money, but it was always one-sided. Once again, Megan must have needed her sister. That had to be the reason for Peggy's absence. Still, why hadn't she taken her purse? Why was the car still in the garage? Peggy must have left a note... somewhere. Jeff checked the kitchen counter, the hall table and night stands near the bed. Finding nothing, he called Megan's cell phone, but got no response. Then, he tried her land line. The phone rang several times before the answering machine kicked in and Megan's melodic voice requested a message.

A jarring thought then occurred to him: the two sisters sounded so much alike on the telephone. Why had he never noticed that before? Moments later and without thinking, Jeff found himself talking on the telephone to his next door neighbor, Janice Sommers, although he had not recalled dialing her number.

"No. I don't want you to come over," he told her. "I just haven't thought this thing through yet," he added quickly. "Did Peggy say anything to you at the party? I've checked everywhere."

Within minutes, Fred picked up an extension and started firing questions. Satisfied that Jeff had made a complete search of the house and grounds for Peggy, Fred asked about Megan.

"I already called both phones minutes ago. No answer on either one. I guess they're out somewhere doing Megan's bidding."

"She told us at dinner that they were stopping at the Crystal Bar for a drink. Don't you remember?" Janice interrupted. "They're meeting some friends."

"I try not to remember anything she has to say," Jeff barked, but quickly regretted making his feelings so obvious.

He tried covering the remark, but was unable to come up with something quick and smart. Instead, he turned the conversation into a cry for help. He knew they would like that.

"So what should I do?" he asked.

"Have you called the police yet?" Fred responded to his question.

"No. I haven't called the police. I really don't think anything happened to Peggy, but I guess that's the right approach."

"You'll tell me if you hear anything," Janice interrupted again.

"Yes. I'll let you know." He housed the receiver.

Taking Fred's suggestion, Jeff phoned the police, only to be told that there was a forty-eight hour waiting period before an investigation could begin. The officer suggested he call back in the morning.

It was only when the conversation ended that Jeff realized an embarrassing fact: he had been running around the house and yard, barefoot and in his underwear.

Chapter 3
Awakening

While Jeff was trying to make sense of his wife's disappearance, Peggy was experiencing a veritable nightmare of her own.

Fear gripped Peggy as she slowly regained consciousness. She felt dazed, confused and totally disoriented. She studied the great kaleidoscope of shapes and colors that danced against the dark background covering her face. She tried to scream, but something around her mouth muffled the sound. Fear struck another cord when Peggy realized she couldn't move.

Why am I tied up? Who put me here?

She wondered why the severe pounding in her head wouldn't go away. She tried to assess the situation, but found logic fractured and useless. Never could she remember feeling so alone, so helpless and so confused. Frightened and knowing the prospect of dying was very real, Peggy suddenly felt determined to regain control of her faculties should escape be possible.

With her wrists tied behind her, Peggy turned on her side and tried to extend a hand to feel her surroundings. Her fingers circled what seemed like a mattress button. Then, after readjusting her body, she extended her tied ankles outward and down. Her shoe rubbed on something gritty. She suddenly understood. A thin mattress had been thrown on the dirty floor solely for her benefit.

But, why?

After moving back to her former position, she reached for the part of the mattress near the button. Her fingers navigated small mounds of very fine crystals that seemed to be scattered. She wondered if someone had accidentally spilled salt or sand on the mattress and then forgot about it. Almost like an involuntary reflex, Peggy began brushing the crystals away from her body.

Suddenly, Peggy heard heavy footsteps approaching and immediately pretended to be unconscious as the door squeaked open. She heard a man make a loud grunt, and mutter something that she couldn't quite understand, before he left the room. From the heavy thud of his footsteps, she thought that he had to be big in stature. His manner of grunting made him sound coarse and crude.

What was it he said? Matches? No. That's wasn't right. No matches or something like that.

He was looking for matches.

But, why would he look for matches here?

The room that held her must have been used as a storeroom. But how did the man know that there were no matches? Did he look in some special place? If so, did he have the ceiling light on or did he use a flashlight? Peggy would never know.

As she lay there, Peggy forced herself to recall the events that led up to her abduction. She had to remember how she came to be in this predicament. Why was she taken from her home and thrown into this room? For what purpose? None of it made any sense.

Her mind wandered back to the anniversary dinner. After their company left, she and Jeff finished the open bottle of champagne before he went to bed. She was to follow, but something happened. Several minutes of blankness passed by before Peggy could finally remember. She recalled washing flute glasses. Then, the bag of trash came to mind. Jeff had forgotten to put the container on the driveway for Monday's pickup. What happened when she went outside? Did someone grab her, while she was tossing the filled bag into the garbage can? It was all a blur.

Have I angered someone?

She thought back to the gift shop. Could some customer or vendor be angry enough to abduct her? Did someone think Peggy cheated them on some big sale or order? As far back as Peggy could remember, she had done nothing to warrant a kidnapping.

She always maintained a good relationship with her customers. Exchanges or refunds never presented a problem. In fact, much of the business rested on those liberal policies. A returned gift usually netted a larger sale. At least, that's what her tracking data proved.

Of course, since the shop was located right in the Village of Williamsville, it was extremely important to have good relationships with everyone. The small business community thrived on goodwill and gossip. The merchants, by day, were friends and neighbors at night. And, while word of mouth spread all sorts of blather, the current climate on the street praised Peggy's new inventory of gift shop treasures. In the dark, she thought of her clientele. She could think of no one who had openly expressed any sort of dissatisfaction with her merchandise or service. Aside from the customers, who else had contact with her? The vendors, perhaps? But their main concern was payment.

Were there outstanding bills?

Nothing came to mind. They were always paid on time. She could not think of one angry vendor. No... The business was current. It had to be something else. But it had to be something related to her. Then she thought of Jeff. Was she taken because of him? She wondered if he could have been involved in some way. She began to think of every viable possibility. She thought of Jeff's promotion first. Could someone have so resented his becoming the new office manager to warrant her abduction? Granted, he did move quickly through the office ranks, at least enough to be noticed by corporate management. But, deserving or not, would someone be that angry to take it out on the man's wife?

Impossible.

People get promoted every day. And every day, someone gets screwed and left behind.

It was only when she thought of Jeff's growing referral network that a sudden realization swept through her. That was the one aspect of his job that she hadn't thought of, but it was important. Her mind wandered back to their conversation after the anniversary party. Jeff told her that he had clients coming in the next day. Had he angered these people? Were they responsible for abducting her? Peggy knew she had to think this thing through logically.

Jeff always told her in advance when an out-of -town client was expected. He was extremely thoughtful that way. Then, she wouldn't worry needlessly, if he decided to stay in the city after a night of entertaining his high-powered guest. But he never mentioned the client's name or the transactions involved. Those things, Jeff had specifically told her, were confidential and off-limits. His clients trusted him with great sums of money and trust was the most important element in their broker-client relationship.

Actually, when it came down to his list of clients, Peggy knew very little about his business dealings. Jeff wanted it that way. The less Peggy knew, the better it was from a legal standpoint. If Jeff were involved in a lawsuit, someone questioning his wife could get no information whatsoever.

Although it seemingly answered his reasons for maintaining the anonymity and the confidentiality of his clients, kidnapping her made no sense. She had very little knowledge of his daily activity. Occasionally, Jeff would mention a particular stock or bond, he purchased for their portfolio, but that was predictable. He watched the market daily and knew which investments were increasing in value. So, Peggy was thankful that, while Jeff kept a close watch on the investments of his clients, he was also studying the growth of their portfolio, as well. In retrospect, she believed they were heavier in stocks and bonds than mutual funds. But did she really know that for a fact?

Why am I thinking of this right now?

She wondered if Jeff had cheated someone. Maybe he lost someone's life savings and this was payback time. Even worse, if he worked with some unsavory people and lost their money, they would have no pity on her if that were true. They would use her as a ransom tool or even take more desperate measures. She dismissed the thought, however. It was too preposterous.

She knew that Jeff would not put her in harm's way. He loved her too much. When he took on new clients, Jeff always discussed the element of risk with them. At least, that's what he told her. But most of his clientele were seasoned investors with large retirement accounts and equally large entertainment requests. At least, that's what she understood... No. That's what she thought.

After thinking back, Peggy began to distrust her own judgment. Was she that stupid or just plain gullible? Maybe she should have taken more of an interest in his work. Perhaps she was too blinded by her love for him.

The one thing, Jeff did tell her, was how much his clients relied on him to make them great sums of money. Of course, they also expected to be entertained when they came to town to review their portfolios. So, as Jeff's referral business grew, his work nights became more frequent, but Peggy never complained. She knew he was doing it for them. Even now, deep in her heart, she believed him. Jeff loved her. She could feel the profound love they shared.

Jeff would remind her constantly. "We have to make it while we can," he would tell her, referring to the commissions from his clients' accounts and their subsequent trades. Still, Jeff did promise to take her somewhere in the fall, although he never revealed the surprise destination. But it was to be a thrilling trip. At least, that's what he said. So, Peggy continued to dream of their being alone together with no telephone interruptions or conference calls. Now, Peggy felt uncertain of ever seeing him again.

She ached to have her husband's arms around her. She wanted him to tell her this was all a bad dream. That it was not real. That he would never allow something like this to happen to her. He loved her too much to see her frightened or unhappy.

"Where are you?" she inwardly asked her husband. "I'm so scared." She felt the tear drops trickle down beneath the eye covering. "I may never see you again."

"Try, darling," she imagined Jeff telling her. "Try to get free."

Peggy wriggled her bound wrists from side to side, but found it impossible to loosen the binding. She continued until her wrists ached with pain. Yet, she refused to give up. After several more attempts, Peggy decided to rest before trying again.

Lying there in the darkness and completely sapped of energy, Peggy's mind filled with memories of Jeff.

She recalled their first meeting.

It had been a Saturday afternoon in June, when she and her sister, Megan, attended the Three Rivers Arts Festival on Liberty Avenue near the Point in Pittsburgh. The two Burke sisters had made it an annual ritual to visit every merchandise booth featured, regardless of their intention to purchase. Year after year, they always followed the same plan.

First, they would shop the kiosks farthest away from the Point, closer to Penn Avenue, and then enjoy lunch at the Hilton Hotel, adjacent the sale booths they had yet to browse. While enjoying their meal, Peggy and Megan would study people passing by, with their newly acquired purchases and make up stories concerning them. Then, after finishing a delicious tiramisu, the two sisters would begin their tour of the remaining kiosks.

At some point, Peggy had wandered into one of the tents and accidentally backed into someone, as she searched through a stack of colored tee shirts. When Peggy turned to apologize, she found herself facing a very handsome man with coifed chestnut hair and dark expressive eyes. Totally embarrassed by her clumsiness, Peggy made some sort of mundane apology to the tall well-built man, and hurriedly left the area to search another kiosk with Megan.

Although the prospect of meeting him again was remote, Peggy could not get him out of her mind. She could only wish... but it was best to forget him.

Two months later, as Peggy and her sister strolled in and out of the Italian stores in the Strip District of Pittsburgh, she saw her handsome man again among a crowd of shoppers at Pennsylvania Macaroni. While she and Megan waited at the cheese counter for their number to be called, Peggy caught a glimpse of him standing in line holding a ticket. When he scanned the crowd and saw her, he hurried to her side and accidently knocked a bag of tomatoes out of Megan's hand and watched them scatter all over the dirty wooden floor. Knowing how unforgiving Megan would be, Peggy hushed her immediately and began gathering the squashed tomatoes along with the handsome man's help.

He insisted on replacing them and instructed Megan to make another selection. While the younger sister was kept busy, the man wasted no time. He introduced himself, asked Peggy for a date and took her phone number. It all happened so fast. Yet, everything seemed so magical from the moment they met. When Megan returned, they were still laughing over their joint clumsiness, both at the Art Festival and then at the Strip. After introducing himself to Megan, he left the two sisters to continue their shopping.

Still, what stuck in Peggy's mind was Megan's immediate reaction to Jeff. Although they had just met, Megan told her sister, in no uncertain terms, that, 'Jeff stunk from his asshole to his eyeballs.' She was against him from the very beginning. And, from that time on, Megan's opinion of him never changed. Her sister's attitude toward the man was something she could never understand. Peggy Burke was twenty-six at the time.

On their first date, Jeff told her that he was a stockbroker with a local company and worked very long hours. But, Jeff insisted on seeing her again. He wanted to be with her. As time went on, they managed to be together more often. He lived in Mount Washington, overlooking the city of Pittsburgh and Point Park where they usually met. They would take the incline up for a more romantic view of the city, have dinner and drinks in one of the upscale Southside restaurants near the Monongahela River, or they would stay in his apartment enjoying each other's company.

She remembered how they made love in his apartment on weekends, both in the afternoon and evening. They didn't need a cigarette, a drink or conversation. All they needed was the loving feel of each other, the soft caresses of two bodies joined together, binding their love.

In retrospect, Peggy longed for those days. Not that their love had eroded. No, her love for Jeff was stronger than ever. What she felt came with age, perhaps, or maybe marriage. She just felt a stronger sense of freedom then. There were no encumbrances, no house, no business, no one to placate. Now, she had a house. Beautiful as it was, it had to be cared for. Her small, cramped apartment was so much easier to clean. Peggy's thoughts soon shifted from the house to the gift shop.

Her wonderful partner and neighbor, Janice Sommers, was the rarest of gems. She had the genteel refinement of a woman who attended a top-notch finishing school. It was her soft spoken way that charmed so many of their returning customers. She imbued a caring interest for each of their many requests and tried to satisfy them in every possible way. Janice was so kind, so giving. Peggy felt grateful to have this wonderful woman for her partner. They had a very close relationship and worked extremely well together. Much of that, Peggy decided, was because both of them were so even tempered.

Although Peggy took care of the inventory and bookkeeping, she discussed everything with Janice. Their business together was based on mutual trust and respect. Of course, the partnership had been drawn up legally, but the husbands were not included in the business arrangement.. Upon Peggy's death, Janice would become the sole owner. For some reason, she was glad of the arrangement. If something did happen to her, Peggy would want Janice to have it. She would make it grow. If the husbands were involved, they would insist on selling the shop to use the money for some stupid investment like stock or bonds. Who needed intangibles when the gift shop did so well? Men could never understand this type of reasoning.

Why am I thinking of these things now? I need help.

'If you don't help yourself, who the hell will?' One of Megan's aphorisms came to mind.

Her thoughts turned to her younger sister whom she loved dearly. Peggy had taken care of her for so many years, happy ones, she hoped. Now, that, too, could be over. Never to see Megan again. She couldn't bear it. Theirs was the closest relationship. The older sister watches her younger sibling while the divorced mother goes to work. It was an old story told hundreds of times.

This one had a different wrinkle. Megan and their mother never got along. Never ever. It went in only one direction as the years passed. It got worse and became a bitter battle of wits.

Their insufferable relationship started long before Megan's teenage years, just before her menstrual cycle began. Older by five years, Peggy recalled a tearful Megan approaching her in the bathroom one day and exposing her armpit.

"What am I looking at?" Peggy remembered asking.

"It's yellow," Megan said, tears streaming down her face. "She said it's the evil coming out. I'm going to die." She came for confirmation, for support, and for the truth.

"No. No. Meg. You're sweaty because you're getting hair. See?"

Peggy removed her blouse and pointed to her own arm pit. "You'll have to shave there," she said, hugging her sister. "You're growing up to be a beautiful young lady."

"With stinkin armpits," Megan added, before she broke into a half-smile.

That particular revelation by her mother caused a war of words that escalated into the banging of doors and the slamming of pots and pans. The only one spoken to and with was Peggy. She often wondered if that was the moment Megan began hating her mother.

After a while, things quieted down. But the quiet calm never lasted long.

Then, a year or so later, when her mother refused to accept Megan's explanation after a horrible incident, their private war escalated to such a pitch that Megan began calling the woman by her given name, Josephine. She no longer deserved the elevation of motherhood.

That was the day the mother/daughter relationship came to its end.

From that time on, Megan refused to discuss the final divide between the two women. But, Peggy had theories of her own, although she never revealed them. What would have been the point? It would have only intensified the situation further when calm was needed. Megan continued to make her mother unhappy. So, the harangue and bitterness just continued incessantly. Their mother tried punishment, but it never worked. It only made Megan more obstinate and sassier, much to their mother's displeasure.

In Peggy's mind, there was only one solution, and that was to move out of the irreconcilable situation as soon as financially possible. That meant living at home for a while after graduating from college and finding a decent job.

A year later, when Peggy was twenty-three and worked for an accounting firm, she had saved up enough money to rent a small apartment in Shadyside, a quaint, upscale area of the city, and she took Megan, who was then eighteen, with her. Her excuse for moving was the proximity to her job. In addition, Peggy told her mother that Megan could select one of the nearby colleges and commute.

In reality, her mother was relieved to see them go. Peggy had always sensed this. By her logic, it would now be Peggy's responsibility to keep Megan straight. Admittedly, Megan was a handful, but Peggy loved her. She knew it would take time and a great deal of patience to care for her outspoken sister, but she had faith that her sibling would come around in time. So, Peggy waited.

After Megan worked a number of dead end jobs, she became totally discouraged. But, with Peggy's help, she finally enrolled at Pitt and then transferred credits to the University of Buffalo when they moved to Amherst. At twenty-seven, Megan married a brilliant and wonderful man, three years her senior, who taught English literature at the university. And now, at twenty-eight, Megan had her college degree and was interviewing for teaching jobs. Peggy was so proud of her sister.

Peggy turned slightly. The throbbing in her head would not go away. Her wrists were sore and her body felt stiff. Still, the spinning in her head continued.

Somewhere in the recesses of her mind, a man slowly appeared out of nowhere. As he came closer and closer, her fear completely dissipated. Peggy knew this man and his kind face. She recognized him, but she couldn't remember where they met. He extended his hand first, and then gathered her into his arms.

"I'm so sorry I couldn't protect you like I should've." He ran his finger over the scar on her upper right arm. "You're a good girl, Maggie pie," he told her. "Look after her til I come back."

Everything faded quickly, leaving Peggy to wonder about the apparition. Was it real or was it a dream? What did it mean? Could it have been someone close to her? Could it have been her father? She had no real recollection of the man. Her mother had taken care of that. The woman had destroyed every family photograph years earlier, when they were too young to object...or too young to realize the importance of family. Now, memories failed and their times together were hard to remember. Yet, Peggy wondered if the apparition was the likeness of her father. Did he call her Maggie pie when she was young? Was that his nickname for her? She couldn't remember. Asking her mother about it would have been pointless. She would have simply suffered memory loss. The woman was like that.

In fact, as years went on, her mother's condition worsened. She would answer no questions regarding the man who sired her children. Peggy always wondered why the woman never spoke of him. It was almost like he was never a part of their lives. As such, he was nonexistent.

She thought about the rest of the man's statement.

"Take care of her til I get back."

What did that mean? Who was Peggy to care for? What person? Megan? Her mother? And when was he coming back? Where had he been all these years? Had he tried to contact her before?

Peggy hadn't thought about the scar in years. She had been seven or eight when it happened.

The two V- formations, one inverted, made the diamond center much more noticeable, than the four stitching lines that faded outward. Makeup never covered it completely, so Peggy decided long ago to accept the scar and forget about it. She treated it much like the birth mole on the back of her neck. However, she could not forget her mother's rage, nor her flinging the glass pitcher at her father, the shards of which stuck Peggy's upper right arm causing blood to spurt everywhere. Peggy remembered being in the line of fire, the subsequent hospital visit that required fourteen stitches and a shot. A lengthy argument between her parents ensued, but beyond that, she recalled little else. She never remembered seeing her father again after that.

Her mother was an entirely different story. She was a woman one would not easily forget. Between her mother's wrath and Megan's fits of temper, life was an ongoing nightmare, days included.

Maybe it was just a dream. Maybe the whole thing was meaningless. None of it made any sense. But in her mental state, Peggy knew the imaginary could be very real.

Imaginary or not, she was afraid of dying.

Thoughts of her mother began to fill her mind. She didn't want to think about her or the man she finally married. The woman always dated losers. Somehow, this one stuck. Donald Egan had been the boyfriend who hung around for years, pretending to go home nights when Peggy and Megan were supposedly asleep. Although they feigned ignorance when their mother's bed repeatedly hit the common wall between the bedrooms, Peggy and Megan would laugh and listen to the stupidity of it all. Of course, once they moved away, their mother and the goon she lived with could fornicate openly.

The sound of loud, arguing voices brought Peggy out of her reverie. Were they arguing about her? What were they saying? Were they coming for her? What were their intentions?

For reasons she could not understand, Peggy was taken from her home, trussed up like a turkey and tossed on some filthy mattress. The heavy lout who entered the room earlier knew her fate was in his hands. But, Peggy was not a stupid woman. She was not prepared to die. Not just yet.

Suddenly, everything became very quiet. Then, she heard loud voices again. One seemed different. Someone else had arrived. Whatever was going to happen to her, it was going to happen now. She heard a loud pounding staccato and realized it was the beating of her heart. She lay there terrified and waited for the sound of an opening door.

Chapter 4
Constraints

The other side of the door was miles away from Peggy's Amherst home on Carriage Hill East. Inside the paint-worn bungalow at the edge of Clarence Center, two burly men had been arguing loudly about the woman in the next room.

"What the hell is wrong with you?" The huskier of the two bristled. "Just how many times did we go over it, Judd? Over and over."

"We're screwed." Mel said, his large hand framing a woman's portrait. "I don't know how we're going to get out of this one. He's beyond mean. You don't make mistakes with him."

He began stroking his beard, as if lost in thought.

"We're dead," Mel repeated his sentiments again, before tossing the photograph on the kitchen table. "There's no way around this."

"Mel, wait," Judd implored. "What if I tell him it was my fault and I'll fix it? Maybe he'd let us go."

From his partner's dark demeanor, it didn't take long for Judd Thorne to realize that he had made the biggest mistake of his young life.

"It wouldn't work," Mel growled. "I'm his only contact. That's how he wanted it from the beginning. Just one contact."

A sudden knock startled the big man who took a step backwards. He slowly slid his fingers inside the pocket of his trousers and wrapped his hand carefully around his gun.

"You expecting somebody, Judd?" He wondered if the dimwitted man compounded his first mistake, by being followed.

"It'd be my brother, Seth," he said, opening the door. "I called him when you were looking in on the woman. You know... to see if she was still asleep."

Judd had to be extremely naïve or totally stupid to tell anybody about the deal they had entered into. Mel eyed the man and decided upon the latter. Not only was Judd slow-minded; he was also stupidly slow-moving.

"What's going on?" Seth Stone asked his younger brother. "You said you were scared."

Although thinner, but more muscular in stature than his brother, the tall, dark-haired man had a quality and presence about him that told people he was not one to be taken lightly.

"This is what's going on," Mel said, grabbing the photograph from the kitchen table and flashing it momentarily. "Your brother screwed up."

"Mel," Judd interrupted, "brought me this deal worth a lot of money. All I had to do was get this woman and bring her here."

"Trouble is, he got the wrong one. Now, we're in a mess because he's so stupid." Mel flashed the picture again, without meaning to give Seth another cursory glance.

"You kidnapped someone?" Seth eyes widened, as he focused on his brother. "That's a felony. You just got out. Now, you'll go away for good."

"He'll be dead long before that," Mel countered.

Although he took time to explain their predicament, the burly man was rethinking a plan to salvage the operation and save himself.

"We'll both die, unless we fix it now," he said.

Without a moment's hesitation, Mel pulled the gun from his pocket and aimed it at Judd, while addressing Seth. "Since you walked into this pile of shit uninvited, I'm going to turn this whole thing around and you're going to help me." Mel cocked the gun, a silent threat to kill them both if Seth refused.

"Now, go into the next room and get the woman," Mel ordered. "Get rid of her and come back here. I've got another plan. If you don't come back, Judd won't see tomorrow."

Seth remained glued to the floor as he watched the man holding a gun on his brother. His legs wouldn't move. He heard what the man said, but he couldn't process the reality of the whole situation; the gravity of it, yes...the reality, no.

Would Mel actually shoot Judd? Why would he do that? What would be gained by killing his brother? Then again, would Seth want to risk that possibility?

His thoughts raced as he tried to assess the situation.

Through some means or another, Judd was hired to abduct a woman. For this, he was to be given a big sum of money and the transaction would be over. However, when Mel checked the woman's identity, he realized Judd's mistake. Now, both men feared being killed by the person who ordered the kidnapping. And, since Judd had been the one to botch the whole thing, Seth was to rectify his brother's error by murdering an innocent woman.

Killing an innocent woman so his brother could live made no sense to Seth. Why didn't they just let her go? What were they hiding from him? On the other hand, perhaps Mel felt by having the woman killed, he would be able to save his own life. Then, at some later date, the right woman could be abducted. Either way, none of this was the thinking of rational man. And Mel, by his actions, was not a rational man.

Finally, Seth broke the silence.

"How did you leave her?" he asked the dirty-looking man.

"Don't worry, she can't see you," Mel shot back. "Besides being gagged, the woman's tied up and unconscious, so she'll be easy to pitch somewhere."

"Put the gun down or we don't play," Seth said, calling his bluff. "I'll take the woman but I want some guarantee that you won't do something stupid. I want the bullets."

Mel placed them on the table and pointed to the next room.

After pocketing the bullets, Seth left the house with the woman and never looked back. He had a plan of his own. Seth would take the woman to his car before making a move. But, he would need Judd's help. Together, they could take the big, burly brute. Alone, he didn't have enough girth to overtake him. Then, through his connections with the police, Seth would get this kidnapping thing sorted out. Seth would tell them the man convinced his somewhat challenged brother to bring the woman to him.

Seth's shoulder began to chafe, and his thoughts returned to the woman he was carrying, grateful that his car was parked nearby. He knew nothing about the woman he held other than she had full rounded breasts and a very solid ass.

As he carefully placed the woman across the back seat of his car, her two high-heels kicked him in the chest as she struggled to free herself.

"Stop!" Seth grabbed the woman's restrained ankles. "I am not going to hurt you. I'm not even a part of this. If you understand, just nod the best way you can."

The woman nodded and Seth closed the car door and moved to the driver's side. "I've got to move the car before Mel gets suspicious," he said aloud.

Seth searched his pocket for his car keys, but soon realized that he must have dropped them somewhere between the house and the car. He hadn't counted on something that stupid to spoil his plan. Seth needed to escape quickly if things went badly.

"I have to find my car keys," he explained to his captive. "I thought I heard something fall when we left the house."

Fearful of being discovered, Seth moved quietly toward the house, sliding his feet softly along the narrow walkway, feeling for a metal key ring. As he stepped closer to the side of the bungalow, he felt something hard under his shoe. He crouched beneath one of the windows and fingered the walkway cautiously for the keys, before grabbing them and sliding them into his pocket.

With a stroke of luck, Seth felt he could use the window to his advantage. One quick peek would tell him everything. Then, he could rush into the house, tackle Mel and, with Judd's help, restrain him for the police.

However, when Seth peered through the window, he was struck with disbelief. He could see the two men clearly. Mel's back was to the window and Judd was facing him. They were arguing, but Seth couldn't hear their conversation. Finally, Seth heard Mel yell something inaudible before stretching his arm forward. Within seconds, Judd's lifeless body fell backwards to the floor, a crumpled ruin where life had existed only seconds earlier.

Instinctively, Seth wanted to rush inside and attack the man who just murdered his brother. Instead, he stood frozen in shock, his mind trying to process what he had just witnessed.

Judd's body lay lifeless in full view and there was nothing Seth could do to avenge his brother's death. The odds were in Mel's favor.

Mel had a loaded gun that he would use if Seth attempted anything at that moment. Another killing would mean nothing to the man who had just committed murder.

Rage coursed through his body, his face frozen with anger. Seth swore he would get even. Somehow, he would develop a plan of his own, regardless of the consequences. Seth quickly raced to the car and sped away, oblivious of the destination or the passenger in the back seat. For the second time in his life, he felt a profound sense of loss and a growing uncontrollable melancholy as he drove along the unfamiliar highway.

Soon, Seth realized he could go no further. He found a side road and parked the car. He rested his head briefly on the steering wheel, and then bolted from the car to a stand of trees and began retching.

Chapter 5
Introductions

Seth leaned against a tall leafy tree to catch his breath and realized his heart had slowed and was no longer pounding. He tried to find a reason for Judd's murder. Why would Mel kill him? Seth's only link was the woman in the car. Was Judd hiding something else from Seth? He hadn't seen his brother lately or even talked with him, thinking back on it now. Judd never returned his phone calls. That was weeks ago.

Seth walked back from the stand of trees and approached the woman lying in the back seat of the car.

"I am not going to hurt you. I'll remove your blindfold and gag, if you promise not to scream. Please," he said softly. "I need your help."

The gentleness in the man's rich, velvet voice made Peggy unafraid. The stranger removed the blindfold and she stared at him, but she could only see his silhouette in the moonlight. After repositioning her body, he then removed all of her restraints and helped her to the front seat of the car.

"Mel just killed my brother and I want to know why."

"If he's the gorilla who kidnapped me, why should I give a shit? I say good riddance." After blurting out her true feelings, Peggy soon realized the crassness of the remark.

The man, who had just rescued her, rested his head on the steering wheel and remained silent.

"I'm sorry," Peggy apologized, wishing she could retract her previous statement. "What do you want from me? I'm the victim here. I don't know anything. I just want to go home."

Seth looked at her briefly and ignored her remark. Even in the dimness of the moonlight, there was a striking appeal about the disheveled woman.

"You can tell me what happened. How did you get to the house?"

"I emptied the trash because Jeff forgot. That's what happened. How I got to the house is a blank."

Her summary was briefer than he had expected.

"What's your excuse?" she shot back.

"Jeff?" He questioned the name.

"My husband. The man who is probably going crazy wondering where I am."

"Did you hear anything?" Seth remained focused.

"Just voices. I heard men arguing when I started to wake up. But I don't know what they were saying. Then, I heard a different one. Yours."

"None of this makes sense." Seth drummed the steering wheel. "There are too many unanswered questions."

Seth sat quietly for a few minutes, and then began to assess their situation verbally, hoping the woman could offer some insight.

"Judd kidnaps you and takes you to a certain address. That was supposed to be the end of it for him. But then something goes wrong. Judd calls and needs my help. When I arrive, this man, Mel, shows me a woman's photograph. He's very angry and he has a gun. Seems Judd kidnapped the wrong person and I was to rectify his mistake by killing you… It doesn't make sense."

Seth continued drumming.

"Wait a minute," Peggy interrupted. "You're telling me this was a mistake? I was kidnapped by mistake?"

"We don't know that," he argued. "The photograph could have been a red herring. This wasn't just your ordinary kidnapping. There is something more involved here."

"Then, take me home. I'll be safe there," she assured him. "My husband will take care of me."

"I wouldn't be so sure about that." Seth looked at the woman. "Contacting the police wouldn't make you any safer either. Just think about it. Mel tells me to return after I dispose of you. We know he's already killed my brother. So, why would he want me to come back to the house? What's the logic in that?"

Without waiting for her response, Seth continued. "Since he thinks I murdered you to save Judd, Mel kills me and every witness to the kidnapping is dead."

"So you're saying Mel will come after me if he knows I'm alive? That's really a stretch," Peggy insisted. "I don't even know what he looks like."

"That's my point. But he would recognize you."

"What if I don't say anything at all? I'll say I spent the night at a hotel."

"It doesn't matter. He can't risk it."

"You're worse off," she conceded. "You know his identity."

"That's true," Seth agreed, "but why didn't he let you go? That's what really puzzles me. Was the photograph I saw for real?"

"I don't follow."

"Since you can't identify him, why didn't he just release you on some street corner? Why was he so anxious to have you killed?"

"You're scaring me."

"I'm just telling you what I think," he said, calmly. "By the way, my name's Seth Stone. Judd Thorne was my younger brother, half-brother, really."

"I'm Margaret, but my friends call me Peggy. Peggy Roberts."

"Well, Peggy Roberts, we have two problems facing us and I need your help."

"Are you saying you won't take me home?" Her face stiffened. The prospect of spending time with someone other than her husband made her uneasy. That this man saved her life was of no consequence at the moment. He was still a stranger.

"I will," he said, appearing to read her thoughts, "After we figure this out. I know I'm going to be questioned when the police find Judd's body. My fingerprints are on the doorknob of the storeroom and the windowsill outside the living room."

The idea of being questioned by the authorities, before Seth had answers, bothered him.

"I need to know what Judd was into, and where you fit in. Either you were the intended victim, or the abduction really was a case of mistaken identity. Either way, you're involved."

Peggy listened quietly, wondering where exactly she did fit into the kidnapping scheme, and how she could possibly help this man who was filled with so many questions. She had no answers.

"We know Mel wasn't smart enough to plan the kidnapping," Seth explained. "Someone else mapped it out, and the sooner we find out who it is, the safer we'll be."

Before Peggy could make any response, Seth started the car and sped along the dark road, before making several winding turns. Reaching a lighted intersection, he turned left and sighed. "Thank God for Transit Road." He heaved another sigh of relief. "I got so lost on Greiner, when I pulled off the side road to vomit. I wasn't sure where the hell we were."

He drove for another fifteen minutes in silence toward Cheektowaga, then glanced at her briefly and chuckled while stopping at a signal light. "I suggest you don't look in the mirror."

"Why?" She pulled the mirrored visor down. "Oh, shit." Peggy pulled at the strands of blond hair spiking in all directions. "I look like a frump."

"C'mon, frumpy," Seth pulled into the parking lot of a large apartment complex. "We're going to search Judd's apartment."

No sooner had Peggy slid out of the car when they heard the rip of her favorite long dress, followed by a rapid flood of loose beads, sequins and pearls bouncing on the ground.

Seth stood by the open car door and laughed sarcastically. "Perfect. Now, the picture's complete."

"Why are you being such a smart ass?" she bristled. But Seth was too busy breaking into Judd's apartment with a credit card to reply.

***

"Jesus." Peggy was struck by the smell of half-eaten food and dirty dishes. She stood dumbfounded, at first, and then walked around the apartment taking inventory.

Newspapers and piles of men's clothing were strewn all over the living room furniture and floor. Scattered on an unmade bed were several pieces of soiled underwear. A trail of used towels led to a dingy bathroom with a heavily stained sink and toilet. A shower curtain, hanging by a few hooks, concealed a tub/shower combination that looked like a laboratory for mold specimens.

"When was the last time you visited?" Peggy asked, returning to the living room.

"I didn't say I visited. I said I phoned." Seth replied quickly, not wanting to face the dirty and disheveled woman directly, for fear of angering her further. He had experienced her flare of temper earlier.

"Your brother needed help. This place is a shit hole."

Startled by the comment, Seth was amused by the comparison and faced her directly.

"I guess I should have warned you. This is how Judd lives...lived," Seth corrected himself.

"Just what are we looking for?" Peggy asked, watching him turn on more lights.

She studied the man who saved her. He was over a head taller than she and, although he was not quite as handsome as her husband, he had a kind face and very clear brown eyes that seemed to notice everything around him. There was a quiet magnetic presence about Seth Stone that seemed to draw her to him. And, although she felt safe with him, his questions were as disconcerting as the shirt that clung to his hard body. She remembered him carrying her. How could a man be tall, thin and still muscular?

Why was she having these thoughts? Quite suddenly, she heard his full, resonant voice respond to her question.

"Some clue that will lead us to Mel's identity. Since Judd didn't have a computer, our only option is the telephone."

Seth switched on the answering machine, but the messages had been erased. "Look for phone bills."

Seth and Peggy went in opposite directions, searching through drawers of furniture, Judd's clothing and under newspapers. They disturbed every nook and cranny for anything that could connect the two men.

"Hey. Look what I found," Peggy said, rushing into the living room, waving a book of matches. "They were in the pocket of Judd's pants. Looks like a bar."

"Find anything else, other matchbooks or notes?"

"Not in the bedroom. I'll try the kitchen." Peggy started to leave the room. "What are you reading?"

"Judd's mail and the un-cashed check I sent. I did find his phone bills," he added. "So I think we should leave."

***

Minutes later, they were headed north along a four lane highway toward Seth's house near Lockport. In what seemed like an eternity, they left the highway, drove up the side of a steep mountain, then along an escarpment before parking in front of an A-frame chalet.

"Do not touch anything when we get inside. We aren't staying long." Seth warned.

When they entered the house, Peggy was overcome by the beauty of exposed wood and expensive décor. The home was filled with teak furniture, vases, wall hangings and paintings. Gleaming crystal and patina like wooden artifacts sat on shelves and tables giving the chalet a rich ambiance of its own.

Seth led Peggy to an upholstered chair, sat her down and disappeared, leaving the woman to wonder who owned the house he claimed was his.

Well, whoever owned it had expensive tastes, she thought.

While waiting, Peggy had time to think. Why was she helping a stranger instead of going home? What made Seth think her husband was a suspect? Was Jeff actually behind the kidnapping? How would that even be possible? Could he have planned her being taken when she emptied the trash, or was the whole thing really a mistake? It couldn't be Jeff. He loved her. He does love me, doesn't he?

The thought brought back memories of her childhood, picking petals from a daisy and saying the same two things. He loves me. He loves me not.

DOES HE LOVE ME? The silence was deafening...

Chapter 6
Motel Guests

"Okay. We're all set." Seth interrupted her reverie. "I've got my laptop, camera and clothes." He held up a large paper bag before taking her arm.

"Where are we going?" Peggy watched him place the paper bag on the car floor behind the driver's seat.

"I made a motel reservation," Seth said simply, never giving it a second thought. "What's with the look?" He waited by the car door.

When Peggy refused to move, Seth hurriedly began to explain. "I will not try to seduce you," he assured her. "But we can't stay here. The police will come to question me when they find Judd's body. They may even think I'm involved with your kidnapping, so I certainly don't want them to find you or your fingerprints at my house."

"Nevertheless, this doesn't look good," Peggy complained. "I'm a happily married woman. Staying with you at a motel gives the appearance of..."

"Impropriety," Seth interrupted. "C'mon frumpy. You're safe." He started the car. "We'll have two beds, but I'm hoping that's the last thing we use."

His last statement left Peggy puzzled. *What exactly did he mean by that?* If he was implying they would use just the one bed, the man was in for a big surprise. Walking would become his number one problem.

Within twenty-five minutes, Seth passed a neon sign and entered the long, treed driveway of the Shady Crest Motel in Clarence. After Seth parked the car, Peggy watched him pull a key from his pocket and enter room three, as she followed closely behind.

Peggy stepped into the room quietly and stood still while he snapped on the wall light switch that turned on a desk lamp. Her eyes swept the large room quickly. Seeing the two double beds with matching patterned spreads and drapes made her sigh with relief. Along one wall sat a long dresser with six drawers and the standard television set. Next to it was a desk with a chair tucked neatly in its center. In the one corner, a small round table sat between two small, upholstered easy chairs.

She assumed the closed door along the back wall was the bathroom. Above the door, closer to the wall center, was a large painting of a landscape. Another companion piece rested on the wall facing the beds. Obviously, they were done by the same artist as part of a contract. It seemed that all motels and chains had similar rooms, furniture and paintings. They bought in bulk. Peggy knew all about saving money that way.

After taking inventory of the room contents, Peggy concentrated on her partner in crime. Seth sat on one of the motel beds and searched his paper bag. He placed the laptop and camera on the large desk, and then tossed the rest of the bag contents to Peggy.

"You should take a shower and put those on. With all that dirt and glitter you look like something on the Syfy channel."

Seth watched a pair of high-heeled shoes sail through the air, as he heard the bathroom door slam and the lock click. So much for trust. He had no intention of witnessing a married woman taking a shower.

Somewhat later, Peggy emerged wearing a white smock and sandals and held a towel in her hands, which she used intermittently to dry her long blonde hair.

"Find anything?" she asked Seth, who sat quietly browsing his laptop.

Peggy tried to read the screen over his shoulder, but found herself glued to Seth's ears and the way they hugged the sides of his head. His crop of dark hair, with its auburn highlights, swept the top of his ears that stood at constant attention. They were so unlike Jeff's. Her husband's ears hung over, but ever so slightly. Why was she even making a comparison?

"Because you never compared any other man once you married your gorgeous husband," said a voice inside her head.

While these thoughts were running through Peggy's mind, Seth was having a few of his own.

With his back to her, Seth could smell the clean, mixed fragrance of shampoo and soap emanating from her body. He turned sideways to speak, but when he saw her in the smock and sandals, painful memories flooded his mind and prevented any conversational flow. He studied her for a moment. She was quite beautiful.

"Well? I know you came up with something," Peggy said.

"I found two phone bills with a number Judd called frequently. After searching the reverse directory I found the name, Nancy Travers. Mel wasn't listed, but it's the same address Judd gave me."

"Maybe she's his wife. You know...to keep everything in her name...so there's no trace of him. No listing. Nothing."

"It's possible," Seth mused. "He could be married to the woman and living somewhere else."

"That's illogical. If Mel had Judd take me to that address why would he live somewhere else?" she asked.

"Because he murdered Judd in that house," he reminded her. "If you wanted to get away with murder, the last place you'd kill someone is in your own home."

The more she thought about it, the more Peggy came to agree with his theory.

"Mel could have moved the body when I didn't come back," he added.

Seth turned away from the computer and casually assessed the woman. The white smock hugged the outline curves of her body and revealed the fullness of her breasts. Her blonde hair, which framed an oval face, swept down to her shoulders. When she turned to make suggestions, the white flecks of her large blue eyes seemed to turn a silver color. They reminded him of a gem store in Sydney that specialized in quality sapphires. He could understand men wanting a beautiful woman, but kidnapping this one made no sense at all.

"Well, frumpy, not only do you clean up well but you smell a lot better." Seth told her, his eyes fixed on her upper right arm.

She caught his stare immediately and raised her left hand automatically to cover the diamond-shaped scar, but Seth's response was too quick and his hand met hers in mid-air. His eyes locked on hers as he held her hand tightly.

"Life is full of imperfections. That's not the way one supposes it to be, but suppositions can sometimes cloud life's reality. It is what it is." He released her hand. "Accept it and move on."

Peggy pondered his comment and wondered about this strange man who spewed his philosophy so freely. Did he give his opinion often? There was only one way to find out.

"You're too damned logical. You must be a shrink," Peggy guessed. She wanted to know more about this man and also of the woman whose clothes she currently wore.

"I couldn't stand the confines of an office, listening to everyone's problems day in and day out. That wouldn't work for me. I'm a painter. How about you?"

"I have a gift shop in the Village of Williamsville," she answered. "In the Town of Amherst," she added, only because he lived in Lockport. "I should say I own a gift shop with my partner, Janice Sommers. She's my next door neighbor and my very best friend."

"And the business: is it successful?"

Although his voice was calm, Peggy caught the underlying innuendo.

"Janice and I are very close. She would never do anything to harm me, if that's what you're thinking. We may be in the black, but it's only by a comfortable margin."

"That leaves your husband? What about him?"

"Jeff's a hair taller than you and has your dark brown hair, without the reddish highlights. He's little heavier, maybe, and very good-looking. When we're out, women always give him a second look."

"I get that too, but it's usually because I have paint on my clothes," Seth laughed at the comparison. "But, I'm not interested in how handsome he is. I want to know what makes him tick. What's the relationship like between the two of you?"

"If you think Jeff had me kidnapped, you've been sniffing too much polyurethane. We just celebrated our fifth wedding anniversary tonight...last night," Peggy corrected herself, after noticing the night stand clock registering three in the morning. "We had a dinner party with my sister and friends."

Recounting the affair suddenly brought tears to Peggy's eyes. She had been so happy. That was less than twenty-four hours ago. She began to cry.

Seth bolted from the desk chair and shook her.

"Snap out of it, Peggy!" he scolded her. "I've been crediting you with some measure of common sense. This is no game. Judd took you to Nancy Travers' house, but what do we know about her? How is she involved?"

Seth sat Peggy down on one of the beds and began to speak softly to her. "I know you want to go home, but we can't risk it. You must understand that when this is over, your life will be normal again, but mine will be forever changed. Nothing will bring my brother back. So, this is not the time for us to cry or grieve."

"I know you're right, Seth." She wiped her eyes and nodded in agreement.

"Let's reconsider our situation," he said. "We know two things. First, someone gave Mel a sum of money to kidnap a particular woman. Second, Mel hired Judd to do the actual abduction for a cut of it. Whether kidnapping you was a mistake is unknown at this point, but until we learn who was behind it, and where Mel is right now, neither one of us is safe."

"So you do suspect Jeff?" Peggy challenged. "That's why you won't take me home or let me call him."

"I think we should stay focused on finding Mel. He will lead us to the person behind all this. That's our only goal right now."

"So maybe we should go to the house where I was held," Peggy offered. "The woman could lead us to her husband."

"I think that's our only option. But we need to scare her into contacting him."

"And how do you propose to do that, Mr. Stone?" She took a mocking tone. "How are you going to persuade a complete stranger to give up her husband?"

"With a phone call. I'll mention Judd's name."

"Do you think she'll know who he is?"

Her question had all sorts of ramifications. It was so absurd. Seth was going to telephone a woman about some stranger with the hope that she would contact her husband who was in hiding. The whole idea seemed ridiculous, but Seth was so sure of himself. That was Seth, focused and on target. Somehow, Peggy trusted him. He was cautious, to say the least, and very, very smart.

"Mel knows and that's all that matters. I think it just might work. Good thinking." Seth said. He was pleased with the plan and satisfied with Peggy and himself.

"If we can discover who ordered the kidnapping," Seth offered, "then we would come full circle."

"What about your brother?" Peggy's mind began to go in a different direction. "Who were his friends? What did he do for a living?"

"He worked as a mechanic in a gas station. Since he got released, he didn't come around much, so I don't know anything about his friends. I left messages, but he wouldn't always return my phone calls. I should have known something was wrong when he didn't cash my last check."

"You sent him money?" Her question brought back thoughts of Megan. That this man cared for his brother impressed her. His feelings for his half-brother, Judd, seemed to parallel hers for Megan.

"He's my brother – was – half-brother or not. It made no difference. After serving time in jail for armed robbery, Judd had a hard time making ends meet. The gas station didn't pay much, but he refused to stay with me. I thought it would be better for him in the long run. To be with me, I mean. Judd was always a little slow. People would take advantage of him. That's how he landed in jail."

"Talk about simpatico," Peggy brightened. "You had Judd. I have Megan, my sister. She married a wonderful man from a very wealthy family. Although he's very generous, Megan spends every penny as fast as she can and then comes to me for a handout. Jeff gets so angry."

Peggy continued to explain her sister's spending problem.

"Megan wants to feel she's arrived...whatever that means. All I know is that she's breaking my piggy bank and causing stress with Jeff."

"What does your husband do for a living?"

"He's works at Pace Securities. Are you familiar with the broker-age house?"

"Heard of it, yes. Familiar: afraid not."

Peggy was disappointed with his response.

Everyone heard of Pace Securities. Maybe he worked with another broker and was embarrassed by her question. No. That wasn't it. He probably worked with someone who dealt in mutual funds. Maybe Seth spent money on furnishing his beautiful house instead of being a smart investor, if of course, he told Peggy the truth, and the property was really his. Then, she remembered. Painters didn't make a lot of money. Seth wouldn't have a portfolio of investments. Peggy should have known better.

"Jeff just got promoted to office manager. He also got a nice bonus to boot. He deserves it, though, with all the hours he puts in, but I don't mind. Sometimes, I work late at the gift shop. It all seems to work out."

"So, you don't have children."

"Not yet. But I'd like four kids."

"And you're how old?" He eyed the woman briefly.

"I'm only thirty-three. How old are you?"

"Old enough to know that twins better run in your family when you're trying to get pregnant."

"I am not that old. I can have babies."

"Not tonight, you can't," Seth said, sitting on the side of the other bed that paralleled hers. "I need my beauty sleep."

He removed his shoes, got under the bed covers and turned away from the woman.

"How old are you?" Peggy asked, snapping off the bed lamp switch before slipping under the covers.

"I'll be forty in November. Now go to sleep. We are going to Nancy Travers' house in a few hours."

"I have one more question, Seth. Where did this smock come from? Who was the woman in your life?"

Seth became disconcerted. He did not want to discuss his personal life with a stranger.

"Her name was Helen. That was a long time ago," he said softly, his tone ending their conversation.

The room fell silent and soon, Peggy was fast asleep, her mouth making soft, little snoring noises into her pillow.

But, Seth lay wide awake with his memories: first, of Helen; and then, of Judd…

***

She was so beautiful…so beautiful and he loved her so much…

But it was all taken away by a reckless teenager on a wild joy ride with his friends.

Why couldn't he have stopped to help her? Instead, he left the wrecked car with her badly injured body inside, thinking he wouldn't be caught. Why didn't the stupid kid call the police anonymously, after leaving the scene of the accident?

Those questions dogged him for the last five years. As he dwelled on these thoughts in the darkness of the room, Seth's mind began to recall the events of that ill-fated night.

They were to meet after work for a quiet dinner at Evangeline's, her favorite restaurant. Seth knew something was terribly wrong when Helen hadn't arrived by six o'clock or answered her cell phone. Although the bank closed at five, Seth knew she always took a few minutes to review the day's transactions on her computer. Helen took her responsibilities of branch manager very seriously.

At six-thirty, when Seth left the restaurant to check the bank for Helen, he was caught in a line of traffic, by the wreckage of an automobile whose scattered parts blocked both northern-bound lanes of the highway. An hour later, Seth received a call on his cell.

It was too late…too late to see her and too late to hold her in his arms once again. All his hopes, all her dreams, all their plans…shattered. Everything in life for them was gone forever.

The face of his dark-eyed beauty faded slowly from his thoughts and yet, the question still remained. Could Helen have been saved, if the young man had taken time to investigate the wreckage, rather than skirt the scene of the accident? The thought continued to haunt him even now, after five years had already passed.

It took less than ten days to identify the three teenagers who were involved in her tragedy. Although the detective was very thorough in his investigation and had gathered a mountain of evidence against the driver, Seth felt the judge's sentence should have been much more severe.

But, Seth knew how the justice game really worked. A local politician's son would get much more preferential treatment than someone less influential and less fortunate. A high-powered lawyer came in, spoke eloquently about extenuating circumstances, and when all was said and done, the judge gave the boy a slap on the wrist with no jail time, two years probation and a year of community service.

As Seth vividly recalled, every family member was unhappy. The whole trial was a miscarriage of justice. A total farce. A charade of the judicial system.

The detective, who happened to be related to the family through marriage, seethed with anger over the leniency of the sentence and over the young driver's history of reckless behavior. Although Seth was not a member of the immediate family, the ones who suffered the loss of their loved one, he was the love of the lost one. And she, in turn, was his.

So whose agony was greater: *The one who left…or the one who was left behind*? Seth bitterly believed it was the latter.

Could I have changed Helen's path somehow? That question gnawed his psyche for years.

What if he hadn't visited Judd? Yet, he couldn't refuse his own brother. They went to look at a truck that was for sale. It needed work but Judd was a good mechanic. Seth knew he would be hit for money but that didn't bother him. So once the dealer agreed on price, the paperwork took very little time.

Seth often wondered. Should he have delayed seeing Judd? Made an appointment for the next day perhaps? Then, he could have met Helen at the bank and driven her to dinner in his car.

Afterward, she could have followed him to Lockport instead of going to her apartment. Since the accident happened on a Friday, they would have had the whole weekend to themselves.

The whole weekend… He had many of those now…but without Helen.

Now, he didn't even have Judd.

The darkened room was a perfect setting for memories of the dead and departed.

In time, Seth fell asleep.

Chapter 7
Megan

Early next morning, the loud ringing of the alarm clock awakened Jeff from a troubled sleep. It was seven o'clock. He turned to face a sleeping Peggy, but found himself quite alone.

He threw on his robe and raced downstairs, half expecting Peggy to be standing in the kitchen with his breakfast coffee. Instead, Jeff found the house the same as it was at two in the morning.

He thought of Megan immediately and telephoned her. Instead of getting the news he wanted, he heard a sleepy voice telling him his wife was not there. Then, suddenly hit with the realization of her sister's disappearance, Megan began a barrage of questions.

"If she's not at home, then where is she?" Megan demanded. Now, she grew seriously concerned. "When did you call last night?" she challenged.

From her confrontational tone, it was obvious that there was no love between them. "Of course, I didn't bother to check messages or caller ID when we came home. That would be ridiculous. Why would I? We were together hours earlier."

Megan listened to her brother-in-law's accounting of Peggy's absence and it was clear that she wasn't buying it. Leaving her a telephone message about Peggy's absence didn't cut it.

She had always considered Jeff a real shit. He never credited her sister openly for anything, not even the slightest accomplishment, such as a beautiful dinner party. But Megan knew better. Peggy was a very smart woman. She ran a business, kept an immaculate house and helped Megan accelerate her college program. And, although Peggy had a degree of her own, Jeff always considered himself superior to her. That was because he graduated from a very expensive and prestigious top liberal university in Pennsylvania and Peggy went to the State's University.

It was always Bucknell this and Bucknell that. There were times Megan wanted to nail the Buck right up his ass. She never discredited the school itself, only the student who attended.

Tuition was another matter of contention. Who paid for this? Good old mom and dad, of course. On the other hand, Peggy had gotten student loans, waited tables, worked at a department store and lived in an old apartment building off-campus where rats traveled the furnace arteries at night, continually scratching the wood of her ironing board closet.

Peggy spent the summers living at home while working in book-keeping at a department store and waiting tables on weekends. She needed the money to continue her college education. Megan knew Peggy's working hours were long and tiring, but her sister was highly motivated.

Her persistence eventually paid off. She was rewarded with a college degree and a bright future. But, a few years later, Peggy's life took a turn and spiraled downward. Megan's only explanation for this was …Jeff Roberts.

Megan's thoughts were brought up short with Jeff's next question.

"If Peggy isn't with you, then where is she?" He was on the offensive.

"You tell me," she responded. "We were with the two of you last night. Now she's gone." Megan looked at the bedroom clock. It was a quarter past seven. "She's not with me and from your account, Peggy's not with Janice. Obviously, my sister's not at home, either, so I strongly suggest you call the police back and report her missing." Megan was angry. She didn't bother saying goodbye. Instead, she hung up on him.

Megan continued fuming as she thought about Jeff's pretended concern. What kind of husband would react like that? If Jeff were really worried, he would have driven to the Crystal Bar or even to Megan's house, since he had not heard back from her regarding Peggy's disappearance. He would have made some real attempt to reach her. What wife goes missing on her wedding anniversary? That didn't make sense, unless something really was wrong.

Regardless of how Megan felt about Jeff, the man did make her sister happy. Peggy adored him. In her eyes, he could do no wrong. Even though he brought her gifts and seemed attentive enough, there was just something about the man that riled Megan.

Maybe Jeff was too overly aggressive. He seemed to have an ulterior motive for everything he did. And yet, he was always more than generous with his wife, always encouraging Peggy with her business. He had clever marketing ideas and clearly helped her. Then too, he was always understanding about her working late hours at the gift shop. And, often times, he worked late himself. Most men wouldn't put up with that. Brad certainly wouldn't.

Megan ogled her handsome husband who was sitting up in their king-size bed, listening to her side of the conversation. Today, his hazel eyes looked green, offsetting the dark coffee-colored hair streaked red in the morning sun. She liked waking up to the spirit of Christmas, as long as the rest of his body remained intact. There were parts of him she did not want changed, ever.

"He must think you're a real bitch," he said, leaning against a pillow.

"Then I'm glad this bitch didn't disappoint him."

The tart reply did not surprise Brad. Megan's sharp tongue and provocative vocabulary always shot to the heart of the matter. She said how she felt about things quite succinctly, most often using profanity to make her point. In her view, profanity was a universal language. Everyone understood what each word meant and its intended usage. No course work needed.

Brad studied his wife. She was a pretty woman. She had laughing blue eyes and golden hair that swept over her shoulders. She and her sister had the same hair and eye coloring, but the family resemblance stopped there. Like him, Megan had high cheek bones, and he towered nicely over her five-foot-three inch frame. Peggy was three inches taller than her younger sister and had more body mass, although she, too, was thin in stature. Where Peggy was even and almost placid in temperament, Megan was difficult and almost volatile on occasion.

Brad's hazel eyes often made him curious about their offspring. Not that their recessive genes bothered him. He questioned being the only Croft with hazel eyes. The rest of his older siblings were brown. His eyes were more expressive and much prettier, according to Megan. She never considered him the runt of the litter and always made her feelings known.

Brad's thoughts went back a year earlier to the New Year's Day party held by his parents at their huge house on Lebrun Circle. At their annual cocktail affair, only the exclusive Buffalo elite were invited, all wealthy friends and business acquaintances of the family.

It was on that occasion Brad sought to introduce Megan to this powerful group. And, while the immediate family thought they knew his new wife rather well through their intimate holiday gatherings, this particular party went down in their family history as an unexpected black omen of things to come. Brad remembered the events vividly. Who could forget it?

Introductions had been going extremely well during the early stages of the party. Megan had simply determined long beforehand to be in agreement with everyone's opinion, regardless of her own true feelings. She would merely nod and smile. So, all conversation flowed freely and without pause, making the consensus of opinion extremely positive. This was an intelligent woman whose views reflected theirs.

Yes, the attractive wife of the youngest Croft fit in nicely and was very charming, although a bit shy. These were the collective thoughts of the guests after Megan left one cocktail group for another in some part of the enormous living room. They excused her shyness, of course, because she was a stranger to them and still a bride, relatively speaking.

Since things had been going so well and, Megan was so warmly received by everyone, Brad decided to circulate among all of the guests, seeking out those she had not previously met and those with whom he had very little association.

Brad was called away for a few minutes shortly after introducing Megan, who was wearing a revealing cocktail dress, to ribald jokester, Winifred Pitts. When Brad returned, however, he was both surprised and highly amused.

In his absence, Winifred made an off-color remark to Megan, while tossing a few ice cubes from his drinking glass down her dress.

In the blink of an eye, Megan Croft clenched her balled fist upward and, after knocking the man to the floor, pulled off the ice cubes stuck to her breasts and brassiere, and hurled them at the mortified man's face.

"How do you like them apples, asshole?" She stood over him, her glaring eyes watching his every move, almost daring him to get up.

The crowd around them immediately froze, mesmerized and temporarily shocked by the small woman's actions. Then, like a swift crack of lightning, they raced to the outer periphery of the room where they remained like frozen statues, fearful of missing any snippet of conversation or contentious exchange should they flee to another part of the house. This was just too juicy to miss.

Winifred Pitts realized his error immediately. The new Mrs. Croft was not one to take an insult lightly. This, he embedded into his brain, as he rose slowly amid the fringed crowd who watched his every movement. Color flooded his cheeks with embarrassment and humiliation. However, the pugnacious woman nearby held her ground and never budged from the spot of combat, her eyes still fixed on his, as if challenging him to make another false move.

That was the day the very wealthy Winifred Pitts met his match.

That was also the day that Megan Croft became a hero to some, namely, the older, less attractive women, who were always targeted by Winifred's cruel jokes, and a villain to others, mainly, the ones who were fearful of Megan's behavioral reach.

Winifred knew better than to let things lie with the new Mrs. Croft. He did try to apologize, profusely. But Megan wasn't having any. She told him flatly. "Take your dirty mouth and leave this house." She wanted no part of him.

The humiliated jokester had no choice. He was no longer welcome.

A huge, thunderous applause from the cheering section of victimized women could be heard as Winifred Pitts swiftly made his escape. Later, as Brad recalled, Victoria Reynolds, a spinster in her fifties who owned huge blocks of prime real estate in the city, approached Megan personally and thanked her.

Within the month, the two women met for lunch and began a friendship by phone or by meeting for coffee.

***

"Now what?" Brad thoughts returned to the present. "You don't really think Jeff's involved with Peggy's disappearance, do you?" He felt certain of the man's innocence. Jeff really loved his wife, adored her. That was obvious to everyone who knew them. He would never do anything to harm her.

"No...I don't. Not really. I guess I don't want to believe it. But, I think the police will consider him a suspect if she doesn't show up soon." Still, Megan wondered if Jeff was holding anything back from her. Not telling her what he really knew.

"I know you're worried, Meg. But I don't know what to do." Brad threw on some sweat clothes. "Let's call Janice," he said.

In reality, he expected the woman knew less than they did. Megan's conversation with her sister's neighbor confirmed Jeff's story. Peggy was gone.

"Now, I am worried," Megan said. "This is so out of character for her. Something's happened to Peggy. I feel it."

In the bright kitchen overlooking their park-like yard, Megan and Brad sat at the table and studied each other in stony silence, thinking things too devastating to discuss openly.

Finally, Brad reached across the table for Megan's hand. "I'm here for you. I always will be." His eyes locked on hers. "No matter what happens, Meg, you can always count on me. I love you."

Megan eyed her compassionate husband and said softly, "I know."

Brad could only hold on to her hand and quietly watch the silent tears stream down his wife's lovely face.

***

Within two hours after Jeff called the police station, a portly man in his mid to late fifties and, somewhat taller than Peggy, appeared at his door and introduced himself as Ben Burrows, the detective assigned to his case. Without a nod from Jeff, the man with heavily sprinkled gray hair and large bulging eyes, walked into the living room, sat in a chair and started writing in his notebook.

"First, I need your wife's legal name and an accounting of the events leading up to her disappearance," the detective said, motioning to a chair directly across from him.

Burrows watched the young husband's nervous body movements and facial expressions closely as he explained his wife's disappearance. Satisfied that he captured the facts of the story, the detective stood up and began checking the house.

"Tell me where your wife was standing before you went to bed." Burrows acknowledged the sink location Jeff provided.

"Now, take me through your two o'clock search. Do not leave anything out."

Jeff led the detective up to their bedroom, then back downstairs again and all through the house. Burrows noticed the purse, ledger and car keys on the hall table. In the garage, he opened the car door and examined the seats and flooring inside before checking the trunk.

"What did you do next?" he asked Jeff.

"I looked in the back yard. I went around the side of the house but didn't see anything."

Jeff led Burrows to the back of the house where he had checked the yard hours earlier. "I didn't see anything here either."

As the two men retraced their steps back into the house, Burrows requested a list of names and addresses of the couples attending the anniversary party.

"And you're saying all six people left the dinner party around the same time?"

"Like I said, Peggy and I had a glass of champagne after they left. I went to bed at ten o'clock. I remember the time because I happened to look at my watch. I told her I had clients coming in today."

"You're planning on going to work?"

Nothing surprised Burrows. He had witnessed this kind of shock time and again. He called it, "the stress factor." Everyone handled it differently, although most people were too devastated to function and usually stayed at home by the phone.

"Just to check in," Jeff gave the detective a card with his cell number.

"A picture of your wife would be helpful."

Burrows watched as the husband calmly pulled a snapshot from a photograph album.

"I'll be in touch." The detective spoke, as they walked out on the driveway together. "Don't expect too much this early. On the other hand, she may be home before the ink dries off the paperwork."

"So, you don't think anything is seriously wrong," Jeff said, looking for reassurance.

"I can't say one way or another until I get all the facts. But, you'll be the first to know if I come up with something. In the meantime, if you can think of anything else, call me." The detective gave Jeff a small white card with his phone number scrawled on it.

As an afterthought, Burrows walked to the end of the driveway and looked up and down Carriage Hill East. Garbage cans lined the street like erect little soldiers.

"You must have been too tired to put your garbage can out last night," he said noting its absence.

"No. I did put it out on the driveway."

They eyed each other momentarily and then, thinking the worst, Burrows raced to the side of the house, popped open the garbage can lid and looked inside.

"You better put it out again," he said, and then watched the man wheel the large green can down the driveway before sliding into his car.

He could almost predict problems with the man in this case. Was Jeff Roberts telling the truth about the trash can or was he lying? Was there any connection between the wife's disappearance and the garbage can, or was it just a red herring?

Burrows would know soon enough.

Chapter 8
Breakfast

Seth crossed the room and studied the woman who lay sleeping on her side. Her profile was quite beautiful. She looked so peaceful and he hated the thought of waking her. Although he was up much earlier, Seth let her rest until he got things organized.

"Peggy," Seth called. He stood over her as she opened her eyes. "It's time to get up."

"I feel like I just went to sleep." Peggy sat up in bed. "What time is it?"

"Seven-thirty. Get ready. You're drinking Poag coffee in ten minutes."

Peggy eyed Seth and wondered if it was something like Starbucks, or a special brand that people on the escarpment drank. She wasn't ready for something that hokey. She pulled down the covers, stood up from the bed and tried to straighten her wrinkled smock.

"I need to splash some water on my face," she explained, slipping into the sandals Seth provided, and closed the bathroom door.

"I'll wait." Seth sat on the other bed.

Why do women always say one thing, but mean something else? Why didn't she just say, 'I have to pee and be done with it?'

Seth pondered this until he heard the toilet flush and then, running water. Peggy opened the door and smiled.

"I feel a lot better now."

Seth chuckled. She probably weighed less, too.

Peggy followed Seth directly behind the motel office into a large bright kitchen that overlooked a huge stone terrace with an expanse of grass that sloped down to a lake. Two large German shepherds lay quietly in the corner, weighing her presence as friend or foe.

"Hello, pretty lady," a man said, pulling out a chair for her. "I'm Poag Fowler."

Peggy sat down and counted four place settings around the table. She took the paper napkin near her dish and placing it across her lap, watched the man pour a cup of coffee from a big aluminum spouted pot and hand it to her.

"Milk and sugar's right there," Poag said, pointing to the center of the table, and then turned his attention to a frying pan cooking something that smelled extraordinarily good.

"Okay, Gabriel." A voice spoke quietly to one of the dogs.

Without a moment's hesitation, a large German shepherd walked over to Seth and sat down. As Gabriel expected, his master's hand ran over the fine, shaded brown and black coat of his head and body.

"I missed you too," Seth said, as he fingered the dog's ears.

Peggy sipped her coffee quietly, dividing her attention between Seth's show of affection toward the large dog, and Poag, the tall skinny man with a weather beaten face, who seemed to be using all four stove burners for a cooked breakfast.

"Hey!" A woman's voice shouted from somewhere outside. Her voice became louder as she came upon them. "Is that Seth's car?"

Gabriel stood up momentarily, turned toward Seth, and then sat down again. Gabriel knew the rules.

"It is," the woman said, rushing into the room and hugging Seth from behind. "You stay in room three?" Her last question no sooner left her mouth when she noticed the newcomer seated at the table.

"Well things are finally looking up," the smiling woman gushed. "You're like a shiny new penny to this boring, old group. God knows we could use some new blood around here." She seemed to address no one in particular.

"Peggy, Clarisa." Poag made the introductions while placing huge mounds of food on the table.

Peggy eyed the big breasted woman who gave her a toothy grin and acknowledged the overture.

"Oh. God. Eggs in the hole with bacon strips and grits," the dark haired woman complained loudly, as she inventoried the breakfast platters. "You gotta start cooking other things."

"I like eggs in a hole," Poag answered. "If you'd leave your husband like I asked, you could make anything you wanted for breakfast."

"Sure, it's not enough that I clean all nine rooms, now you want me to be your cook," she chided. "What's the benefit in that?"

"After breakfast, we'll go to room five and I'll show you," Poag laughed. "I may be long, lean and gray, but I still have what it takes to make a woman happy."

"Yeah, yeah, yeah. Keep eating those egg yolks," Clarisa snapped back, "and I'll bury you in that Jacuzzi."

"What I want buried, isn't in the Jacuzzi," Poag corrected, "and the king-size bed would add a helleva lot to my comfort."

"That's in room five, too," she whispered to Peggy.

"I take it back. Don't leave your husband," Poag scolded, "the man's probably one hen-pecked son of a bitch."

His remark, while causing laugher among the three of them, left Peggy somewhat bewildered. Catching Peggy's attention, Seth quietly pointed to his ring finger.

"I can't believe that." Peggy caught his signal. "I'll bet they really enjoy each other."

"If you knew her husband, you wouldn't like him," Poag replied.

"Oh, I don't know. You two might be a lot alike," she needled. "Ornery and horny."

"I like this woman," Clarisa told Seth. "Where have you been hiding her?"

Clarisa's simple question drew a sudden burst of laughter from Peggy and Seth.

"Don't ask." Poag warned the woman, before turning to Seth. "I think you should take some food and water with you. It could be a long day."

Apparently, Poag knew the whole story. He knew where they were going and their hope for a positive outcome with Nancy Travers. Peggy wondered about Seth's relationship to this man. What was Poag to Seth that imbued so much trust?

"Where are they going?" Clarisa demanded when the breakfast was over. "What's going on that I don't know about?"

"I want you to fix them a picnic basket with sandwiches, water and fruit." Although he met the woman's silent stare, his demeanor spoke volumes.

"Oh." She followed Poag's lead. "Something is going on. Is Judd in trouble again?"

"That's what we're trying to find out." Seth was being honest with the woman. "We just don't know the situation at this point."

Clarisa eyed Poag and began wrapping the sandwiches which she placed in a box that contained bottled water.

"They can eat these while they're waiting." Clarisa gave Poag the box.

"What makes you think that?" Poag demanded.

"Listen, you old coot, I know your ways. If Seth needs a box of food, I know damn well he's not going to Sherkston Beach. He's either going on a trip or he's waiting somewhere for something to happen."

After addressing Poag, Clarisa turned to Seth, a worried expression on her face. "Are you two in trouble? What can we do to help?"

For some inexplicable reason, her overly concern and compassionate manner hit Peggy like a ton of bricks. Tears streamed down her face and shaken with emotion, she rose to embrace Clarisa.

"That's the kindest thing we've heard in twenty-four hours," Peggy cried.

"Ah, honey, don't you worry," Clarisa patted her back gently. "Whatever it is, Seth will take care of it. He's a good decent man, not a bit like Poag."

Withdrawing her arms, Peggy stood a few inches away from the big angular woman and began to laugh hysterically.

"I needed that," she told Clarisa. "It's been a difficult time for both of us." Then Peggy eyed Seth. "We're leaving now, aren't we?"

"It's time we get on our way," Seth agreed.

He led Gabriel to the corner of the room and sat him beside the other German shepherd who never moved from his spot.

"Stay with Reese," Seth commanded. "I'll be back for you later." He gave Gabriel a final pat.

Peggy approached Poag and faced him directly. "I want to thank you for everything. It was sweet of you to take us in." Peggy reached up and kissed the man's cheek.

Turning to Clarisa, Peggy embraced the woman and smiled. "Maybe you should give Poag another chance and leave your husband."

"Then he better do more than take me to room five," she laughed. Clarisa turned and kissed them both with a final warning to Seth. "You call us if you need the other sign."

***

When they approached the car, Peggy questioned Clarisa's comment as she watched Seth place the packed food box on the car floor. "What was that all about?"

"Fishing." Seth pulled out of the driveway and turned right toward Clarence Center.

"Fishing?" Peggy repeated.

"Poag uses the 'Closed for Remodeling' sign when he wants to go fishing," he said.

"Does he do that often?"

"He remodels about three times a year."

"So, when he and Clarisa go on a fishing vacation, they post a remodeling sign?" Peggy asked. She wanted clarity.

"No. When Poag goes fishing, Clarisa visits their children. One lives on the west coast, somewhere around Los Angeles. And the other, lives in Portland, Maine. Clarisa likes to see the grandchildren. Everybody works, so it's tough for them to come here. But, they do every few years."

"Well then, who fishes with Poag?"

"His brother-in-law usually goes with him. Sometimes I tag along."

Peggy began storing the information Seth gave her. He and Poag were obviously very close friends, maybe even relatives. When Seth needed a safe place to stay, he went to Poag's place. The fact that it was a motel was irrelevant. That's why he seemed so unconcerned about impropriety. It was obvious that Seth told Poag about Judd, the kidnapping and the police. So, Poag knew their relationship was one of survival. Poag even knew about Nancy Travers and their attempt to scare the woman into producing Mel.

"Is that why you have a key to room three?" Peggy continued her questions.

"What do you mean?"

"I saw you, Seth," Peggy exclaimed. "I saw you use the key to open room three."

"Poag gave it to me a long time ago. Yes, I keep a key. When we go fishing, I sleep at the motel, so we can take off early. Then, I crash when we come back. I also go there when I want to be with Poag. Most people have a spare bedroom in their house. Poag doesn't. His guest bedroom is in the motel."

"So he keeps the room just for you?"

"It doesn't work that way. When I want to visit, I use the room if it's vacant. Poag always tells me beforehand."

"How convenient," Peggy sounded judgmental.

"No. It is what it is. Poag runs a business. He can't leave most of the time. So, if I want to see him, I do the visiting. Instead of sleeping on their couch, I use one of the motel rooms."

"Room three."

"Ninety-nine percent of the time, but, I've never been in room five," he laughed. "Come to think of it, I wonder if Poag and Clarisa ever slept there."

"And the other one percent?" She pushed for an answer.

"His God-awful couch."

"You seem close."

It seemed like such an understatement, but she wanted to understand their relationship. There was something between them that went deeper than friendship. Peggy could feel the chemistry between the two men. What tied these two totally different men together? They had to be related in some way. There was no other explanation.

"We have been for a long time," Seth replied, ending their conversation.

Chapter 9
Interrogations

Burrows slid behind the wheel of his car a little more slowly, realizing the Beef on Weck that he enjoyed eating so much, was beginning to showcase a paunch. As he checked the names of the three couples who attended the anniversary party, he found Jeff Roberts' list not only curious, but very telling. He began to recap the man's story of his wife's disappearance.

A husband wakes up to find his wife missing and calls his sister-in-law and next door neighbor. After failing to find her, the husband notifies the police who then assign a detective to the case. Enter Ben Burrows.

In police work, it was common knowledge that the people closest to the missing person would be questioned first. Or, in this case, Burrows would question the wife's sister, Megan Croft, after speaking with the husband of the missing woman. Yet, Megan and her husband, Brad Croft, appeared third on Jeff Roberts' list of names. Dead last instead of first. Why?

Even more curious were the names of Alice and John Beck whose names topped the list, although they apparently had no knowledge of the woman's disappearance. Jeff Roberts never phoned them, according to Burrows' notes.

His many years as a detective taught Ben Burrows to study the constants present in each and every case: facts, body language and modified behavior.

And Jeff Roberts' list was very telling.

That he placed Megan Croft third indicated a lack of close family ties, a strained relationship or one that escalated with his wife's disappearance.

Burrows totally dismissed the second placement of Janice and Fred Sommers. Still, listing the names of John and Alice Beck, first, puzzled him. Was it unintentional, work related, or did Jeff Roberts hate his sister-in-law that much?

***

Pulling out of the driveway, Ben Burrows took a sharp turn off Carriage Hill East and decided to call upon the first couple on Jeff Roberts' list. It came as a surprise that John and Alice Beck lived so close by on Carriage Hill West. Then he remembered. Janice Sommers lived next door to Peggy Roberts. Burrows found the housing proximity of the three couples rather interesting. It was the sister, Megan Croft, who lived farther away from the group of invitees to the anniversary party. He made a mental note of that.

As he approached the Beck address, he noticed a small thin woman walking from the side of her house toward the front door.

"Can I help you?" she asked him.

Sliding slowly from the automobile, Burrows immediately identified himself. "You must be Alice Beck," he said.

She was one of the most beautiful women he had ever seen – long black hair, delicate white skin and large dark chocolate eyes that studied him from under her noticeably long eyelashes.

Inwardly, Burrows felt embarrassed. The detective knew he had been staring at her far too long. He wasn't certain whether or not the woman noticed.

"I came by to ask you and your husband a few questions," he said, as calmly as possible.

"Is something wrong?" Alice Beck ushered him into her living room. "John's out of town and won't be back until tomorrow evening."

"You might be able to provide me with the information I need," he said lightly. "How well do you know Peggy Roberts?"

"We're very good friends. I've known her since they moved here four years ago," Alice replied. "We were at their house last night."

"Did anything seem out of the ordinary to you?" he asked.

"No. Everything was lovely. We celebrated their fifth wedding anniversary over a delicious dinner. Why?"

There was no question of the woman's sincerity. She knew nothing of Peggy Roberts' disappearance.

"Her husband reported her missing."

"Oh, my God!" she gasped, "When? We were just with her...them." She sat down. "I can't believe it. Megan. Did you call her sister? She and Peggy are very close. If anyone knows where she is, it would be Megan."

"Mr. Roberts already did that," he answered. "Where were you after the party?"

"We came straight home. John had to leave early this morning for a meeting with some clients. He went to bed but I watched a little TV before turning in."

"Where is the meeting? In what city?"

"He was driving to Chili, near Rochester. Why?" A frown crossed her face. "You can't believe John was involved with Peggy's disappearance."

"Oh, no," Burrows reassured her, as he continued writing in his little notebook. "This is just part of my follow-up. But, I'll need to know the person or persons he met there. It's just routine."

He stopped writing momentarily to recap the beautiful woman's story.

"So for all intents and purposes, the two of you came home after the party. Your husband left early this morning for a meeting and won't be home until tomorrow evening. Is that correct?"

"Yes," she agreed with his timeline.

"This morning, I showered and did the breakfast dishes. I have to run a few errands before going to work. I'm on the afternoon shift at Millard Medical."

"You're a nurse?"

"Been there seven years," Alice Beck said proudly. "It's a great hospital."

Ben Burrows closed his notebook, thanked the woman and left the house.

Now that's what I'd call a great piece of ass. Burrows thought to himself, as the woman stood in the doorway and waved goodbye to him.

As Burrows edged down the driveway, he noticed the placement of Alice Beck's garbage can along the side of her house. Obviously, the woman was returning it to its rightful place when he drove in. Still, he noticed the other trash cans on the street still lining the driveways.

It caused him to remember Jeff Roberts' story regarding the placement of his own garbage can the previous evening. The man must have been very distressed by his wife's disappearance.

Ben Burrows dismissed Jeff Roberts' story completely. The man had simply forgotten to set it out.

***

After his normal Beef on Weck lunch at Harry's local drive in, Burrows parked at the Municipal Building in Williamsville, and then walked casually down Main Street to Mill. He stopped in front of a large store window and took inventory of the various displays of perfume, gifts and scented soaps.

The shop sign that read *Gardenia Place* was not a misnomer. An overwhelming fragrance enveloped him as soon as he opened the door.

"God, this place smells sweet," he murmured.

"That's us, Ben. We're very sweet people," Janice Sommers greeted him. "It's mostly the soap and candles that smell, but you're not here to buy. You want to talk about my partner, Peggy Roberts. What do you want to know?" She was very direct.

They were good friends, approximately the same age, somewhere in their fifties and both starting to turn gray. She had the refined look of an educated woman with a moneyed background. Soft-spoken and quite intelligent, she was a genteel sort of woman with a graceful figure and clear brown eyes.

He, on the other hand, was more direct, perhaps a little coarser, but someone who knew how to deal with people tactfully enough to get the wanted response to his many questions.

"I don't know anything about Peggy Roberts. What can you tell me about her?"

"She's a very smart business woman with an uncanny knack of knowing what sells. Peggy's very even-tempered and extremely easy to work with. She lives next door to us."

"Would she just go off somewhere?" Burrows said, and then caught himself. He had not meant to phrase the question that way.

Janice questioned Ben with her eyes, but remained silent.

"You know what I mean," he said.

"No. She would not go off on a toot in the middle of the night," she answered coldly.

"How do you know?"

"Because I know her. It's not the kind of thing she would do."

"And the husband? You told him to call the police."

"Fred talked with him and suggested he call. Fred thought he sounded rattled and wasn't thinking clearly."

"You disagreed?"

"I thought he sounded angry because Megan wasn't home when he phoned. He forgot she was meeting people at the Crystal Bar."

"I get the feeling you aren't that crazy about him. Why?"

"No," she corrected him. "That was not my intention. He's given us some good ideas for the shop. I have to credit him for that."

Janice fell silent for a moment.

"What aren't you telling me?" He studied her response carefully.

"Peggy adores the man. In her eyes, he can do no wrong. But, I wish he'd make more of an effort to get along with Megan. Peggy is like a referee sometimes."

"But you think their marriage is sound enough and strong enough to survive."

"Jeff loves her. I never questioned that. They are wonderful together. He would never do anything to hurt Peggy."

"So what do you think happened? Why did she disappear? Could she have been angry enough to leave home?"

"Ben, I run a gift shop. It's your job to find out what happened to her."

"That may be true," he quickly agreed, "but if you are so close to Peggy Roberts, why are you so calm about her disappearance?"

Intentional or not, his comment hit a very raw nerve. Without a moment's hesitation, Janice raced to the front door of the shop and waved him out in anger.

"For a detective, you don't know shit about the workings of people. She's like a daughter to me and you better find her."

Before she could slam the door shut, Ben broke into a broad smile.

"Now that's the kind of reaction I was looking for," he shouted.

"Well, when you see Fred at Planning, you tell him I kicked your ass out of my shop!" Janice slammed the door on him.

"Oh, my God," Janice murmured, as she leaned against the framed entry way, "I'm beginning to sound like Megan." The thought was very, very unsettling.

***

There was a light sprint in Ben Burrows' step after his interview with Janice. Now, he had some real insight on the case. His first presumption, that Jeff Roberts disliked his sister-in-law, Megan, proved to be true. She was the main source of tension between Jeff and Peggy Roberts. Janice had just confirmed that. Otherwise, according to Janice once again, the couple had a good strong relationship.

Now, there was only one question that remained, as there always seemed to be in domestic cases, and it was a question that Ben just had to determine. Could something have caused Jeff Roberts to kill his wife? He was the prime suspect. But, did he do it? More important still, could Burrows come up with evidence to prove it?

Burrows had no facts. He had no information that would even hint of a domestic quarrel. He had nothing other than a five-year marriage that was saddled with a quarrelsome sister-in-law. End game. Burrows had nothing. Soon, his light sprint became the slow methodical step of someone lost in thought.

Burrows found himself back at the Municipal Building on Main Street and started walking toward the back parking lot. He turned suddenly, entered the building and took a flight of stairs down to the Planning Department.

"Thought I'd drop by to say hello," Burrows greeted the gray-haired man who was part of his monthly poker group.

"No, you didn't, you old rascal," Fred Sommers answered. "You talk with Jeff?"

"This morning, but didn't get much. He hasn't a clue to his wife's disappearance."

"I know that trick," Sommers laughed, "but I don't think he'd do anything to hurt her."

"Janice said the same thing," Burrows answered.

"You saw her? Janice, I mean." Fred caught Ben's nod.

"I just left her."

"How was she?" Fred's concern was glaringly obvious.

"Clear, coherent and very calm. Is there something I should know?"

"She was a wreck this morning. They are very close. The business may be in both names, but Janice couldn't make it without Peggy. I can't explain their relationship. She wanted to close the shop until you found her. I talked her out of it."

"Well, you did one helleva job. She kicked me out of the place."

"She didn't." Fred said, his face frozen in shock.

"I was to tell you that she kicked my ass out of the shop," Ben repeated Janice Sommers' statement.

"Oh, my God," Fred met Ben's stare. "She's been talking with Megan again."

"The sister?" Ben understood Fred's meaning. "I plan to see her shortly." He turned to leave.

"Take your gun," Fred advised, as he watched the door close behind him.

Silently, Fred Sommers was amused, not because his wife was becoming influenced by Megan's vocabulary, but because she had just thrown their friend out of the gift shop. It was so unlike her, so out of character. Yet, it was wonderful that Janice stood up to Burrows when she believed she was right. He was so proud of her. His fingers nimbly dialed a number.

"Hi," Fred said, after he heard the voice of the woman he loved. "Ben just left. He told me what you did. You bet I'm proud. In fact, I'm going to grill you the best steak in town…What?"

Fred stared down at the mouthpiece in disbelief. "Before dinner?" He housed the receiver and began humming. Maybe Megan was a better influence than he realized.

***

When Ben left Fred, he did not go directly to the Croft residence to interview Megan. Instead, Ben did what he always did, when puzzled by a case. He crossed Main Street and walked down a path leading to a working mill that was overly busy in the fall selling cider. He found a bench near a small noisy waterfall, and watched the rushing water ripple swiftly over the large uneven rocks and small flat stones. Occasionally, he'd spot a small fish swimming by.

The deserted area and the sound of rushing water seemed to relax him. He needed time to think. He needed to sift through his written information before interviewing Megan and concentrate on what was relevant to the case. She was the only relative who could provide pertinent information about her brother-in-law. But would she? Could he get her to divulge anything? What would he say to her? What questions could he ask?

He had no clues to her sister's disappearance. Nothing seemed to stand out. There were no calls for ransom. Therefore, the case did not have the hallmarks of a normal kidnapping, where some family member was usually contacted within a twenty-four hour period.

So the question still remained. Did Peggy Roberts simply vanish or was she murdered?

He glanced down at his watch. It was four o'clock. Rather than call this infamous sister for an appointment, Ben Burrows decided to make a surprise visit.

Chapter 10
The Frog Prince

In his line of work, nothing shocked Ben Burrows. He had seen everything and met all types of people; those who commit crimes, the victims left behind, and the so-called upstanding citizens who used the law to shield their corrupt money grabs.

So, there was nothing Megan Croft could say, or even perhaps do, to astonish, unnerve or surprise him. His years of detective work had steeled him for everything or so he thought.

As he walked up three steps of the lovely, pillared home on Los Robles Street, Ben expected to ring the doorbell and be ushered into the house by the woman whose reputation was notorious. Instead, a small young woman opened the door before his finger hit the chime and pulled him inside before banging the heavy door closed.

"Where have you been?" Megan Croft demanded. "I've been waiting for you all day."

When Ben pulled out his credentials, Megan shoved them aside.

"Janice told me you looked like a frog, so you seem to fit the bill. Not that your bulging eyes surprise me. You're shorter and more... pudgy than I pictured you to be. But I didn't expect the double chin or the peppered gray hair."

"Well, don't stand there, come in and sit down. I need to ask you some questions." Megan pointed to the living room where she offered him a chair.

"For starters, where is my sister? Do you know why she disappeared? Did Jeff start a fight with her?"

Megan fired a barrage of questions at the detective, never giving him a chance to respond.

"That's it, isn't it? You don't know a damn thing." She threw up her hands in desperation. "So, what do you do, when you don't have anything to go on?"

"You're right. I don't have anything. I came here last instead of first, hoping there was something you could tell me."

"Nice try, Burrows. It is Ben Burrows, right? I wrote your name in my tablet. The kind you carry. Instead of playing me, tell me what you have." Megan wondered if the pencil and notebook he always carried were extensions of his hands.

"Virtually nothing," he said, eyeing his notes. "Your brother-in-law detailed the events of last night's search for his wife, his phone calls to you, the neighbor and police. This morning, after he spoke with you, Mr. Roberts reported your sister's disappearance to the police once again. Since this is so out of character for your sister, I thought I'd take an early look."

He didn't want to tell the woman that he knew Peggy Roberts was Janice Sommers' partner at their gift shop. Her name would come up regularly with Janice's, when Fred mentioned something about them at their monthly poker games. So, instead of waiting the full forty-eight hours, as he should have legally, he started the investigation as a token of friendship for Janice. It was the least he could do.

She had been there for him at the most desperate time in his life. Janice Sommers, the genteel woman, who always looked so prim and proper, had dived into blood, defecation and tears and cleaned up everything, while staying the course. If the Roberts woman turned up, nothing would be lost but his time; the time he would have given freely, since there was no other way to repay Janice for everything she had done.

If, on the other hand, something did happen to Peggy Roberts, then it would be time well spent. He'd have an edge. He would have been there at the start of the case.

He recalled Janice kicking him out of the shop. He had played the hand well. She would think the right amount of time had passed for the start of his investigation. She wouldn't know. Fred was another matter. He was a counter. But, Fred wouldn't tell his wife. He would just thank his poker partner with a six pack of Budweiser.

His thoughts changed immediately when Megan Croft spoke.

"So, you did talk with Jeff this morning," she mused. "Funny, there was no answer when I called the house this afternoon."

"He did mention going to the office for a little while. Something about meeting clients, I think."

"My sister goes missing and he runs off to work. What an asshole."

"Going to work is not uncommon when something like this happens. People handle stress in different ways." Burrows tried to explain. "I told him I'd contact him if something comes up."

"So, you don't suspect him of doing anything to Peggy? I mean," she sighed. "You know what I mean."

"I don't rule anything or anyone out." His implication was clear.

"If you're including me, get over that thought. My sister means everything to me. If that son of a bitch did anything to her, I'll kill him myself."

"It would help my case if I could understand the bitter relationship between the two of you."

Their eyes met briefly after his statement and he noticed a shift in her body language.

Megan eyed the man's ring finger. "Do you love your wife more than life itself?" she asked.

"Excuse me?"

Her question gave him pause. It was so illogical and irrelevant to her sister's disappearance. Yet, Burrows determined if he wanted to get the information he desperately needed, it would be much better to let her digress.

"It's a simple question, with a very simple yes or no."

"Where is the relevancy?"

"That's what you don't understand. It is relevant. And, obviously, your answer is no."

"You're wrong, Mrs. Croft. I would have given anything and everything."

"Megan," she corrected, and then followed his muted response with a question. "Is your wife no longer living? I'm sorry," she said, catching his nod.

"Was she ill?" Megan asked, in a much softer tone.

"Julie passed away six years ago. Pancreatic cancer."

There was a great deal of sadness in his voice. And, as he sat on the living room chair holding his pencil and tablet, Ben Burrows looked very small and extremely pitiful.

"You loved her." Megan said simply.

"Indeed, I did," he agreed.

"Then, you can understand the relevancy. Jeff does not love Peggy that way. I know it. I feel it. Everything in their marriage is slanted his way. So, I don't have to tell you where all the love and adoration lies in that union."

Megan was on a roll.

"He must have fifteen suits and a dozen pair of shoes. He gets the best of everything –the best clothes, the best portions of food, control of the remote and Peggy gets crap. He is so into himself: a real egotist and a sadistic one at that."

She was adamant. "I know. I lived with them. I saw what went on."

Suddenly, Megan leaned forward, almost touching Ben's face. "You must think I'm a real bitch. Well, maybe I am," she said, standing up. "Come with me to the kitchen, I want to show you something."

When they crossed the front hall, Megan hesitated in front of a long wall mirror, as if she had suddenly remembered something relevant about her brother-in-law.

"Every time 'Boy Beauty' comes to the house, he always stops here to comb his hair and check his teeth. A real class act."

Megan ushered the detective into the kitchen and poured coffee from a carafe. A plate of cookies sat in the center of the table.

"The coffee's fresh, but I can't vouch for the cookies. They've been drying out all day for you," she laughed.

Megan sipped her coffee slowly.

"She never bought much for herself. The rag Peggy had on last night was the same thing she wore for Christmas, New Years and just about every holiday in between. But, she always looked nice at the shop. That's only because those clothes were part of her trousseau."

"But, other than material things, there was no abuse or anything like that," Ben concluded.

"Of course, there was abuse. It was all mental. I saw it." Megan went on to elaborate.

"He graduated from Bucknell in Lewisburg, Pennsylvania. Some residents regard it as their own prestigious Ivy League University. In many ways it is. I mean its ranking and programs. Like Penn is thought of. Only Philadelphia's Penn is a lot bigger and more well-known. "

Making certain she still had his full attention, she continued.

"Peggy went to Penn State and he always rubs her nose in it when they are out with a group for drinks. He'll say, 'Penn State is only known for its football team, which doesn't say much for its sports or academics.' Intellectually, he considers Peggy his inferior. Her degree means nothing in comparison to his. He is such a shit."

"Maybe so. But, Jeff didn't discourage her starting a business," he interrupted. He gleaned that bit of information at their monthly card game when the girls first started their operation.

"Well, that's because he couldn't. We came up with the idea at Janice's house one night when he was working late. We had already checked the rental. It's a prime location."

Megan continued enthusiastically about her sister's project.

"Besides, Peggy worked in a gift shop department when she went to college. So, she had a lot of experience in collectibles and that sort of thing. And, given that she is really good with numbers, it was a no-brainer."

"Still, you've given me nothing to suspect Jeff Roberts of his wife's disappearance."

"Unfortunately, that's true. But, he doesn't love her like he should. And, I think she's too easily swayed by his good looks, his charm and his bullshit babble."

"Not loving her enough does not make him a suspect of foul play. By your standards, he may not be the greatest husband in the world, but who's to judge? The woman loves him. She may think they have a great marriage."

Ben knew he could not convince her. She doggedly disliked the man. Nothing could ever change that. But, he had to make Megan understand, that at some point, she would have to accept Jeff Roberts, if only for the sake of her sister's happiness.

"They've been together for five years," he continued. "Obviously, he must be doing something to make her happy. Maybe their relationship is not the problem: maybe it's the divide between the two of you."

With that remark, Burrows expected the plate of cookies to be thrown at him.

"No," she disagreed, as if lost in some train of thought. "Sometimes, I think there's something wrong with her thinking. She's so giving and he's so...selfish." Megan wiped a tear with her napkin. "You've got to find her."

"Aside from her husband and you, is there anyone else, some other family member?"

"Only Josephine. Josephine Burke, our witch mother in Florida, but Peggy wouldn't be with her. The woman never cared about us. She was always too busy doing her own thing."

"And you're sure of that?" He wrote the woman's name on his pad.

"Why would I lie?" Megan challenged. "The woman said dreadful things and hid everything from us, including our father. I found an old letter of his in the garbage one day stained with tomato sauce. I must have been in my teens at the time. When I confronted her with it, we had one helleva fight."

"I never told Peggy. So, why am I telling you?" She faced him directly.

"I haven't the slightest idea," he shrugged, "but you didn't answer my question. Could Peggy be with her now?"

"Absolutely not! She was as anxious to leave home as I was."

"You're sure I shouldn't call her, your mother I mean?" Burrows asked, somewhat confused.

"That would only bring me grief. Believe me, life with Josephine was a living hell."

Burrows became silent, waiting for an explanation.

"Aside from being totally nuts and man-crazy, I think the woman's bipolar. If she were a monkey, she'd be swinging from tree to tree, searching for someone to screw. The real screwing, you understand, would come after the sex."

As if she were talking to herself, Megan added, "The woman should have an hourglass tattooed on her forehead."

Ben listened closely to Megan's cynical description of her mother. There was no love for the woman she portrayed. The story seemed so familiar. He had heard it so many times before.

Yet, aside from the hatred she spewed for her mother, there was still the loving sister, a surrogate, perhaps. All through the conversation, Burrows sensed something even more sinister, a despair, of sorts, vastly similar to those deep, inflicted wounds that often appear within a very dysfunctional family. These were the wounds that come from depending on someone who was supposed to protect and love you, but instead, turned on you for other more enjoyable pursuits.

What painful circumstances caused this young woman to react this way? Had Megan's mother ruined her formative years when she needed nurturing most? Or was her father to blame? What happened to him? Was he still alive? Could Peggy be with him? He considered each of these questions.

He studied the young woman, and immediately felt a great deal of empathy for her at that moment. Her seminal years could not have been easy. Whatever trauma took place in her young life left its permanent mark. She learned to deal with it head on and become stronger for it. Obviously, it had happened long ago.

"Maybe," she pondered aloud. "No. It's been too long. She could even be dead." Then, Megan went on to explain her statement.

"We did have an Aunt Gwennie, Josephine's sister, but she moved away when I was real little. We were never close after that, although I don't remember why. She was so much fun."

"Is there anything else you can tell me?"

"Only if you keep it to yourself; it has nothing to do with the case."

"Then, perhaps, you better not discuss it." Ben had no interest in her family secrets or closet skeletons that were unrelated to the case.

"Listen, dammit, I want to tell you," she objected. His calm disinterest was beginning to annoy her. She felt that, although the information may not have been relevant to her sister's disappearance, it would help him understand how much she loved her sister. How close their relationship really was.

"I want your full attention," she demanded. "This is very important. You will hear or have already heard that I am the biggest spendthrift in Williamsville or perhaps all of Buffalo."

Megan stood on her chair and reached the top shelf of the china closet. Hidden behind a porcelain teapot was a bank book, which she placed on the table after jumping off the chair.

She moved closer to the detective.

"Jeff will tell you that I never give him any leads. You know," she went on to explain, "the names of people who might be interested in buying stock. That's true. I haven't. Hell will have to freeze over first, and then the answer would still be no. He can go pound salt."

Through all the vitriol spewed by Megan Croft, Ben wondered where this was all heading. He sipped his coffee silently and continued to listen to the woman's harangue.

"You'll also hear that I borrow money from Peggy and never give it back. That's true…to an extent."

Megan displayed a bank book. The names of the two sisters appeared on the account. In neat columns, there were deposits made on different days in varying amounts. The current sum read $7000.14. The latest entry was over a week earlier.

"This is all Peggy's money. I run in and tell her I'm short of money for a pair of shoes or some stupid thing and then I deposit the funds."

She stopped abruptly.

"Gotcha, didn't I?"

Surprise was written all over Burrows' face.

"I plan to add ten thousand to the account when I get a nursery school job. She got me to where I am today and I owe her."

"Why are you telling me this?"

"Because a large part of me is hurting. She always looked after me. Took care of me. And, unless you find her, my world is shattered."

A tear dropped down her cheek. Megan paused momentarily. "Can you possibly understand how much I distrust him? I wanted Peggy to have something to fall back on, in case their marriage failed. Obviously, I have no faith in their union."

"So, she doesn't know about the bank book?"

"Only three people know: Brad, me and now, you."

"Brad is so supportive. Whatever I want to do about paying back my sister is fine with him. He's offered to give me the money, but I want to do it on my own, if I can. Peggy didn't know she was signing the bank card. I ran into the shop one day and said I needed her signature on a student loan that had been repaid. So, the rest was easy."

"Maybe I should be watching you," Ben said, putting away his tablet and pencil.

"I expect you here at noon, tomorrow," she said. "I am not letting you off the hook that easy, Ben Burrows. You can bring me up to date over lunch."

"You're serious?"

"Well, for Christ sake, you have to eat somewhere, so why not here? You think I'm incapable of making a sandwich?"

If Megan Croft were a man, Ben would have said he had a pair the size of bowling balls. The woman came on like an unexpected avalanche, making demands and heaving accusations everywhere. Her continued attack against her brother-in-law had no real bearing on her sister's disappearance. They were more behavior-oriented than substantive. Yet, if Megan Croft had her way, Jeff Roberts would have been strapped to a gurney, given a lethal injection and then, had Peggy reappear, big as life. The trial, previously held, would have already taken place in the courtroom of her mind.

Burrows continued to sit silently, not wanting to commit to lunch the following day.

"Okay, I won't wait until tomorrow for my confession," Megan said, simply.

"You have a confession?" Burrows echoed.

"Janice never said you looked like a frog. She said you had very large eyes which accounted for your being such a good detective."

However, Megan disagreed with that assessment. "Personally, I think that's a lot of crap," she said. "Big eyes do not a good detective make. A good detective is like a hunting dog in pursuit. He never gives up until he gets his prey."

Their conversation was suddenly interrupted by Brad Croft's entrance into the kitchen.

The tall, curly-haired man kissed his wife and then introduced himself to Ben.

"Any news on Peggy?" Brad asked.

"I've been at this all day. No one has seen her and..." Burrows stopped. "We have no other reports," he said, rising to leave.

He gave Megan a small, white card with a phone number scrawled on it. "If anything changes, call me."

"Tomorrow, at noon," Megan reminded him.

Ignoring her reminder, Ben turned to Brad. "If you can think of anything that Megan hasn't covered, let me know."

"You can't be serious," Brad said, breaking into a grin.

Ben caught the implication immediately and chuckled. Megan Croft was never short of information. In fact, the woman covered more than he needed to know.

When the three of them crossed the hall, Megan stopped both men in front of the long viewing mirror, and then, after moving in closer for a better reflection, bared her teeth.

"Let's do it right," she directed them. "Who has a comb?"

Understanding her reference to Jeff, the two men eyed Megan sideways and began to laugh. Within minutes, Ben Burrows was off to his parked car.

He thought about the woman he just interviewed. Regardless of her reputation as a hard nose, there was something poignantly sweet about her on things that mattered...a love greater than life itself and the communion of marriage, permitting two people to grow as one.

Did Megan actually believe this or had she read Romeo and Juliet too many times and decided on her own interpretation?

Clear to him was Megan's love for her sister. Even clearer was her dislike of her brother- in-law. But, what rang clearest of all was Megan's succinct vocabulary. The woman had the simplest way of making him understand her every meaning.

Although he wasn't planning on joining Megan for lunch, he really enjoyed their conversation. Yes. He liked Mrs. Croft very much. She was the raw pearl in a sea of oysters.

Then, he thought back to a specific part of their conversation and broke into a broad grin.

Preschool mothers had no idea what they would be getting in Megan Croft, nursery school teacher. Would their children acquire an expanded vocabulary of the English language or simply repeat what they heard at home?

As Ben Burrows slowly slid into his car, he heard the bank clock on the corner of Main and Los Robles chime five times. He could not remember when time passed by so quickly during an interview.

***

After Ben left the Croft household, Megan sat down to ponder their meeting. The detective had questioned everyone at the anniversary party about their relationship with Peggy. But he waited to interview her last. Instinct told Megan he was collecting clues to determine an underlying motive for Peggy's disappearance. And, she wondered if he might be considering Jeff's involvement. Maybe he was considered a suspect. It would not surprise her.

She always hated her despicable brother-in-law for seeing Peggy as intellectually inferior. In Megan's eyes, the smarter of the two was her sister. Unfortunately, Peggy's brains went south when she fell in love with Jeff. The physical attraction had been too great. That would explain her sister's stupidity. Peggy let her hormones do the walking, right into that asshole's bed.

Her thoughts went back to Ben Burrows. She was not a suspect. Of that, Megan was certain. However, throughout the interview, nothing escaped those bulging eyeballs, or the words she uttered, which he continuously copied on his note pad.

Megan thought about the sneaky little man who unwittingly wormed his way into her heart. To invite him to lunch on their first meeting was a first, even for her. Never had she done anything so stupid before. Even worse, she told him about the bank book for Peggy. Why did she do that? Nothing came to mind. But, somehow, she knew her little frog would never divulge the secret they shared. There was something about him that seemed to fulfill a need of hers. It was like a communion of sorts. He would find Peggy...one way or another. Megan had very deep feelings about that. His calm demeanor gave her the reassurance she so desperately needed. A kind of empathy between them seemed to exist. It was real. She felt it.

In a way, he would be the hero in her fairy tale, but it would be in reverse. Normally, the princess kisses the frog to incur a structural change, to a handsome prince of sorts. No matter how many times Megan would kiss Ben Burrows, he would still be a frog. And yet, if she could be privileged to have one single fantasy, Megan would ask for a Frog Prince of her own, existing just for her, in some imaginary kingdom. A pudgy, bug-eyed Frog Prince of her very, very own.

In the quiet room of her thoughts, she fancied the idea with a great deal of relish.

Suddenly, as if a great magic force erupted, Megan Croft was swept from the living room chair through the gigantic hall mirror and into the realm of her own private kingdom, a vast, but colorful manicured garden of stately trees and flowers. Then, walking along a stone path which led to her throne, she turned slowly to face the duty before her.

She was dressed in a red velvet long-sleeved ceremonial gown, banded at the neckline with multiple chains of gold, and on her head sat a golden tiara sprinkled with diamonds. Princess Megan stood tall and reserved, before tapping the golden wand, crusted with rubies and diamonds, on the shoulders of a kneeling figure. Moments later, the kneeling figure rose and silently withdrew from the throne room mirror.

A FROG PRINCE IS CHRISTENED

Later, when Megan relived her fantasy, she wondered if a princess could actually christen someone to be a prince or if he had to be born into a royal family.

"Who gives a shit?" she told herself. "It's my fairy tale and I can do whatever I want. Right now my Frog Prince is on a quest to find my sister."

Chapter 11
Remmy's Tavern

Seth was silent as he sped along the highway toward Nancy Travers' house in Clarence Center. Conversation was not needed. They were both lost in thought, each with a different perspective.

To Seth, Nancy Travers was the means to Mel. Once the man was found, Seth would quickly accuse him of Judd's murder. Then, Seth would tell the police he actually witnessed the shooting death of his brother and detail everything he saw through the window. Once the police verified the information, he felt certain the man would go to prison.

Peggy's thoughts were completely different. Once Nancy Travers led them to Mel, everything would be resolved. He would be convicted of murdering the man who kidnapped her and sent to prison. Seth would then acknowledge her husband's complete innocence and she and Jeff could go on with their lives.

More than anything else in the world, Peggy wanted to go home. She wanted the safety of her husband's arms around her, his strength protecting her. Peggy wanted her world to be normal again.

Jeff had told her so many times he would always take care of her. Peggy needed to hear him say that again. In turn, she wanted to tell Jeff how much she loved him...missed him... yearned to be with him. She dwelled on these thoughts until they reached their destination.

***

When they finally arrived in Clarence Center, Peggy noticed how little the small community had to offer in terms of shopping conveniences. Aside from the few bars sprinkled along Main Street, the highway that fronted the housing subdivisions, there seemed to be no supermarkets or drugstores nearby. Still, there may have been a shopping center farther east, somewhat closer, but in the opposite direction. Peggy had never traveled out that far or that way. In fact, she wasn't certain of anything beyond Clarence Center Road.

Seth turned down a two-lane street and searched for an address on the postage-size lots. He passed Nancy Travers' house deliberately and seemed to be looking for something else.

On the opposite side of the street, two houses down from the Travers' address, was a vacant lot, strewn with cans, wheel-trodden snack bags and weeds, helplessly waiting for someone to come with a tool set and manicure it. The faded For Sale sign, with its remnants of cardboard, was partially torn from its post and sat leaning downward, kissing the yellow dandelions in the gentle, blowing wind.

Without a moment's hesitation, Seth pulled into the vacant lot and turned the car around to face Nancy Travers' house. He carefully maneuvered the car and parked close to an adjacent house, making it appear as part of a normal landscape when someone came to visit.

"We're here," Seth pointed up the street. "That's her house. Now, we wait and watch."

Sitting there, Seth wondered if his mind was playing tricks on him. He hadn't remembered the bungalow that way. By daylight, the house appeared weather-beaten and shabby, as if a coat of paint had not touched the wooden frame in years. A down spout, loosened from its housing, stood vertically against the concrete block foundation, adding another facet to the unkempt appearance of the property. The grass had not been cut and seemed immeasurably high.

Still, it was night when Seth visited the bungalow, so his knowledge of the house exterior and grounds would have been negligible. The only things he could recall correctly were the walkway and the windows above the low foundation.

Seth removed his camera from its case, hoping to catch a shot of the woman at some point.

"I don't see her car. Maybe she parked it in the garage," he said, looking through a multi lens that enlarged his view of the house.

He dialed the woman's phone number and listened to the ringing of her telephone. "Her answering machine is off. She may not be home."

"So, we just sit here and wait?" Peggy asked.

"Unless you can come up with a better idea." Seth removed his seat belt and hit a button to push back the front bench seat, jolting and startling her simultaneously. She said nothing, but was obviously surprised by the sudden movement without warning. Her shocked look surprised Seth. Moving back the one-piece front seat never bothered Gabriel. So what was her problem?

"Get comfortable. We may be here for awhile."

Peggy followed Seth's lead for comfort by slipping off her sandals.

"How long have Poag and Clarisa been married?" Peggy changed the subject.

"Listening to them, it's hard to tell. They've been together as long as I can remember. But when they got married...I really can't say. I've known Poag for about eight years."

"What about you?" Peggy was curious. "You said Judd was your half-brother. You have family?"

"Everyone has family: some more than others, some less."

Seth knew where this conversation was headed and he felt uncomfortable. Under no circumstances would he divulge any personal information or bare his soul to this woman. The chances of meeting her again anywhere were slim to none, once they found Mel. At that time the police would take over the case and he and the woman would part permanently.

"So where do you stand in this pattern?" She pushed for an answer.

"I have Gabriel," he cut her off, refusing to offer any further information.

Peggy picked up on the sharpness of his reply and wondered what he was hiding. She couldn't force him to talk about himself, or for that matter, have an extended conversation relating to his friends. And, it was more than obvious that he wasn't interested in knowing anything further about her or her extended family.

It didn't matter. Once they found Mel, the whole kidnapping-murder thing would be over. The police would take it from there and she would never see Seth again. Did anything connected to him really matter, when all she really wanted was to be in Jeff's safe arms again? Conversation, at that point, was totally unnecessary.

However, she did wonder how Seth knew about the vacant lot. She remembered feeling the car make a very quick turnaround the previous night, when she lay in the back seat as his temporary prisoner. This must have been his parking spot. She was surprised that he remembered it, considering his emotional state with the death of his half-brother.

As they sat in the car and waited for Nancy Travers to come home, Seth became more and more aware of the soft, intermittent sounds breaking the silence.

Peggy Roberts was snoring in her sleep.

***

At ten minutes past twelve, Seth shook his companion gently and focused his camera on a car pulling into the driveway of the house under surveillance.

"What?" Peggy eyed the man aiming his camera. "Oh, she came home."

Peggy watched Seth shoot several pictures of the woman pulling grocery bags from the trunk of her dark blue Ford.

"Are you going to call her?"

"Let's give her twenty minutes. Just enough time to put the groceries away before we ruin her day."

A short time later, Seth checked his watch and waited for the woman to answer the ringing phone.

"Hello." A distinctive voice answered.

"Hello, Nancy." Seth said in a warning tone. "I know about Mel and Judd's illegal operation."

"What do you mean?" The woman could be heard screaming, as Seth pressed the end button on his cell phone.

"She's totally bewildered!" Peggy exclaimed before realizing something was terribly wrong. "What have you done?"

Seth sat far back in his seat with his eyes closed and heaved silently, never responding to her comment.

Peggy had witnessed that same stony silence before...

The shock of the killing came first, long before the realization of it had set in. She knew what was going on; she could understand it all.

They were parked at the scene of the kidnapping. They were watching the house where a violent crime had taken place. A crime he witnessed. Now, Seth was reliving the murder of his brother all over again.

"Seth," she said, shaking his arm. "Seth. You have to stop this. Do you hear me?"

"I can't believe he's dead. I don't want to believe it. I was supposed to take care of him and I failed." He moaned in disbelief.

Peggy noticed the moist glisten of his eyes and knew she had to act promptly. He could not dwell on the past twenty-four hours. He had to focus on their job at hand.

"Listen," Peggy scolded. "I wanted to go home last night, but you asked me to help find the man who killed your brother. So, if you want to do something for Judd, you have to find Mel."

"You're right," Seth soberly agreed. "Do you trust me, Peggy?"

"This is a helleva time to be asking that question."

"What if we find Mel and don't learn who ordered the kidnapping? Your life could still be in danger." His concern was genuine.

"I don't believe Jeff ordered the kidnapping. There would be no reason for it. I know it sounds silly but the man really loves me."

"We'll see," Seth said simply.

"What is that supposed to mean?"

"Let's see what happens first. I may have someone who could help us."

"What's Poag going to do, keep me sequestered in room three?"

"Then, I can visit both of you." Seth began to chuckle.

"Show me how to use the camera." Peggy ignored the remark. "You may want me to take pictures."

Seth moved closer to the woman to explain the mechanics of his camera and found her hair was softer than he imagined. As time passed, they ate the sandwiches Clarisa packed for them and waited for Nancy Travers to leave the house.

"What is taking her so long? Do you think she saw us? Maybe she called Mel to keep him away from the house." Peggy was becoming more and more skeptical of the plan's success.

"No." Seth reassured her. "She needs to see him. Watch his expression. She wants to know about this Judd person and what their operation consisted of. More to the point, whether or not something illegal is going on. The truth. That's what she needs to witness."

"What makes you so sure?"

"Few people surprise me, Peggy. That's how it is. Murder may be an entirely different matter, but I don't think so."

Seth said nothing further. The camera rested on a used Ziploc sandwich bag that sat between them, while they watched silently and waited for Nancy Travers to make a move.

***

Later that afternoon, Nancy Travers slid into her blue Ford and drove to the outskirts of town, unaware that Seth and Peggy were following her at a safe distance.

Within twenty minutes, they watched Nancy Travers pull into the parking lot of Remmy's Roadside Tavern and walk into the building.

"Judd's book matches," Peggy whispered. "Mel must come here."

"Why are you whispering?"

Seth parked carefully between two cars along one side of the painted red building. From there he could view the tavern's equally red front door and check the license plate of every car entering the unpaved lot.

"I don't know," she whispered again. "But, now that we have a clue, we might be on to something."

"I think you're right." Seth reached for his camera.

As they waited for a glimpse of Mel, Peggy's frustration began to mount.

"I don't ever remember spending so much time in a car, watching some old house or some shabby-looking saloon, just waiting for something to happen," she sighed. "This place must be a hundred years old. They don't make structures with vertical boards anymore, do they?"

Seth remained silent, letting her continue to vent.

"When you think about it, we are so far out of our league. We have no legal authority. Just what do we hope to accomplish?" Her question demanded an answer.

"Give it time and we'll soon find out."

"Barf."

"You sound like Gabriel."

"That is one big German shepherd. He does listen to your commands, though, I'll give you that. Did you train him?"

"To a degree. He was a police dog before I got him through some budget cuts. But, make no mistake, Gabriel's a guard dog. If crossed, he will attack."

"Oh," she said, quietly. That was more than she needed to know.

Peggy thought about Gabriel. Although he was beautiful and had gorgeous coloring, she would never feel safe around the large, muscular attack dog. To be honest with herself, she was afraid of him, of his size, his demeanor...of his teeth. Fortunately, Peggy would never have that problem, once she was at home with Jeff.

She felt Seth's hand touch her shoulder and point to a car entering the parking lot. The two men who occupied the car seemed to linger in conversation before exiting the stationary vehicle. Nevertheless, recognition was instantaneous.

Seth aimed the camera as Mel left the passenger's side of the car and began to snap several pictures in succession. When the driver exited the vehicle to remove his jacket and place it in the back seat, Peggy lunged at Seth spontaneously and slammed him hard against the car door. She began to scream like a wild woman under attack, unnerving him completely.

"Picture! Take his picture! Both men. Quick! Quick! Before he gets back into the car."

"Okay! Okay!" Seth responded painfully, his hands and arms still upright taking pictures.

As he tried moving away from the door handle scraping his butt, he felt Peggy's body banging hard against him again, crushing him further under the steering wheel.

"More! I need more pictures!" she bellowed, watching the man enter his car.

Seth could not determine her actions or her mood. Was she excited or angry? Either way, if she continued to squash his body with hers under the steering wheel, his testicles would be flattened for life, and his penis would forever resemble cooked rigatoni.

Still holding the camera, Seth tried to lower his arms. "Either you move or drive the car. You can't do both," he said angrily. Their heads faced each other nose to nose. "Move," he demanded. Everything from his chest on down ached.

"Don't you see? It all fits." Peggy inched away from him finally. "It's John Beck! He's behind all this."

The revelation came as a surprise. The fact that she recognized the stranger with Mel put a different perspective on their whole operation.

"And you know him, how?" Seth was skeptical and sore.

"He works for Jeff. Well, now he does. I told you Jeff just got promoted. John and Alice were at our anniversary party last night... whenever." Peggy found the timeline confusing.

"What's the connection?"

"What do you mean?" she insisted. "It's clear to me."

"Quick. Get down!" Seth pushed her head below the dashboard.

Peering from the lower portion of the windshield, they watched Mel and Nancy Travers exit the bar. John Beck had already driven away. Then Mel and Nancy Travers entered her vehicle. The woman was never given the opportunity to meet the man who drove Mel to Remmy's Roadside Tavern.

"What do you suggest we do now, Mr. Stone?" Silly as the question seemed, Peggy needed some sort of guidance.

"We need to talk. Something doesn't fit." He responded quickly.

Seth looked at his watch. It was four-thirty. They had spent the entire day watching and waiting. Whether or not they had all of the answers would depend on the information only Peggy could supply.

"You hungry?"

"Not another sandwich," Peggy pleaded.

"We can't take the chance of being seen," he reminded her.

"Then, I suggest you think of a place to eat, but I need the hall pass first," she said.

Given the directive, Seth eyed the woman in amazement. Peggy Roberts was no shrinking violet. She made her wants known – very clearly. Yet, he did not find her uncompromising or difficult. Peggy was just as interested in getting her kidnapping resolved as he was in having Mel arrested for his brother's murder. They were a good match in that respect. Nothing else mattered to either of them. They had this one priority. They were on the same page. Everything else was peripheral.

Chapter 12
Betrayal

When Seth drove out of Remmy's parking lot, he had no idea where to take Peggy after they made a quick stop at the gas station. His home on the escarpment was out. He couldn't chance meeting the police if Judd's body had been found. And, by now, the police could actively be looking for Peggy. In both cases, it would be better if they could escape scrutiny until they determined John Beck's role in the kidnapping.

He thought of Tammy's Table. The restaurant was known by the locals as a great place for good food. Also in its favor were the tall wooden booths that gave diners a feeling of privacy.

The only drawback was its darkness. A small candle lighting their meal may have been romantic for couples in love, but he needed to see the woman's facial expressions. And he had to watch her body language.

When all was said and done, Seth had to question Peggy Roberts to determine John Beck's motive for the kidnapping. He felt certain Peggy had information that could help them, but didn't know it.

"Where are you taking me?" She noticed the mileage sign to Depew. "We're heading south, aren't we?"

"I think it's safer," he replied. "I don't think we'll run into anyone we know."

"We looked in Elma for a house when we moved to Buffalo. I think it was on Chairfactory Road. The streets have the strangest names. The one that really got me was Girdle Road," she laughed.

"And where do you live, Mrs. Green?" she asked an imaginary figure.

"Oh, my dear, Mrs. Smith, I found the most beautiful house. You must come to visit us at 124 Girdle Road."

"I wonder if the women who live on Girdle Road wear corsets," she said aloud. Peggy heard Seth chuckle although he never responded.

Seth listened to her prattle on until he reached the Henry Hayward Inn in East Aurora. He turned into a long treed driveway, that half-circled a pond filled with ducks enjoying the blue-green water, and then parked in a nearby lot.

"This is beautiful," she exclaimed, delighted with his restaurant selection.

Before Peggy could say anything further, Seth ushered her up the veranda steps to a table overlooking the pond.

"We need to talk."

"And we will, just as soon as you feed me."

This was not the response Seth expected. He eyed the woman first and then the menu. At that point, he knew it was useless to bring up any subject until they ordered.

"I want something substantial," she said.

Seth gave her a knowing smile and wondered how she would react if he told her to order one of everything on the menu.

Within ten minutes, Peggy was enjoying a buttered roll and ready for his questions before their steaks arrived.

"How do you know John Beck?" Seth questioned her again.

"I already told you. He works for my husband."

"Is the relationship between them strictly business?"

"God, no," she shook her head. "We're close friends. We met John and Alice four years ago when we moved here. That's when Jeff started working at Pace."

"So, if John Beck worked at the company before you moved here," Seth mused, "shouldn't he have been promoted?"

"Instead of Jeff?"

"He had the seniority," Seth was quick to point out.

"I don't think it's a problem. He acted fine at the party."

"That's not surprising," Seth dismissed the remark. "Anything else would be interpreted as sour grapes."

"I don't believe it."

"Right now, you shouldn't be defending him." Seth reminded her. "He is the one responsible for your abduction and possible murder."

At that precise moment, the waitress brought their dinners and Peggy refrained from answering his remark until they were alone.

"Do you really have to spoil my dinner?" she groused. "John Beck has always been a friend. I don't think he meant to harm me."

"Regardless of intent, you would have been killed. Get that through your head. This wasn't a ransom-type kidnapping. The man wanted the woman dead. We just don't know whether you or someone else was the intended victim."

"And just how are you going to determine that, Mr. Stone?"

He read the sarcasm in her voice and knew she was unhappy, but not with him, although it seemed that way.

Still, Peggy knew he spoke a truth that she found hard to accept: a four year friendship had been broken in twenty-four short hours.

She knew what John had done. But what had she done to him? Why would he want to kidnap her? Why was it necessary to kill her? After all those years of being together socially, did she really know the man?

"Money could be a motive," Seth said, pointing a piece of forked steak in her direction. "Who has the money, John or his wife?"

"That's absurd. Money's not an issue. They're loaded."

Now they were getting somewhere. Money and motive often went hand in hand. Granted, there were other motives for murder – revenge, power, another woman in his life – but, Seth wanted to explore the money angle first.

"So? Which of the two has the money?"

"John does, of course. He has a tremendous clientele list, according to Jeff. I'm talking big investor blocks. He's been networking and expanding for years. Why?" Peggy looked confused.

"What about his wife? What does she do?"

"She's a nurse at Millard. Her shift changed six months ago and she hates it."

"What's their relationship like? Are they close? Happily married? Are they still in love?" He placed a great deal of emphasis on his last question.

"I really don't know. They seem happy together, but I was never privy to their bedroom performance, so I can't give you a testimonial. But, she did complain to me."

Seth ignored her saucy comments and hooked on her last statement.

"You mean he's tight with money?" Seth pressed.

"She's angry because he no longer helps her around the house. Then too, Alice always wanted to move to Wellington Woods, which is a more prestigious address, but John refused."

"So, what happened?"

"Nothing happened," Peggy replied. "They're still living on Carriage Hill West. And we're on Carriage Hill East, still getting their mail by mistake."

Peggy took a sip of water and stopped talking. Seth was no longer eating. He sat quietly, looking lost in thought, while staring at the pond of water filled with waterfowl. Peggy wondered if he remembered her sitting across the table from him.

She folded her arms calmly, trying to capture Seth's mood, and followed his stare.

A large mallard followed by five little ducklings fluttered single file across the water. As if on cue, ducks, of different colors and families, fashioned together and joined the procession for a glorious pond parade. The ducks were smart. They knew food was coming.

"What does she look like?" Seth spoke suddenly.

"Who?"

"Alice. Alice Beck," he repeated.

"She's quite beautiful and a really good friend. When we moved here, I needed so much help. You know, doctors, banks, post office, that sort of thing. Alice was always there for me."

"Have you noticed anything different about her?"

"Her hair is darker now. I didn't remember it that way before."

"She has dark hair?" he asked, recalling the picture Mel showed him briefly. "What else can you tell me about her?"

"You'll think I'm jealous."

"I won't think anything of the sort," he said, and then thought to himself, *this is how women always preface their bitchiness.*

"It's her clothes. Nipple line and short."

The simple remark caused him to laugh. Describing another woman's style of clothing was not what he expected. Yet, why would she be so affected by some friend's change of wardrobe and hair color? The thought that Peggy might be jealous tickled him. What he sought was a behavioral change, not something cosmetic. Nevertheless, Seth found her comments intriguing and thought he would play along. Something of importance could shake out during the conversation.

"And how long have you noticed this change in Alice?"

"That's just it. I don't know. I mean, she's always been beautiful, but I never really looked at her that way until the party," Peggy said. "She just looks different."

"Does her husband seem to like the new Alice?" Seth waited for her response. He had to determine John Beck's place in his wife's new look.

"I wouldn't see why not," she offered. "As I said, she's a beautiful woman."

"That could be a reason."

Seth left her wondering what he meant by the cryptic remark.

Peggy was totally unaware that she and Seth were thinking on two different levels. Every scrap of information she offered, Seth absorbed and used, as if he were piecing together a giant puzzle. Fortunately, he was able to sift through all the data she provided to determine how the kidnapping occurred, and perhaps a plausible motive. Now, he had to learn which woman was the intended victim.

From Peggy's perspective, the information she gave Seth meant nothing. It was all common knowledge. Who worked where? Lived where? Had money? In the long run, what did it prove? Nothing! The only thing that really mattered was John Beck's appearance with Mel at Remmy's Roadside Tavern. That fact, alone, proved he was involved with her kidnapping.

"I have two more questions for you," Seth said. "How much money does Jeff Roberts have, and would he pay John Beck to have you kidnapped?"

Peggy gasped. She clenched her teeth and curled her fists into a ball. She was so enraged she couldn't speak. She wanted to smash his face.

"How could you even think that?" she roared openly.

"You think this is fun for me?" he exploded, complimenting her rage.

"My brother was murdered because you were taken, and I was dragged into this mess because Judd called for help. Mel knows I made the phone call today and will come looking for me," Seth growled, his fury increasing tenfold. "Right now, everyone's a suspect in my book, so get off your high horse and let's get on with it."

The sudden outburst had a sobering effect on Peggy. She knew how Seth felt from the very beginning. He trusted no one. That fact was very evident. And so was his temper.

That Jeff was a possible suspect in her abduction was made very clear when they had their first conversation. When they found Mel with John Beck, it confirmed her husband's innocence in her mind. So, why did Seth continue to suspect Jeff? Had something occurred that she wasn't aware of? But, more important, would he tell her?

Peggy thought about the substance of their conversation over dinner and through dessert.

He had asked a multitude of questions. Some probed deep into their personal life. Others questioned the motives of their friends. Now, it seemed like Seth was on a crusade to uncover even more secrets. Suspecting Jeff was totally ridiculous. He would not do anything to harm her. The man across the table needed serious help.

"Well, do I get the honor of some response?" Seth baited her.

"If my sister were here instead of me, she would have thrown a glass of water at you."

"Wrong again," he corrected. "Megan would never have been taken in the first place. She would not have married Jeff. Anyway, you're stalling, which means you have doubts about my questions," he said.

"I don't actually know our net worth. But, I think we are quite comfortable, financially. What I mean by that is: we come and go freely, take vacations, eat out, that kind of thing." Peggy felt satisfied with her financial summary.

"I find that strange," Seth told her.

"What's so strange? I think we're doing great."

"Someone, who owns a gift shop, has to know to the penny where she stands in the operation. Yet, this same individual has no idea of her own personal worth. I'd say something is very strange here. Don't you and Jeff talk?"

"Of course, we talk. Jeff takes care of the household expenses and naturally, our investments. That's his business."

Seth continued to stare at the woman.

"As far as I'm concerned, there is no basis for the second question. Jeff and I have a good solid marriage. We love each other very much. He would never harm me." Peggy could not be swayed into thinking otherwise.

"You're convinced of his innocence?" Seth asked again.

"Of that, I am certain," she insisted.

Peggy never pretended to know all the financial details of their accounts and investments. Although she knew where the financial records were kept, Peggy seldom checked. It never mattered. When she needed money, Jeff was always there with cash or a check. He never asked for an explanation, unless the money was for Megan. And Peggy used her credit cards freely enough. So, why was Seth questioning her again about her husband? Seth wasn't privy to their business. He had no idea how secure she felt with Jeff. It was time she went home to her husband.

"I needed to hear you say that again," Seth said, quietly.

When he caught the waitress' attention, Seth requested she bring a blank sheet of paper to the table. Peggy wondered what he had in mind for her this time. Shortly afterward, he had her make a drawing with his pen.

"You can't be serious," she said.

"Think about it. Where were you when it happened?" He continued to study her. "What were you doing?" Seth had her relive the abduction.

"That doesn't make sense."

"It does, when you factor this east-west housing area with identical numbers," he pointed to a section of the drawing. "If your mailman can get the address mixed up, Judd could have done the same thing. Remember, he wasn't the shiniest penny in the pond."

Then, Seth continued. "Judd must have been watching your house instead of John Beck's. Poor bastard was waiting for the right moment to grab you. That mistake cost him his life."

"So, you think my kidnapping was definitely a mistake." She wanted reassurance.

"Between the mail mix-up and the picture Mel had, I'm certain of it. If you recall, I wondered why they didn't release you somewhere. You never saw Mel's face or Judd's for that matter." Seth caught her nod.

"Now, I know," Seth added. "John Beck wanted his wife to be found dead after the kidnapping. But, I still don't know why. Maybe money was the motive."

"And I was the mistake? But, that still doesn't explain why they had to kill me." Peggy reminded him.

"I told you yesterday. There could be no witnesses, remember? Mel kills Judd. I murder you and Mel shoots me when I return to the house. I understand now why that was necessary. There is going to be another plan."

"I don't follow you. What plan?"

"You can't recognize Mel. At least that's what he thinks, so he moves freely. And, you know nothing about John Beck's involvement in all of this. No one saw us at Remmy's Tavern. So, months from now, Mel and John Beck will hatch another plan to get rid of Alice. It won't be a kidnapping this time. It will be more of an accident. They'll have to make sure that Judd's body is not found, at least for now. Judd would simply disappear without telling anyone. That way, I wouldn't get overly suspicious. Remember, Mel doesn't know I witnessed the murder."

Seth stopped talking momentarily. "Still, something's not right. The reason has to be money." His fingers drummed the table.

"Maybe John found someone else and doesn't want to split his money, if there's a divorce," he added. Adultery was a more satisfactory explanation.

"Shouldn't we warn Alice?" Peggy asked. "At least tell her what happened to me. We can say we saw John with Mel. That should convince her."

"If she came to you with this story, would you believe her?" Seth waited for an answer.

"No. I wouldn't. I'd want some kind of proof and we don't have any," Peggy said, totally disappointed.

"We have pictures. We can show her those," Seth reminded her.

"We can't wait." Peggy became impatient. "We have to go to the hospital when her shift's over. John's supposed to be out-of-town, so we know he won't be with her tonight." Then she detailed Jeff's conversation with her about John's schedule.

"We'll go somewhere and talk. She has to be told," Peggy insisted.

"Oh, God," she suddenly remembered. "You're still in danger. Mel will come after you."

"Once you're safe, Mel's no longer an issue. Gabriel will see to that."

Seth moved the empty dinner plate away from him and watched Peggy sip her coffee.

"Would you like something else? More coffee? "

Seth knew the woman had to be more than satisfied with the meal. She had eaten her salad first, and then proceeded to the entrée, wiping the plate clean with two dinner rolls, before devouring a large piece of pecan pie. He wasn't taking inventory of her food intake. He was wondering how she could eat so much and still be thin. Did she exercise or jog every day or almost every morning like he did? Maybe her metabolism accounted for the caloric intake. Why was he having these thoughts? They were so ridiculous when he had far bigger things to consider. Still, she had beautiful body lines. A sculpt artist would find her an interesting subject.

"I need to be excused," she said, interrupting his thoughts, "How about you? Don't you ever pee?"

Seth chuckled at the remark and watched her walk toward the back of the restaurant. As soon as Peggy disappeared, he left the table and entered the men's room near the bar.

Minutes later, Seth watched a group of mallards swim the rim of the pond in single file. Another family of ducks sat on the thick bed of grass under the shade trees and waited for some occasional diner to throw crusts of bread their way.

"This is a beautiful restaurant." Peggy took his arm. "I'd like to show Jeff this place."

Seth made no comment. Someone like Jeff had probably been there already, many times.

***

Seth took the long way back from East Aurora, knowing they had a great deal of time on their hands.

"You seem to know your way around here," Peggy remarked. "Do you go to the Henry Hayward Inn a lot?"

Then, Peggy remembered and wished she hadn't asked the question. Painters didn't make much money and the restaurant menu was rather pricey. She never thought about it when she ordered the steak.

"Not really." She heard him reply. "I thought it would be a good out-of-the-way place for dinner."

Seth made a sudden turn, throwing Peggy's body toward him.

"Sorry. I just thought of something. Somewhere down here, there used to be an old fashioned ice cream parlor. Start looking."

They drove several miles before Peggy spotted a drive in.

"Is that it?" Peggy pointed.

"It doesn't look familiar." Seth drove into the parking lot. "Let's try it anyhow."

"What kind of ice cream do I like?" she asked, surprising him.

"Butter pecan," he answered, without a pause.

"How did you know that?"

"Everybody likes butter pecan."

"People like you spoil things for people like me. Are you aware of that?" she asked.

"That was not my intention," he chuckled, as they walked up to the sliding glass window of the ice cream shop.

"Two waffle cones with two scoops of butter pecan ice cream," Seth said to the clerk.

"And two Bah Humbugs," Peggy added, catching the young man's quizzical look.

The teenager ogled Peggy for a minute and decided to ignore the crazy lady.

"Coming right up, sir," he addressed Seth.

The two of them sat on the bench of a nearby pagoda and enjoyed their waffle cones, never thinking about the past twenty-four hours. By the time they reached the hospital parking lot, it was after ten o'clock and quite deserted.

"I think we should park near the door to wait for Alice."

"Are you sure she comes out this way?" Seth questioned.

"I'm sure. We don't want to miss her."

"Drive around the lot," Peggy directed. "Over there," she said, a few minutes later. "That's her car. She has to come this way."

Seth drove up a parallel lane and parked the car facing the building. From that angle, they could see the building's entrance and still have a close view of Alice's car.

Shortly after eleven, a small figure emerged.

"It's Alice," Peggy whispered. "Let's go."

Peggy hurried to exit the car, but felt Seth's hand restrain her.

"What?" she groused, and then followed the direction of his pointed finger.

A man stepped out of the shadows and caught Alice in a long, passionate embrace. They exchanged a few words and, within minutes, the woman slid into her car and waited. As soon as the man's car appeared, Alice drove in behind it and followed his lead down the highway toward a strip of motels along Transit Road, completely unaware of Seth's car tailing her.

"That son of a bitch," Peggy fumed. "Work late my ass! How could he do this to me? I go missing and he finds comfort in some other woman's arms. John must have known. No wonder he wanted her killed. I am so pissed."

"Just follow them. Please, Seth," she said after a moment, her voice cracking with anger.

"Jeff?" he asked, wondering if the shock of seeing him with someone else caused her to tremble, or if it was the pure rage of infidelity.

"My wonderful husband who loves me," Peggy answered, reaching in the back seat for the camera.

"Peggy. No!" Seth warned. He knew the woman's thinking was muddled. "You may regret it later."

"No way in hell. I am going to get that son of a bitch if it's the last thing I do. So, don't give me any shit. Oh, Christ, I sound like Megan," she ranted.

Peggy was not ashamed of venting her true feelings at that particular moment. Nor was she embarrassed by the string of profanities she spewed in front of Seth. The man would not think less of her. In fact, since they had experienced so much turmoil in the last twenty-four hours, this outburst would probably seem like a natural reaction to him. The man understood her completely.

Seth smiled. He had to meet this sister. She was the scrapper who wouldn't take any shit. He liked that. Yet, there was nothing he could do to assuage Peggy's anger, much less her pain. Seth felt helpless. After all the poor woman had been through, her husband's infidelity was the last thing she would have ever expected.

Throughout her whole ordeal, she believed in him, loved and adored him and stayed steadfast to her belief of his innocence. This was the man who said he loved her...who would take care of her for the rest of their lives. And, this was the same man who just stabbed her in the heart and left her in a mountain of pain. Still, Seth could do nothing for her. What words of comfort could he give her? Were there any, really? Ones which were truly believable?

"Pull in here," she pointed to the motel parking lot, "Park behind that truck."

Peggy waited until Jeff registered and had the room key, before snapping pictures of the couple locked in an embrace, as they stood on the outside stairway that lead to their room.

She waited a few more minutes, took the camera and bolted out of the car, leaving a puzzled Seth behind. Peggy raced up the stairs and banged on the motel door. "Pizza delivery," Peggy disguised her voice. "Pizza delivery," she shouted again.

A half-undressed Alice stood directly behind Jeff, when he answered the door and exposed his bare chest and boxer shorts.

"Smile, you cheating son of a bitch! You and your closet whore," Peggy yelled as she snapped a few pictures before racing down the stairs to Seth's car.

"Quick, drive away!!!" she ordered.

***

By the time Peggy collected herself, she realized Seth was driving north on Transit Road, before turning east on Main Street, the very long road that ran from the heart of Buffalo, through the many different boroughs of Snyder, Williamsville, Clarence, and Clarence Center.

"Where the hell are you taking me?"

"I called Poag. Room three's empty. We'll go there and settle this. His brother-in-law will help us."

"What exactly does that mean? This has been the worst twenty-four hours of my life."

Peggy began to cry hysterically.

Seth pulled into a fast food parking lot.

I don't want a hamburger," she wailed. Tears flooded down her face, causing her to take the hemline of her smock and wipe her eyes and nose.

"I'm not buying you one."

Seth put his arms around her and felt the softness of her body against his. He could still smell the scant scent of shampoo as she buried her head on his shoulder. The longer he held her, the more the chemistry between them intensified. He knew how vulnerable she was at that moment – how vulnerable they both were. Feeling the firmness of her breasts against him, Seth realized he was in very dangerous territory and had to break the intense mood of their bodies molded together.

"If you want to cry it out, I'm here for you. Just don't get my shirt all snotty." He was able to capture the right tone.

"How do you do that?" Peggy laughed, suddenly moving away from him.

"What?"

"Say something so incredibly stupid to make me laugh."

"Is that what I did?"

"Oh shit, I give up." Peggy began to giggle.

"You're right. You do sound like Megan." Seth pulled out of the parking lot and drove away.

Chapter 13
Evidence

The entry lights above the motel rooms were the only source of illumination when they entered Poag's long driveway shortly after midnight. Seth turned on the room lamps and left Peggy resting comfortably on one of the upholstered chairs. When he returned with Gabriel and a wrapped package under his arm, Seth found her weeping uncontrollably. He quickly tossed the package on the bed and pulled the sobbing woman to him. Seth embraced her closely, and in trying to comfort her, he placed Peggy's head on his shoulder while gently stroking her hair.

"You don't know what it's like for a woman," she said, between sobs. "It would have been better if I had been killed. At least there's no rejection in death. That's exactly how I feel, rejected and miserable."

Tears streamed from her swollen eyes, as she continued to express her thoughts.

"Men always have the upper hand." She choked between gasps. "If a man gets bored, he just moves on to another woman. That was obvious tonight."

"That is not true," Seth said, pushing her gently away while meeting her stare. He could feel the anger growing inside him as he disagreed with her assessment of men. Seth could not believe someone so intellectually gifted could be so stupid. Categorizing the entire male sex for her errant husband's mistake was totally wrong.

"You are a strikingly beautiful woman. If that asshole you married doesn't appreciate what he has, then he doesn't deserve you. Think about that for awhile."

Seth eyed the pitiful woman and tried to make her understand the options open to her. "If you want to be stupid and feel rejected, go live in a cave somewhere and hide. But, if you're smart, you can take this opportunity to move on with your life. Grow your business. Travel somewhere. Enrich your education. There's a lot you can do."

"I feel so humiliated." Peggy swallowed hard. "I am so hurt, Seth. I am so hurt that he did this to me. And he did it when I went missing. It shows how little he cares."

"Listen to me. You will get through this and be a much stronger person for it. I've had my share of grief. So I know."

A frown crossed Seth's face. She was not convinced. He could see it in her eyes.

"Believe me, Peggy, when I say this, not all men cheat. So, don't rubber-stamp the male universe with your husband's behavior. It doesn't wash."

"Then why?" she asked. Tears ran along the side of her nose and, without giving it a second thought, and much to his surprise, Peggy used the bottom of Seth's collared polo shirt to blot them. "He knew how much I loved him. Why did he throw it all away?"

"I can't answer that. But, someday he'll come to regret it." His reply only made the situation worse. She continued to sob in his arms.

While holding her, Seth felt a noticeable tremor running through her body. He pulled Peggy much closer to him and tightened his arms around her back while pushing her head gently on his shoulder. One would think that he was burping a baby.

"Take a deep breath," he said, gently. "Listen to me, Peggy. Do it. Now. Good. Another one. I won't let you fall. You're not going to faint on me, are you? I'll be wearing my balls on my nose, if Clarisa thinks I did something to you."

"You did it again," she began to laugh.

"Am I in trouble?"

"I can see why they like you so much." Her eyes met his. "You have a quiet way of sneaking into people's lives."

Seth felt uncomfortable with the direction the conversation was taking and, while gently pushing Peggy away from him, he led her back to the upholstered chair. Seth grabbed a box of tissues from the bathroom while ever-astute Gabriel, who had been watching them from a corner of the room, walked to the seated woman, stood very still and faced her silently. He stood inches away from her face. Fear swept through Peggy. Would Gabriel sense her uneasiness? Would he know she was deathly afraid of him? Gabriel made a soft crying sound and continued gazing at the woman, his nose nearly touching hers.

"Gabriel knows you're unhappy. Open the palm of your right hand slowly and extend it to him," Seth instructed. "And, whatever you do, don't move." Seth watched Gabriel closely.

When Peggy opened the palm of her hand, Gabriel extended his paw and placed it dead center.

"Just stay still. He's testing." Seth hoped he knew his large guard dog.

Peggy followed Seth's instruction, but felt the only thing Gabriel was testing was whether or not she would taste good. Gabriel removed his paw, and then placed his face up to hers.

"He wants you to pet him behind his ears. When Gabriel starts to move away, he no longer wants to be stroked. He'll go sit somewhere." Seth hoped he wouldn't eat her fingers instead.

A man may think he knows his dog, but man's best friend still has a few surprises for his owner. Soon after Peggy petted Gabriel, the dog elected to sit at her feet in a very protective manner.

"So much for rejection," Seth muttered to himself, but his thoughts were interrupted by a loud knock before the door opened.

"I brought some coffee. Rather, Poag suggested it. He also made it." Clarisa shuffled into the room and placed the coffee pot on the dresser. Poag followed his wife, holding a basket filled with paper cups and an assortment of cheese filled crackers.

They were dressed in dark blue matching robes which covered their equally dark blue pajamas. They had the appearance of having been awakened from a deep night's sleep. Yet, they seemed downright cheerful to be meeting Seth and Peggy again, if only to bring them coffee.

Clarisa moved toward Peggy, who stood up immediately.

"Move, Gabriel," she addressed the dog then hugged the young woman.

"People are such shits, aren't they?" she said, to Peggy's surprise. "Seth told Poag about your close friend. Although it hurts to know he did this to you, it's good you found out. Now, you can have him arrested."

Clarisa turned to Poag. "She can have him arrested, can't she? I mean, there's this Mel guy too."

"That's for the law to decide," Poag answered. "All they can do now is report it. I think they should definitely do that." Poag poured coffee for Seth and Peggy.

"Maybe they should get a lawyer," Clarisa interrupted.

"It would be a lot easier if they were connected to the Mafia," Poag replied.

"Oh, hush," she hissed, trying to quell him. "Now, you know the kind of thinking that goes on here." Clarisa spoke to no one in particular.

Seth and Peggy enjoyed listening to their banter. Within twenty minutes, they gave various opinions on how Seth and Peggy should proceed with the information they collected earlier at Remmy's Roadside Tavern. But, neither of them knew anything about her husband's infidelity.

Seth felt the woman's personal anguish was hers and hers alone. If Peggy wished to share her husband's betrayal with them, that was her choice, not his. The matter was out of his hands.

"Sorry about Judd. If there's anything," Poag took Seth aside.

"I know," he answered quietly, and then added, "I plan to spend the night."

Before Poag could reply, they heard a soft rapping before the door opened.

"Thanks for coming," Seth greeted Ben Burrows.

"You people keep the damndest hours," he answered. "Why do crimes always have to occur after midnight?"

"Yeah, like you have a big social schedule with something better to do," Poag reminded his brother-in-law. "Quit bitchin. We stayed awake just to see you."

"Right," Burrows replied dryly. "Like you and my sister didn't want to know what I was doing here."

The short, squat detective turned his attention to Peggy. "So, you're Peggy Roberts. A lot of people are worried about you. Seth tells me the two of you experienced a lot of bad things the last twenty-four hours. So, where should we begin?"

He sat on a chair opposite Peggy and placed his pad and pencil on the table between them, waiting quietly for someone to begin speaking.

Poag took Clarisa's arm. "We better leave so they can tell Ben their story."

"I'll call to go fishing," Ben said. "That is, if I can pry you away from room five. Is she leaving her husband or what?"

"He doesn't make that decision," Clarisa told her brother. "I do."

After they left the room, Ben Burrows listened to Peggy Roberts tell her story of kidnapping, broken friendships and a husband's betrayal.

When she finished speaking, Seth took the package from the bed and placed it on the table.

"Peggy wore these clothes when she was kidnapped," he told the detective. "I had Clarisa box her dress and shoes in case you needed them."

"We left them behind when we went to Nancy Travers' house," Seth reminded her.

Then, Seth described his own encounter with Judd, Mel and Peggy. Afterward, he gave a visual account of his brother's murder. Much of it was brief. Seth reported, witnessing from the bungalow window, what seemed to be an argument between both men, before his brother fell back and collapsed when Mel shot him.

He reached inside his pocket and pulled out a handful of bullets, which he gave to the detective. Ben silently examined the hollow point bullets...ones for the magazine and chamber. They would kill any target in the line of fire, doing so by mushrooming inside the designated victim and damaging the surrounding organs. Death would come quickly.

A three-eighty caliber bullet. He began calculating the type of semi-automatic used. According to Seth's account, the gun was in Mel's pocket, so it had to be small enough and light weight. A Ruger LCP came to mind, only because Burrows happened to own a modified one, but there were other semi-automatic pistols that would fit into a pocket just as nicely.

His thoughts shifted, as he listened to them recount their escape from Mel, and he wrote continuously on his note pad. When they finished speaking, he surprised them both with a flood of questions.

"Let me understand this clearly," he addressed Peggy first.

"Did you actually see Judd or Mel when you were kidnapped? And did you see any part of the house where you were taken?" His first question was immediately followed by the second one, making Peggy somewhat apprehensive with her response.

"No. I didn't see anyone," she answered honestly. "And, I didn't see any part of the house either."

"In fact, there could have been more than two people in the house where you were taken. Is that correct?"

Peggy nodded.

"The only reason you know the house location is because Seth took you there the next day. Would that be an accurate statement?"

"You make this sound like I'm lying." Peggy grew angry. "I am not making this up. We have pictures of everyone involved."

"I believe you, Mrs. Roberts," he assured her. "But, you must realize what an experienced lawyer could do to your story if this ever came to trial. It's all hearsay. No witnesses."

"What about Seth? He met Mel at the house."

"That's another story. We could arrest Mel possibly for holding you in the house against your will. But, who knows what sordid story he would come up with? Telling Seth to kill you? I think not. It's Seth's word against his. Seth saw Mel kill Judd, but we have no body. So, I can't arrest Mel for murder. And, you have absolutely nothing on John Beck. What we need is evidence."

Peggy looked dejected. "Dammit to hell. I'm the victim and Mel gets a free pass. Poag was right. Justice would have been better served with the Mafia."

Her comments stopped Ben Burrows dead in his tracks. Peggy's way of phrasing profanity reminded him of her sister. And, at that very moment, he was more than grateful that the woman was found unharmed. He would have dreaded facing Megan had the outcome been different.

"I won't let this go away, Mrs. Roberts."

"Call me Peggy. I plan to make a name change shortly," she told the detective.

"Your husband's infidelity is out of my hands," he said, unequivocally. "But, I do intend to investigate Mel and Nancy Travers very quietly to see where it takes me."

Burrows continued to study the woman's body language as he spoke. "I'll do the same with John Beck, particularly if his wife has an unfortunate accident. Still, I think they'll go their separate ways eventually. There isn't much choice for any of them after your pizza delivery photos."

He turned his attention to Seth. "I don't know what I can do about Judd. I will keep you informed if..."

"I understand," Seth said, quietly. "It's just hard to believe there nothing we can do." The man clearly understood Ben's reference. He would be notified if Judd's body was found.

"Just give me time," the detective told him. "It's like fishing. Once my hooks get locked onto something, I won't let go."

"I appreciate your coming out tonight." Seth told his friend. "I talked with Poag about Judd and Mel, confidentially, and he thought you should be the one to help us."

"Good." Ben put his notebook and pencil away. "When you have time, drop off the photographs."

Ben eyed Peggy. Given the situation with the abduction and her husband's philandering, he felt she should stay with her sister, but was loathe suggesting it. The decision had to come from her.

"So, what do you want to do now, Peggy? Shall I take you home?"

"Can you call Megan for me? I'd rather stay with her tonight. I'm sure she's worried."

"She's very worried about you and so is Janice Sommers. I visited both of them earlier today," he said, pleased with her decision.

"Seth and I thought we shouldn't contact anyone until we knew who was behind the kidnapping. Not that it will do us any good, I guess."

"We'll see about that in due time," he said, as he dialed a number.

Instead of saying hello and waiting for an answer, Megan bombarded the detective with a stream of questions. She wanted to know if he had any leads to her sister's disappearance.

When Ben held the phone in the air and refused to answer, Megan became silent. At that point, he told her to be quiet and listen to what he was saying. After learning Peggy was spending the night with her, a gleeful Megan told Ben Burrows she didn't care if he did look like a frog, he would always be her prince.

"She really could screw up a one car funeral." That was his only remark when the phone call ended.

Ben shook hands with Seth and took the package. "Maybe we can get out in the next two weeks. I'll call Poag." He walked to the door and left it partially open in case they had another question for him.

Peggy stood by the dresser and studied the tall, handsome Seth with his dog. The time for leaving the man who saved her life had come and she didn't quite know what to say or do. She couldn't just give him a simple thank you. Through it all, he protected her, was respectful of her and encouraged her while her life was falling apart. They had shared so much together and now it was time to leave. It was time to move on for both of them.

"Seth," she began, walking slowly toward him. "I don't know what to say." She started to cry. "You've been..." She couldn't continue.

Seth put his arms around her. "It's going to be okay. Trust me." He gave her a slip of paper. "Call my cell, if you want to talk." In turn, Peggy offered her number, before kissing his cheek. "I don't know what's going to happen, but I do want you to paint my house."

"Goodbye, Gabriel." Upon hearing his name, Gabriel approached Peggy and stood still.

"Pet him," Seth told her. "Then, say goodbye."

Peggy followed Seth's simple instructions, left the room and never looked back.

***

As Seth watched the door close, a flood of emotions swept through him. Once again, he felt a sense of loss, the kind that comes with the death of a loved one. It had all come down to this again.

Would there ever be a sustainable relationship in his life? Had another chapter of his life just close? Did it always have to end with separation or death? Was there no reprieve…ever?

Two strangers thrown together under extraordinary circumstances were forced to join forces, not only to survive, but to identify and outwit those who would do them harm. Seth recalled their journey together. He could still remember her reluctance to stay with him at the motel. But, she soon learned to trust and respect him as a man who would not overstep the marital boundary. He remembered her excitement at watching the pond ducks at dinner and how she delighted in the experience of something very new and different. Peggy had been so happy. At that time, John Beck was the culprit while Jeff was clearly innocent. She relished the thought of going home to her husband, or so she thought. All of that changed by one chance encounter.

Still, they would go their separate ways. He would go back to his quiet, uneventful life while she pursued a new and different journey. He only hoped she would stand fast and not forgive the man whose moral compass was nothing but a sham. Seth had seen his kind before, aggressively pushing his way to the top, and stealing ideas from his weaker colleagues to present them as his own to those in charge. How many bodies had he left along his path to success? Was John Beck one of them?

Seth then thought of John Beck. The man knew the kind of game Jeff Roberts played. Not only was he smart about office politics, John Beck knew that in Jeff's path to success, the man felt entitled to all of the company perks, which, of course, included his wife, Alice. After all, they were the closest of friends. For one brief moment, Seth wished he could punch Jeff Roberts, right in the face.

His thoughts went back to Peggy. He felt so close to the woman, yet he could not determine why. He had initiated nothing substantive with her. She was a married woman. The intimacy between them developed in their pursuit of Mel, he told himself. He asked and she stayed the course for him. Now, he had to face it. Their time together was over. Whatever her decision, Seth hoped she would be happy. In the end, that was the very thing everyone wanted. Still…

Why was he having these thoughts? There had been no exchange between them, no knowing look and no words. There was nothing to indicate interest on either side. And, he totally avoided her questions in the beginning, keeping his life private. There was only one priority at the time… finding Mel.

What had changed? He asked this question over and over to himself. Did he feel this sudden emptiness because their accelerated time together was over and he would miss her company? Or was it because she discovered her husband's infidelity and he felt sorry for her? Doubt no longer lingered in his mind. It was a combination of both. Seth felt satisfied with the assessment.

He eyed Gabriel. "I'm going to bed."

It took Seth a long time to drift off, but Gabriel sensed his uneasiness, and lay quietly beside his master, waiting and listening for the small, intermittent sounds of sleep.

***

Megan wasted no time in spreading the news when she hung up the phone. She jumped on her husband, who was still lying in bed and, shaking him excitedly, repeated her conversation with Ben Burrows. Greatly animated that her sister was alive and well, Megan pulled the comforter off the poor man and demanded they both get dressed in preparation for their company. Robes and pajamas would be acceptable dress for Peggy, but not – definitely not – for her hero, Ben Burrows.

Megan ran downstairs to make a fresh pot of coffee. When she checked the pantry, the only cookies to be found were those she served almost twelve hours earlier. Would her Frog Prince remember? Of course, he would, very little slipped by those big bulging eyes. He would not mention the stale cookies though. He was very kind that way.

Brad joined her in record time and grabbed her at the kitchen sink. "Next time you jump me in bed, you won't get off so easy."

"Next time I jump you in bed, I won't want to get off," Megan said, impishly. "I'll want to play in your pen."

"My kind of girl," Brad grabbed the cups and saucers from the china closet. "When are they getting here?"

"I have no clue. I don't know where Peggy's been or exactly what happened to her."

"So, you didn't speak to Peggy."

"Burrows never gave her the phone. We'll know the details when she gets here, but I think that asshole she married is involved somehow."

"Is that because she's coming here instead of going home? Is that what you mean?" Brad asked. He needed clarification.

"Think about it. She disappears suddenly. No one knows where she is. All her stuff's left behind. What would you think?"

"Something happened, I grant you. But, Jeff wouldn't do anything to harm her."

"I'm not so sure," Megan disagreed. "They could have had a fight and he won't admit it. Still, I can't see Peggy fighting with him. She wears blinders when it comes to her husband. In her eyes, he can do no wrong."

"Before condemning him totally, I think we should hear what Peggy has to say. If nothing else, Burrows will fill in the details."

After Brad completed his thought, he watched his wife take the cordless phone from its cradle and start dialing a number. He knew it was useless to discourage Megan from calling anyone at that late hour and decided listening to the conversation was much better than asking her a lot of questions.

"Hey! When did you get in, you staying long? Oh. Well maybe." Megan spoke to the woman who answered the phone, then clarified the conversation for her husband's benefit.

"Amy's in town. Fred and Janice's daughter," she nudged him. "She's here for a wedding."

"Do me a favor," Megan continued the conversation, "get Janice for me. I really need to talk to her."

While Megan waited for Amy to awaken her mother, she continued talking with Brad. There were a few things the two of them overlooked. Peggy's election to stay with them might have meant that she was afraid to go home. Could Jeff have threatened her? Was that the reason she disappeared? Maybe that's why Ben Burrows did all the talking. Peggy didn't want her whereabouts known, wherever that was.

"What happened, Megan?" Janice spoke nervously. "What have you heard?"

"Ben Burrows called. Peggy's coming here instead of going home. That's why I needed to talk to you."

"I don't understand," Janice replied. "Doesn't she want to come home?"

"No. She doesn't." Megan answered dryly. "That's why I'm calling. I think Jeff must be involved somehow."

"What can I do to help?" Janice offered.

"If Jeff asks you about Peggy, tell him you don't know anything. This, of course is true. But, that's what you tell him. I'd like you to keep an eye on the house though. You know how much I trust the S.O.B."

"If I see your car in the driveway tomorrow, I'll come over, otherwise I'll phone," Janice said.

"One other thing," Megan added. "I told Ben Burrows you think he looks like a frog."

"You said that?" Janice took an angry tone.

"That's what I told him, but afterward, I confessed that I lied."

"Oh. No!" Janice cried, thinking back to his visit. Having never made that statement about Ben, Janice became very cross.

"Calm down," Megan insisted. "I told him you thought he was a brilliant detective and that you were glad he was handling the case. He was so pleased I thought he was going to wet himself."

"You must be joking," Janice replied coldly.

"I never joke at this hour of the morning." Megan housed the phone abruptly, leaving Janice Sommers, a totally bewildered woman.

Then a spirited Megan waltzed to her husband's side and threw her arms around him. "I don't know what I would do without you." Her eyes glistened as she spoke. "I love my sister. We're blood. But, you are my world now and everything I could possibly want in life."

Brad embraced his wife and kissed her gently. "I will always be here for you, Meg. Always. I know I'm too quiet sometimes, but my love runs deep. Remember that."

She looked at him playfully. "Can I remind you of that tonight?"

"Counting on it," he shot back with a wink. Suddenly, his conversation was interrupted by a noise from the street. "I think I hear a car in the driveway."

Chapter 14
Explanations

While Seth was feeling melancholy over her departure, Peggy sat in silence and watched the trees sway and dance in the wind. She felt completely alone and abandoned. No longer would Jeff be there for her. Earlier, she thought he would be, but she was wrong. All wrong. Completely wrong. How could she have been so stupid? So blind? So naïve?

She seemed unaware of the detective who was speeding toward the Village of Williamsville to an awaiting Megan. But, being with her sister was not part of her thoughts now.

Peggy wasn't sure she wanted to leave the safety net Seth had provided for her. She was hurt, humiliated and frightened, but Seth always found a way of making her feel better. He took a very different view of things. And, her thoughts shifted back to their first meeting and the events that followed her abduction.

Within twenty-four hours, a horrible mistake had changed her life completely.

Tears slowly trickled down her cheeks as she thought about all that had happened. Only through the kindness of a stranger had her life been spared. Someone, without pity or moral compass, would have killed her just as easily as Mel had murdered Judd.

Seth told her at the outset he would not hurt her. He knew she was frightened. By agreeing to help him find Mel, Peggy believed he would allow her to go free.

Then, little by little, Peggy came to know and respect the man who saved her life. In fact, she began to enjoy their time together. No longer was she afraid. And, her input to their search counted. She was not dismissed as some ineffectual woman with nothing to offer. Seth made her feel intellectually important and Peggy hadn't felt that way for a long, long time.

Peggy thought of Seth and the people she met through him. Poag and Clarisa obviously cared for the man who occasionally slept in room three. She wondered how their relationship began. Maybe, he met them through his painting business.

Painters were like undertakers, Peggy thought. *They were always needed.*

But that still didn't explain the friendship or their seemingly close bond.

What was his relationship with the detective? They also seemed to have a close personal connection...something that brought them together. Maybe it was Judd's arrest. And, Burrows did say something to Poag about getting together in a few weeks. Was Seth really included in their outing? How often did he go fishing with them?

Although Seth never spoke of himself, people seemed drawn to this quiet, soft spoken man. She could see why. He was so different from anyone she had ever met. Seth was always there for everyone. He was so dependable and unselfish. That would characterize him. The man was nothing like Jeff.

The comparison triggered her thoughts and Peggy began to dwell on her situation closer to home. Burrows told them they had nothing on John Beck, so the man who masterminded the kidnapping would be allowed to go free. Of course, John would not be aware of Peggy's having this knowledge. Would that make her safer from him? She wondered.

Then too, the detective would watch Mel. Not just because he was involved in the kidnapping. No. That wasn't the chief reason. Seth witnessed a murder and Burrows wanted to find Judd's body.

In retrospect, finding Mel with John Beck had other rewards. By finding them, she found Alice...with Jeff. John must have known about the adulterous relationship. But, did he really want Alice killed? How long had she been seeing Jeff? How much would Jeff deny? Would there be a scene, a confrontation of some kind? Peggy was too tired to think. Everything was happening too fast. Just thinking of the last twenty-four hours was giving her a headache.

She turned her face toward Ben who kept his eyes glued on the road.

"I know you'll have to call him. Jeff, I mean. To tell him you found me," she explained.

"It's part of the job," he said, simply. Notification was always a part of his routine. The news of finding someone alive was much easier to convey than the other alternative.

"You've been doing this for some time, haven't you?"

"A long time. But, it doesn't get any easier. Crimes just get scarier and people, meaner."

Peggy found his manner very direct. "It's faster today. The pace, I mean," she said. "People become dissatisfied too quickly."

"Too much technology, no patience and a lot of drugs," Burrows explained a part of the problem, but he knew her veiled inquiry was just a preliminary for the many questions to come.

"You must meet a whole gamut of people," she started.

He immediately caught the subtle underlying question of her statement. He called it, 'Women's Fishing 101.' Peggy wanted information about Seth, but did not want to ask him directly. She wanted Ben to volunteer it.

"You were lucky Seth rescued you," Ben said, giving her the opening she wanted. "He's a decent man. You might not have been so fortunate with someone else."

"It was the worst night of my life," she agreed. "I'll never forget it."

"That will be true for awhile, but the worst of it is over for you. Seth still has to live with it. Remember, he saw Mel shoot his brother. Until I find Judd, there is no closure for him."

"Who is Helen?" Peggy changed the subject abruptly. "Seth mentioned her once."

"She died five years ago...almost a year to a day...," his voice trailed off.

"She was his wife, wasn't she?"

"No. But I think a wedding may have been in their plans. There was no announcement of it, though. I think it was just understood. They really cared for each other."

"How did Seth meet her?"

Peggy thought if she asked the right questions, the detective might be able to give her some answers about the woman in Seth's life. Still, he was not one to divulge information easily.

"I don't know exactly. You'll have to ask Clarisa. Helen was Poag's sister."

A bell went off in Peggy's brain. Bingo. Helen was the connection who cemented the relationship between Seth and Poag. She was the dead woman in Seth's life, the one he mentioned when they spent the night together in room three.

Ben was determined not to reveal anything further. There were certain things Seth would consider private and therefore, an intrusion of his personal life. It would be better if Peggy got the information about Helen from him or perhaps, Clarisa.

"Didn't Seth tell you?" Burrows questioned.

"No. All he told me was her name. I wanted to know whose dress I was wearing."

"And, you didn't notice anything in room three?" he asked.

"Like what?"

"What do you know about Seth?"

"Only what he told me. He has or had a half-brother, Judd, who worked as a mechanic. He just got out of prison for some kind of robbery. Seth did tell me he was a painter."

"So, that's where you got the idea to have him paint your house," Ben laughed, when he thought about the conversation he overheard. "You couldn't possibly afford him."

"You think he'd be too expensive. Is that it? You're wrong." She was becoming very annoyed with his continuous laughter.

"I don't think Seth Stone would ever overcharge me. He would never take advantage of me financially. He's not that kind of person."

The more indignant Peggy became, the harder Ben Burrows laughed.

"Peggy! Peggy! Peggy! Unless you are into painted landscapes, Seth Stone can't possibly help you."

"What do you mean?" she frowned. "Oh. No!" The realization had finally set in. "Why didn't he tell me?" She smacked her forehead. "I'm so embarrassed."

"He did. You said he told you," Ben repeated.

"When someone tells me he's a painter, I automatically think house painter. He didn't say he was a different kind of painter. Is he any good?"

"He's very talented. The prints in room three are his. Of course, they're copies."

Peggy closed her eyes. She spent a few minutes reflecting his paintings.

"When I thought Seth was staring into space and thinking of our next step, he was really looking at the paintings. The female figure in the companion landscape was Helen. Am I right? I remember now. She was wearing a white dress...this dress. These must be her sandals."

She eyed Ben, and then continued the conversation.

"Now, I really feel stupid. It must have brought back so many memories seeing me in her clothes. He never said a word. Poor Seth: first, Helen; and now, Judd. Stupid! Stupid! How could I be so dumb... about everything," she chastised herself.

Tears spilled down Peggy's cheeks. "Everything I touch turns to shit lately."

"You shouldn't think like that. If Seth wanted you to wear those clothes, he had his reasons."

Burrows knew he couldn't change the woman's surly mood, so he took a new approach. "If it makes you feel any better, drop them off at the station next week. I know that's when Poag plans to go fishing. Seth will probably join us. We've shared room three before. Poag refuses to add another bedroom to his house. Did Seth tell you?"

"Yes, he did," she said, confirming his statement. "Seth uses room three, if it's available. He said that it's Poag's guest room. I guess it beats sleeping on the couch."

"Exactly put, unless, of course, you like sleeping in a valley. The couch sags in the middle like a two-humped camel, and the springs on one couch pillow died last March." Burrows gave a slight laugh. "I almost think Poag refuses to buy a couch, because he'd rather have us sleep in room three... in the motel units outside his house."

"I wonder if Megan will have a room three for me," Peggy said, half aloud. "I am going to hate tomorrow."

"Right now, you should be thinking about what you're going to tell her," he cautioned. "It has to sound convincing."

"What's that supposed to mean? Why can't I just tell her what happened?" Peggy couldn't follow his logic.

"For your own safety, you do not mention Mel or John Beck," he warned. "Tell her Seth saw a photograph, but it wasn't you. Do not mention Alice as a possible victim or that you were at the hospital."

"Then, how did I catch them together?"

"I suggest a slight modification of the truth. As you were driving toward Amherst after being rescued, you recognized both cars stopped at a signal light and decided to follow them. It's quite understandable. You were suspicious, particularly at that hour of night."

He studied her briefly. "It's all true, only the sequence is changed. But, you can't start from the beginning anyhow. The house in Clarence Center is off-limits in any conversation, as is Nancy Travers. That could jeopardize my investigation."

"So, I was kidnapped by mistake and Seth saved me. If that's my story, Megan won't buy it."

"She will, if you tell her Seth's brother called him, because he was in trouble. Remember, he took the wrong woman. Now, he's missing or presumed dead. Nobody knows what happened to him. Of course, you were blindfolded and drugged, so you weren't aware of anything."

The detective looked at her briefly. "It doesn't really matter whether or not she believes you. When she learns how Jeff betrayed you, she'll be enraged."

"I know she dislikes him."

"After tonight, she'll think castration's too mild a punishment for his philandering."

"I know she sounds like a loose cannon sometimes," Peggy replied. "But, I love her dearly."

"Your sister has the vocabulary of a steelworker and the heart of a romantic. But, when it comes to your husband, the Spanish Inquisition wouldn't be harsh enough for him. But, I must say I like her. She hasn't fixated on being politically correct and still enjoys the adventure of a young life."

"Are you sure you're not related to Seth? You have a euphemistic way of saying my sister is crude and coarse and yet, has a sweet notion of ideal love."

"You've got it all wrong. The one thing I do know is people. That hard façade Megan wears is nothing but a protective shell. Whoever hurt her did one helleva job."

"What do you mean?" Peggy asked, surprised by the comment.

"You know exactly what I mean." He shot back, unloading his thoughts.

"Her affection for you is deeper than sisterly love. You're too protective of each other. Did you look after Megan when she was growing up? Where were your parents?"

"I had to with Megan and Josephine. That's what Megan calls our mother. They never got along, never ever." She emphasized her last two words. "As for my father, I have no idea of his whereabouts. Megan was two and I was seven when he left. Everything connected to him is gone. I can't even remember what he looked like."

"You never searched for him?"

"No. I never did," she replied, quickly.

"Why not, do you know why he left?"

"No. I never had any information about him. Mother refused to tell me anything. As it was, I had to save all the money I made for college. Then, later, we moved out."

"We, as in you and Megan?" he asked, catching her nod.

"After getting my degree, I got a job and lived at home to save money. We moved when Megan graduated."

"She's got a lot of rage inside her. Do you know what triggered it?"

"I'm not really sure. Mother was never there for us. She always worked extra hours or took occasional side jobs to pay the bills. Still, there was always someone around to help."

"You mean boyfriends?"

"More like a revolving door. She finally married her last live-in."

"Think back in time. Did Megan ever fight with your mother about any of them?"

"I think she was responsible for chasing someone away. I wasn't there when it happened, so I don't know the full story. She refused to talk about it. But, then, Megan was always fighting about the men mother brought home," Peggy continued. "The yelling between them was fierce. But, I really think one of them crossed the line, and it was the events of that day, that caused Megan to begin calling mother, Josephine."

Peggy thought back.

"She was a teenager when it happened. I mean the name switch. I didn't see it then. Megan didn't go into detail, other than swearing at my mother."

"What exactly are you saying?"

"She had to learn to protect herself from mother's parade of boyfriends. That's why the war between them got so ugly."

"So, you two lived together until you got married?" he asked, urging her to continue. For some reason, Ben had a need to connect the parts of Megan's broken childhood to better understand her. The young woman had wounds that never healed.

"No. Megan continued to live with us after we got married. She attended Pitt, and then transferred her credits when we moved here. She met Brad at UB. He was getting his doctorate at the time. They married in her senior year."

"And you're happy with the marriage?"

"Absolutely. He loves her dearly. I know that. Even more important, Brad understands Megan. He knows her volatility and does not try to smother her. In turn, she adores him. It's a terrific match."

"Whether you realize it or not, your sister has a great deal of street smarts. Maybe that's why she's so protective of you and hates your husband so much. Jeff reminds her of your mother's lotharios, or at least one of them."

"I don't know what you mean." His remark had surprised Peggy. "Jeff would never do anything to Megan."

"Of course not. Jeff's too smart to try anything on her. I'm with your sister. Your husband's an asshole to have thrown it all away."

Ben said nothing further, as he pulled into Megan's driveway.

Chapter 15
Megan's House

Approaching the Croft house, Ben Burrows felt like it was Trick or Treat night on Halloween. The home blazed with lights everywhere – the grass, on the walkway, the front porch globe and all the other house lights that faced the street.

As they walked up the front steps, Megan raced out on the front porch, threw her arms around both of them and began jumping up and down.

"You're safe! You're safe!" she shouted, hugging her sister. "Thank you, thank you," she kissed Ben's cheek, and then drew them into the kitchen where Brad stood to greet them.

"I'm so glad you're safe." He gave Peggy a hug, "We were so worried about you. Megan wanted to call Mr. Burrows every fifteen minutes."

"Try nine messages," Burrows interjected, dryly. "After answering the first, I gave up. I told your sister I had no news." He faced Peggy and shook his head. "She doesn't give up easily."

Megan gathered them around the kitchen table, while Brad served coffee and the stale morning cookies.

"What happened? Where have you been?" Megan began.

Peggy carefully narrated the abduction but omitted Mel Travers and John Beck completely. She concentrated on being saved by Seth, his missing brother and the discovery of Alice...with Jeff. She focused heavily on the last point.

During the question and answer period, Megan's eyes shifted between her sister and Ben. In the back of her mind, she wondered if they concocted the story for her benefit, or were withholding information, because the Frog Prince felt it necessary for Peggy's welfare.

"If the kidnapping was a mistake, who was behind it?" Megan raised the expected question.

"I'm working on that," Burrows interrupted, before she could ask about the intended victim.

"But, you don't really know at this point," Megan insisted.

"At this point, no," Ben echoed her remark.

Megan studied her sister and shrugged. "I don't get it. Is Peggy in any danger?" Her eyes shifted to her little frog.

"At this point, I don't believe she is," he said sincerely.

"Then, who is this Seth person, and why is his brother missing, if he's the one who called for help?"

Megan fixated on both of them. "You two better come up with a better story," she said frankly.

"Megan," Burrows snapped back with sudden urgency. "It is what it is. All you need to know is that Peggy's safe. She's gone through a very bad time."

"You mean, because of that slime ball she married. We'll handle that in the morning...at the house first and then, the bank."

"You and Brad can take it from here." Ben Burrows rose from his chair. "Thanks for the coffee."

"Not so fast." Megan halted him. "I know we're not supposed to ask Peggy any more questions. You've already counseled her on that. For safety reasons, I suppose."

She caught a faint glimmer in his eyes. "You are protecting her! Thank God someone is. Now, tell me about this Seth person. I want to meet him."

"I'm not sure I can help you with that. Seth Stone is a very private person."

"Seth Stone, as in Seth Stone, the artist?" her eyes widened.

"I thought he was a painter," Peggy frowned.

"He's an artist!" Megan repeated, and then, grabbed Ben Burrows' arm and marched him into the living room.

Not wanting to miss the excitement, Brad and Peggy followed.

"See?" Megan pointed to the print on her wall.

The idyllic scene depicted a stand of leafy green trees overlooking a running brook of sparkling water. A figure of a woman wearing a white dress appeared to be holding a basket of colorful flowers, while enjoying the view with two other women. The faded sky-blue background encapsulated the painting completely.

Peggy eyed Ben Burrows knowingly and then shifted her attention to the painting. It was a print of the companion piece in room three.

"It's quite beautiful."

"It cost a small fortune, but we love it." Brad agreed with Peggy's assessment.

As the four of them quietly studied the painting, Ben broke the silence with his intention of leaving.

"I'll be in touch," he told Peggy, as he crossed the front hall. "You have my number if something else comes up."

"I appreciate everything you've done," Peggy said. She approached him quietly and took his hand, "Everything."

Then, as an afterthought Peggy added, "I'll check with you next week."

Megan and Brad thought Peggy referred to the kidnapping case, but Ben knew otherwise. The woman planned to return the borrowed clothing.

Megan walked her Frog Prince to the front door while Brad and Peggy stayed behind.

"You came through for me, Ben Burrows. You brought my sister back to me." She placed her arms around him, as a tear spilled down her cheek.

Surprised by the display of emotion, he patted her gently. "It's going to be alright, really it is."

"Promise?" her eyes locked on his.

"You can count on it." The detective inched away from her. "But, you have to help your sister."

"How?" she brightened.

"Two ways," he said. It was important that Megan fully capture the seriousness of the situation. To a degree, it would be a reversal of roles...the younger sister caring for the older one.

"You have to remember, she was bound and blindfolded, alone and very afraid during the abduction. Peggy had no idea what was happening to her. When the heart is pounding with fear, the mind floods with all kinds of memories, because you feel death is near."

Ben knew he had her attention now.

"So, you see, Megan, Peggy will relive this experience over and over again. It's not the kind of thing one forgets easily."

"Is that what actually happened to her?" Megan caught his nod. "Peggy never mentioned that part of the story. Oh, my poor sister!" she cried.

"Then," Burrows continued the narrative. "When Peggy thought she was finally free from the kidnapping, Jeff's betrayal demoralized her completely. Her self-esteem is shot. She needs encouragement. So, don't keep telling her Jeff's a shit."

"But, he is," Megan replied. "You already know that."

"So, does she," he agreed. "Don't talk. Just listen and be supportive. Those two things are very important now."

"I can do that," Megan nodded. "I won't say anything. I'll just listen."

"That will be a first," the detective snickered. "But, you're a good sister. You have a big heart."

"And, so do you. That's why I need you." She caught him by surprise again.

"I'm not sure I understand." Two vertical ridges appeared above his nose and he wondered what she had in mind for him now. With Megan, he could always count on the unexpected.

"When the time comes, I want you to do something for me. It has to stay between us because it might not materialize. And, Peggy's been hurt enough. I really don't think he's still alive."

"You're talking about your father. You want my help in locating him, if he is."

"You're the only one who can help me," Megan pleaded. "You have access to all kinds of things for investigative work. I would have asked Miss Quigley, but she can't help me with that kind of thing."

"And she is?"

"The librarian at UB. She helped me so much with my term papers. She always dresses nice, but I wish I had the guts to tell her. I owe her a lot."

"You're not talking about your father now, are you?" He tried to follow her unpredictable train of thought.

"Why would I do that? I just told you she can't help me," Megan scolded. "I'm talking about her saggy tits. They make her look older, just resting there. She needs to buy a sturdy new brassiere and I don't know how to tell her that."

Burrows exploded with laughter.

Megan's unexpected concern over some woman's breasts captured the right ending to a very long night. The thought was so ridiculous, so surprising, so very like Megan.

Burrows opened the front door. "Megan. Megan. I don't know what I'm going to do with you." He crossed the front porch and stood edging the front steps.

"You can be a grandfather to my children." She followed him, "You and Peggy for me."

"What are you saying?" he asked. "I can't do that."

"Why not," her blue eyes misted. "Beside Peggy, you've done more for me then anyone I know. Brad has a family. Why can't I, with you and Peggy? You can be the family I never had."

In the detective's world, things were black and white. Facts were facts and there was no room for shades of gray.

"It doesn't work that way. You're born into a family. You don't just pick and choose at random."

"That's crap and you know it!" she hissed, angrily. "Tell that to the kids who have been adopted. Tell them they don't have a family," she insisted. "So, why can't I adopt you?"

Ben studied Megan silently. Deep inside, the young fragile woman was starving for the affection one gets from belonging to a loving group...a real family. And, this young woman hungered for a father figure. She already had a substitute for Josephine, and Megan needed Ben to complete the family circle, particularly if her father really was dead.

"When the time comes, Peggy and I will take care of it," he reassured her.

Then, he thought about the prospects of finding her real father. "You're a good girl, Megan Croft. We care about you. Remember that." Ben knew that he would help the young woman, but it had to be on his own time.

Ben's parting words left Megan with a profound sense of peace. She couldn't remember ever feeling like that. In fact, never in her entire life could she ever remember feeling that way. She watched him saunter down the steps and drive away. Moments later, Megan turned off all the outside lights. She began to smile, as she thought about the grandfather for her children, and a papa for his daughter.

Papa Frog Prince

The title had a nice ring to it.

Chapter 16
Burrows' House

When Ben Burrows entered his home on Ayer Road, he followed a routine of someone accustomed to living alone...car in the garage, keys, wallet and cell phone on the nightstand and gun inside, the usual resting place for a weapon.

Aside from those items specified in the bedroom part of the house, were other work-related articles that needed his perusal before retiring. A notepad and pencil lay on the kitchen table waiting for a nightly review, while a sports coat idly hugged the arms of a captain's chair. But, as was his custom, he also needed the necessary fortification to clarify his thinking.

After pulling a bottle of single malt scotch and a glass from the kitchen cupboard, Ben placed them on the granite counter and reached for the phone. He hated making the call, but not because it was bad news. On the contrary, the detective wished he could bring this kind of message to every family missing one of their members.

The fact that he knew the man's shallow character really annoyed him. The false concern for his wife riled him even more. Of course, his dislike for Jeff Roberts may have been triggered by Megan's assessment of her brother-in-law, although, as it turned out, the woman was right on target.

Jeff Roberts really was an asshole.

The philandering of men was nothing new to Burrows, or the cases he followed, but to actively screw around when his wife went missing was a real first. At least, for him it was. If Peggy Roberts had been found dead, the husband would have been knee deep in it. As it was, Jeff Roberts had been the prime suspect when he first filed the report. Now that Peggy surfaced, he was no longer someone of interest.

Now, the case moved in another direction: finding Judd's body and the man, Mel, who murdered him. Arresting the person behind the whole boondoggle would come later, much later. Right now, he had nothing except the return of a woman who was reported missing.

Having made this kind of phone call hundreds of times before, Burrows knew exactly what to say. He would start first with apologizing for the hour. Then, he would go on to briefly explain the good news.

"Yes, she's fine," he spoke into the phone. "Mrs. Roberts had been abducted, but was later rescued. No injuries. She asked to be driven to her sister's house. What do you mean?"

Burrows knew exactly where the man was coming from, but he wasn't getting involved in their marital affair.

"I have no idea," he told Jeff Roberts. "That's the address she gave. My concern is the case and the fact that she is safe. But, I will need to question her again. This, you understand, is an ongoing investigation."

Jeff Roberts raised several more questions, but was frustrated by the detective's cool non-committal answers. The conversation was over in minutes.

"*He's pissed.*" Burrows poured a drink and scanned his notes briefly.

"Read my report," he told an imaginary Jeff Roberts, "then kiss my ass."

He eyeballed his glass of scotch. *If Judd's body doesn't turn up soon, I'll have no case to speak of.*

Within the hour, the detective had turned off the lights, crossed the darkened living room and stumbled on the way to his bedroom.

"Son of a bitch," he said aloud, hurting his foot. "I left the table in the middle of the room."

"*Poker was three days ago,*" an inner voice reminded him.

"Screw yourself," he answered and slipped into bed.

He should have moved it back to the corner of the living room when the game was over. Maybe he shouldn't have bought the table in the first place.

"*Seth bought it,*" the inner voice corrected him. "*The men got tired of moving your kitchen table to the living room every month. It's oval anyhow. Poag wanted a round table for poker.*"

That was true, Burrows recalled. He found the table sitting in the middle of the living room, when he came home from the station one day, courtesy of Seth. There had been a note on it that read, 'Poag thinks this might improve your game.'

Later, he learned Poag actually selected the table and both men planted it there. That they entered his home without his knowledge came as a surprise. But, it could not be construed as criminal trespass. Burrows had given his sister a key to his home years ago, when Julie was alive...when she lay dying.

Normally, the group moved the table at evening's end. That did not happen this time. It was so late when the game broke up and everyone was anxious to go home. So, Ben said he would take care of it. Moving the table was no big deal. He could handle it by himself. But, maybe they should start playing earlier. He would check with the guys.

The monthly poker game had always been held at his house after Julie died. But, he wasn't the careful housekeeper she was. Nor did he pretend to be, as his mind wandered back.

Before her demise, they played bridge with Fred and Janice Sommers every month, alternating houses. The girls initially met at some library club and struck up a friendship that included a restaurant dinner with the husbands. When it was discovered all four enjoyed bridge, the calendar was set for a monthly game. Then, within a short time, the foursome seemed to meet more and more frequently, whether it was going out for an evening, or watching Sunday football and eating chili afterward.

Whether it was gradual or sudden, Ben couldn't remember. He couldn't remember, even now. Julie began to lose weight and felt happy to shed a few pounds, until she felt the sharp pain of cramps. It was only when the stomach pains grew severe that she agreed to a physical. Afterward, more tests were scheduled. The news came a week later, and the results crushed their hopes of enjoying a long life together.

Ben remembered the nightmare vividly. She wanted to die at home, refusing any suggestion by the doctor for a hospice stay. Ben tried to be with her as much as he could. Clarisa helped when she was available, but the motel took much of her time.

The full brunt of caring for Julie fell on Janice, although she never complained. If Ben was needed on a case, Janice would rush over to care for her friend in every way possible.

While Julie slept, Janice cleaned house, did laundry and cooked meals that could be frozen for a later time.

Without question, Janice Sommers was a remarkable woman. He could not have managed without her. Fred was a lucky man to have Janice, despite her kicking him out of the gift shop earlier that day. Janice Sommers had spirit. Genteel as she was ninety-nine percent of the time, the remaining one percent was like a house fire, once the flame got started.

His thoughts returned to Julie.

It was too quiet when she left him. He held her hand as he always did at her bedside. His eyes were glued to hers and he remembered the small, quiet gasp before the final hand of death touched her. He remembered Janice patting his shoulder.

"She's gone, Ben. I'll leave you alone."

He knew what she meant. Ben needed to tell Julie goodbye. He needed to tell her how much she meant to him….how life would be so deplorable without her…how he wanted to go with her…to whatever destination there was after death. Wherever the place, he wanted to be with her.

Ben remembered it well.

He rested his head on Julie's still warm hand and wept profusely. It was only when the undertaker arrived that Ben released it. He sat in their room, a broken, lonely man waiting for the bony hand of death to touch him, too.

Janice and Fred followed through with all of Ben's scheduled funeral arrangements. They were kind. They gave him time to make peace with himself and time to accept death.

After a few months passed by, Fred suggested they start a monthly poker game. With a confusion of mixed household schedules, nothing went well, at first. Then, Poag coaxed Ben into using his house permanently for the monthly game. Between Fred's friends at Planning and Ben's cronies at the police station, they had an oversupply of willing players.

Poag played occasionally, but only when business was slow. Seth, of course, never made it. He spent his evenings with Helen. Later, he found it too unbearable to play cards. He detested the hand life had dealt him.

Thinking of Seth brought his thoughts to the present case. Before he could start questioning anyone about Judd, Seth would have to file a missing person report. He didn't need the forty-eight hour wait. Judd had been missing for two days so he could start an official investigation now and begin to question people of interest. He would question Judd's co-workers first, a waste of time, of course. But, that had to be done before he could question Nancy Travers to find Mel. Linking Nancy Travers to Judd was a piece of cake. He had access to Judd's phone records.

Ben pulled up the bed covers around him. For some inexplicable reason, he thought of Megan.

If they could have had children, he would have enjoyed a daughter like her. God knows they tried. A smile crossed his face. The nursery school mothers were in for a real treat.

Within minutes, the Frog Prince was fast asleep.

Chapter 17
Sisters

Later that night, when Peggy was getting ready to retire, Megan entered the room and sat on the bed beside her sister.

"Is it okay if we talk for a few minutes? I mean, while we're alone?"

"Sure. What's up?"

Although Peggy responded quickly to Megan's request, she hoped there would be no more questions about the kidnapping. She had to evade any question that would lead her to mention Mel Travers or John Beck. Yet, she felt fairly certain Megan's questions would concern Jeff. However, Peggy was very surprised when Megan requested something very different.

"I'm not stupid, Peggy," her sister began. "And, I'm smart enough, not to ask you any more questions about the case. I know there's more to this kidnapping than you can tell me right now. But, I'd like you to promise me something."

"Like what?" Peggy took her sister's hands. "What do you want?"

"I want your promise that after everything is over...the case, I mean. You'll tell me what happened. All of it."

Peggy studied her sister and smiled.

"Only if you tell me what happened the day you started calling mother, Josephine."

"You still remember that?" Megan made an ugly face. "Yuk."

"I might not have been there for the battle, but I certainly was there for the bloody aftermath. No surrender, as I recall."

Peggy's mind shifted back again to Megan's teenage years.

She remembered the constant fighting that went on between her mother and Megan. After the armpit episode, the battle just continued to escalate. Then, after work one summer day during the college interim, Peggy found Megan sitting on the front stoop with a frying pan in her hands. At that point, she knew the verbal battle had spiraled into something more dangerously physical. Then, Peggy became afraid. How could she attend college and still protect her sister?

She remembered hearing Megan spew each and every profanity on record, along with some relatively new provocative slang, whose meanings only high school students could understand. But, Peggy never knew the exact cause of her sister's anger…what precipitated it. Still, neither of them would tell her the circumstances that triggered the event. They refused to talk to her.

Peggy could only guess, after learning her mother's current boyfriend left the house permanently…and fuming with rage. Peggy knew then what she had to do. Getting her sister away from Josephine's quagmire of men was Megan's only real chance of survival.

"I can still see you on the stoop," Peggy reminded her. "You were holding a cast iron frying pan."

"My weapon of the moment," Megan replied. "That was decision day for me."

"Megan, I am sorry I wasn't there for you. Maybe I shouldn't have gone away to school."

"You couldn't be with me every minute," she insisted. "It wasn't easy for you either," she quickly added. "You worked every summer for college money. Graduating was the only way you could get us out of that hell hole we called home."

Megan caught her sister's puzzled look. "What don't you understand?"

"What really happened? I know she hurt you."

"She didn't believe me. Josephine took his part. 'I enticed him.' That's what she said. Can you picture that? Skinny little me enticing her current find?" Megan explained her dilemma.

"I thought it was something like that. But, I wasn't sure. No one would tell me anything." Peggy was not surprised. Her mother always had some stray male around to service for making major house repairs.

"He made a move on me in the kitchen and I tried to hit him in the balls with a frying pan. But, I must have hit his chest instead. Anyhow, while he's yelling in pain, I ran out of the kitchen just in time to meet the house witch. She walked in right after it happened and found him crouched on the floor."

Megan was on a roll. It was unlikely that she would forget that day.

"He was the ugly one with a beard. Remember him? He always looked dirty and smelled like beer. You know who I mean, the one who put up the back fence. Josephine always called him, Fergie. I think his last name was Ferguson."

Then, Megan continued her story.

"When I told her he tried to get into my pants, she started screaming at me. I was to blame for the attack. It was entirely my fault…my doing… my encouragement. So, I thought, screw it. If my own mother takes the word of some pervert over her own daughter, then she's no longer deserves the title. That's when I started calling her, Josephine. You took better care of me than she ever did." Megan eyes became misty at first, and then, she broke down completely.

Peggy threw her arms around her little sister and held her until the sobbing began to ebb. She knew there was more to the damning confrontation with Josephine, more details than Megan told her, but the gist of it was quite clear.

What part of intended rape couldn't her mother understand?

"No one is going to hurt you, Megan. I'll always be here for you. And Brad loves you very, very much. He would not allow any harm to come to you, believe me."

"I know. I love him, too, Peggy. I really love him." Megan stopped suddenly. She had completely forgotten about Peggy's own suffering.

"You're a very lucky young woman," Peggy reiterated. "You have a husband who adores you, a loving sister and a fan who thinks you're terrific."

"What? Who? You're making this up." Megan gushed.

"No. I'm not. Ben Burrows really likes you. He told me."

"For sure?"

"Absolutely," Peggy replied.

Megan was too excited to respond. That Ben Burrows truly liked her made Megan ecstatic. It didn't matter how much his eyes bulged, he would always be her Frog Prince.

"I believe in Fairy Tales," Megan said, wistfully, a soft smile breaking into her train of thought. "If you wish hard enough, and long enough, things you dream about will come true."

Peggy watched her sister with interest. The fantasy trip she had just finished had been more of a living nightmare than a daydream paradise. Nevertheless, she did not want to break Megan's euphoric mood.

"That means you found your Prince Charming," Peggy nodded reassuringly.

"He's so much more than a handsome prince, he's magic." She emphasized his importance. As she turned to leave, Megan reminded Peggy of her promise.

"I will, Megan, when the case is over."

"I'm glad you're safe. We were really worried."

"I know," she nodded.

Peggy watched her sister leave the room, but quite suddenly, Megan dropped her hand off the door knob, and turned abruptly to face her once again.

"What's he really like?" she asked.

"I think he's a very competent detective and a very nice man."

"Not Ben Burrows," Megan interrupted. "Seth Stone. What's he like?"

Peggy was slow to respond to her sister's question.

What could she say about Seth? The man saved her life. She owned him everything, but he expected nothing in return... wanted nothing. Since he was not a house painter, the prospect of their meeting again was zero. They lived in two different worlds. Yet, she would miss him. Aside from rescuing her, Seth had become her friend.

"He is probably the most honorable man I have ever met." Peggy felt it was an honest assessment. Saying anything further could be misinterpreted.

"You mean he's boring," Megan corrected her.

"No. He's very interesting. Seth's extremely intelligent and quite articulate. You'd like him."

"So when do I meet him?"

"You don't," Peggy discouraged her. "Don't push it, Megan. Let the case run its course."

"Oh. I wasn't thinking." She opened the bedroom door, "I'll see you in the morning, Maggie Pie."

"What did you say?" Peggy asked.

"I said I'll see you in the morning." Megan closed the bedroom door.

***

As she walked down the hall to her bedroom, Megan thought about her conversation with Ben. They talked about so many things. Would they come to fruition? She could only hope. Ben told Peggy he liked her. The fact, that someone other than her husband and sister cared, made a difference. And she felt good about being liked by someone worthy of her.

It was a good feeling knowing that someone outside the family cared for you. Now, if she could get her Frog Prince inside the family, Megan would have it all. She needed to work on that.

***

Down the hall, Peggy wrestled with her own thoughts. What prompted Megan's comment about fairy tales? What was she babbling about now? Of course, Peggy knew her sister's Prince Charming. Brad Croft was a wonderful man and an adoring husband. He certainly would fit the bill in Grimm's or anybody else's fairy tale. Megan could be strange, sometimes.

Then too, what prompted Megan to call her, Maggie Pie? Where did she get that nickname? Is that what her father called her? Did her sister remember something Peggy forgot? Instead of talking about Josephine, Peggy needed a conversation with Megan about their father. Yet, if Peggy couldn't remember the man, how could Megan? She was so much younger when he went away. Megan couldn't have been more than two or three. Was remembering him even possible...at that early age?

Her thoughts wrestled that question as she slowly drifted off to sleep.

Chapter 18
Kitchen Talk

Early next morning, Peggy made a determined effort to grab a quick cup of coffee and have Megan take her home as soon as possible. Jeff would be waiting for her with expectations of some dramatic or explosive scene. Any mention of his tryst with Alice would be pointless. There could be no denial.

Remaining between them were two options: forgiveness or divorce.

But she was not in a very forgiving mood. If Peggy were more like her sister, she would engage in some furious shouting match, while throwing things to maim or injure his manhood. But, Peggy was not Megan. However, the thought of injuring that specific area did seem to have merit.

But, something had changed deep within her. She felt different. Yet, she didn't know why. Maybe the abduction caused it...the fear that set in when she was alone, frightened and afraid of death. Whether it was her stream of consciousness or her psyche, a change of consequence had occurred. She began to see things from a different perspective.

Perhaps the change came when Seth saved her and Peggy knew she had been given another chance at life. Or it could have been the stark realization that Jeff was more interested in promoting his own sexual wantonness than feeling real concern for his missing wife. That was the biggest hurt of all. Was he always that way? Was he always for himself? Had love blinded her so completely that she was devoid of having any rational judgment?

When he worked late, was Jeff really doing his job for Pace or was he at some local motel? Why hadn't she seen this side of him before? Had she caught a glimpse of this behavior, sometime earlier, and simply refused to believe it, erasing any suspicion from her mind?

There was no point in berating herself. Everything had finally surfaced. There was no going back now. The trust was gone; the love, eroded. In Peggy's mind, the marriage was over. Now, it was important she control her emotions when they met. Regardless of how she really felt, it was necessary to maintain a calm presence.

"So, do you think the scumbag's home?" Megan asked, as she parked in the driveway. "His car could be in the garage."

"He's waiting for me." Peggy was quick to reply. "Don't interfere with our conversation, Megan. Go to the kitchen or somewhere else in the house. Please."

"I think that's a dumb idea. If he comes after you, I'm grabbing a poker."

The picture of Megan choosing a poker instead of a frying pan made her smile.

"Don't worry. Deep down inside where it really counts, Jeff's a coward."

Peggy's insight surprised her sister.

"The last thing he wants is a public confrontation," Peggy said, turning the front door knob slowly before entering the house.

"I've been waiting for you," Jeff greeted her from the living room sofa. "I see you brought your bodyguard with you."

Peggy watched Megan enter the kitchen, and then turned to face her husband.

"I wouldn't go down that road, if I were you," Peggy spoke calmly. "At this point, you have too much to lose."

"That sounds like a threat," Jeff replied, interpreting her remark.

"No. I'm just not in the mood for one of your mind games."

Peggy ignored him, as she wandered down the hall toward a small office adjacent the family room. Although she heard his footsteps following her, Peggy had no idea how much her cool composure disconcerted him.

Jeff's mind was a jumble. His wife looked too calm and he wondered what she had planned for him. Something about her seemed different. But he couldn't interpret what it was.

Would she make him suffer and exact her pound of flesh? That's what women did when men wronged them in some way. If that was her plan, it wouldn't work. Not with him. It was too transparent. She needed to come up with something better than that.

He would admit to the mistake with Alice, since she caught him in the act, so to speak, and then, he would go on from there. Still, Peggy was not a stupid woman. He had hurt her deeply. Now, he would have to pace himself if they were to continue the marriage.

She walked over to the desk. After taking an expanding folder from the bottom drawer, she filled it with selected papers, two bank books, a ledger and two safety deposit box keys.

"Where do you think you're going with those?" Jeff demanded. "You are not leaving the house with our files."

"Then, come with me. I'm having everything copied. The attorney will need a record of our finances when I file for divorce. I want half of the estate plus the house. The terms are not negotiable."

At that moment, Jeff knew it was going to be very difficult getting Peggy to change her mind about divorcing him. He blamed Megan, his nemesis, for his wife's tenacious attitude. His sister-in-law would anticipate the dissolution of their marriage with glee. Oh, how she would gloat and try to belittle him. Her hatred of him began long before the day of his wedding, although Jeff could never ascertain when it actually started. Yet, he felt the growing strength of her loathing during their years of living together, and any attempt to ease that situation failed.

When Megan finally married and moved out of the house, Jeff felt they had been given a second reprieve at life. But that only lasted temporarily. Megan found every possible excuse to be around her sister, regardless of the day or hour.

While Jeff was lost in thought, Peggy waited silently for him to raise some sort of objection to her settlement terms. However, Jeff surprised her when he referred to something she had mentioned earlier.

"I can make copies at the office," Jeff replied, "and you won't have to pay for them."

"Sorry. Trust is not your long suit," Peggy interrupted. "I could always use our printer, but I prefer going to Mr. Copy."

"You know we can work this out, if you'd only give me another chance. It didn't mean anything," Jeff pleaded.

"It did to me." Peggy brushed him aside. "Death would have been kinder."

"I want you to forgive me, Peggy. You know I love you. I always have. I'll do anything you ask. Anything. I never meant to hurt you. I know I made a terrible mistake."

Peggy met her husband's stare. The man was so pathetic. Was he really sincere or putting on a good show? She suspected the latter. In either case, it didn't matter anymore. They could never go back to the way they were.

"Then, don't make another one," she suggested. "We can end the marriage like two rational people or start slinging mud in the courts. In either case, you will not win."

"Don't be too sure of that." His attitude changed suddenly. Women always threatened when they were on the losing side of an argument.

"Oh, I think the judge will side with the wife whose husband was out screwing around when she was abducted from her home."

"When Burrows phoned last night, he said you were kidnapped, but he never gave me any details. He just told me you were safe and wanted to stay at Megan's," he said, avoiding her comment.

"It doesn't matter now. We both know what went on in my absence. As far as I'm concerned, we're done."

"Is this what you really want?" Jeff thought she might soften with a little cajoling. "We've been together five years and for one mistake, you're going to throw it all away?"

"No. Jeff. You did that. You threw it all away." She corrected him. "Just like so much garbage."

Peggy continued to meet his stare.

Inwardly, Jeff was puzzled. He had never remembered her this way. This was not the same woman who walked down the aisle with him five years earlier. She was warm and loving then. This woman's temperament was vastly different. She was so cold, so unforgiving and so determined to end the marriage. It was precisely then that Jeff realized there was nothing more he could say to change her mind. But, he continued to hope, she would have a change of heart later, when things settled a little more...when she looked at all the alternatives.

"I'm contacting an attorney today with instructions on our estate. I already told you my terms." Peggy reaffirmed her position. "I will give him a copy of the files, so he can start the paperwork."

"And, if we don't reach an agreement?" Jeff continued to think ahead. If he delayed long enough she might consider reconciling. Jeff needed to derail her immediate plans, but how could he do that? So much was at stake.

"Well, then, there are the pictures. John would learn of your extramarital romp and Pace would no longer want you in management, if they wanted you at all. Breaking the rules with a co-worker's wife could be a job killer."

"You've made your point, but I am not moving out of the house until this is settled." Jeff turned to leave.

"Your things will be moved to the guest room. Just so you understand."

"I don't care if you sleep with your bodyguard; I have no interest in touching you." He stormed out of the house.

Peggy had finally pushed the right buttons.

***

"The fault, dear Brutus, is not in the stars." Megan rushed to Peggy's side, quoting Shakespeare. "You were brilliant."

"I don't feel brilliant, I feel numb." Peggy sat on a kitchen chair and began to cry. "I didn't want it to end this way. I never thought my marriage would end in divorce. I thought we were happy. I was happy. Where did I go wrong?" Peggy sobbed uncontrollably.

Megan hated seeing her sister suffer this way. Yet, there was little she could do. She knew Peggy would be much better off without Jeff, but for now, she had to be supportive. Ben told her this would happen. He also told her, not to remind Peggy she married an asshole, or something on that order. What could she possibly do to help her sister?

Megan didn't know what to do, so she decided to make a pot of coffee. She thought Peggy would like that. As she set out the cups and saucers, she heard someone knocking on the front door.

"I'm so glad to see you!" Megan exclaimed, pulling Janice into the living room. "She's a wreck," she whispered. "The kidnapping is only the half of it." Megan took Janice's hand and walked her into the kitchen.

"Look who I found on the welcome mat," Megan addressed her sister.

"Oh. Peggy!" Janice rushed to embrace her. "I was so afraid when you went missing. Let me look at you."

Janice studied Peggy's tearful face. "Something is seriously wrong here," she addressed Megan. "I want to know what caused this breakdown and whom do we hold responsible?"

"Whom...as in Jeff," Megan answered quickly. "That's whom."

"Pour the coffee, Megan." Peggy swallowed hard between tearful gasps. "I want Janice to know the whole story. Confidential or not, I know it won't leave this room."

Peggy knew from past history that anything she told Janice in confidence never came back to haunt her. And, while she trusted the woman completely, Peggy had to be careful how she handled the story of her abduction. She also had to make certain the story duplicated the one she told her sister.

Peggy carefully reconstructed the kidnapping, giving the story the same details that she had given Megan. Neither Mel Travers nor John Beck was mentioned, although Peggy did credit Ben Burrows for his thorough investigative work. Then, when she told Janice about Jeff's infidelity, the woman became grief stricken.

"Oh, Peggy, to suffer an ordeal like that and then to experience outright betrayal at home. That skinny little slut! Does John know?"

"Who's going to tell him?" Peggy replied. "Not me. I just want out of this marriage." Peggy dried her eyes.

Janice studied her for a moment and wondered if the woman had given her marriage enough thought. Was she merely moving toward divorce because Jeff cheated on her? Had she weighed her years of happiness with the man she loved, against the future years of living alone? Had she carefully considered every aspect involved with the dissolution of her marriage, both financial and emotional? The final decision could not be taken lightly. Divorce was a very serious matter.

"I'm a lot older than you, Peggy, and I want you to think about something before you see your attorney. If you still love your husband, can't you find it in your heart to forgive him this one mistake?"

"Could you, if Fred slept with someone else?" Peggy challenged.

"I think I could," Janice answered, without a second thought. "My life is much better with Fred than without him."

"Yes, but you've got at least twenty years on Peggy," Megan interrupted. "Pickins get slimmer as you get older."

"Thanks Megan, I really needed your running commentary on my age," Janice quipped sarcastically. "But, you know what I mean," she said to Peggy.

"I do, but then, I can't. I don't know what's in store for me, but truth be told, I can't go on with Jeff. I know now my original suspicions were correct. I feel it in my heart."

Both Megan and Janice were puzzled by her statement. They watched her walk down the hall, pick up her shop ledger and return to the kitchen table. Peggy flipped to the back pocket and slowly pulled out two ticket stubs to a past production at the Shaw Theater and placed them on the table.

The two women eyed the ticket stubs in silence and waited for Peggy's explanation.

"I've never been to Niagara on the Lake, let alone the Shaw Theater." She referred to the Canadian tourist town on Lake Ontario that vacationers visited annually.

Her comment took Megan by surprise. For a solitary moment, she was left flabbergasted and speechless. This was so unexpected. Even for someone like Jeff. Janice was bereft of words, thinking of Jeff's visit there with someone other than Peggy. Nevertheless, they were mesmerized with her next revelation.

Peggy slid her hand once again inside the ledger pocket and pulled out two small signs that read, 'Second Seating.' She placed them carefully on the table.

"I've never been to Opal's for dinner at Niagara on the Lake," Peggy said quietly, but was startled suddenly by Megan's loud rebellious outcry.

"That sneaky son of a bitch!"

Megan's anger reverberated throughout the room, the house, and most probably, the neighborhood. That she was consumed with total rage was much more than an understatement. Had Jeff Roberts still been at home, Megan would have surely attacked the man with the fireplace poker, banging his genitalia first.

Peggy placed the ticket stubs and signs back into the ledger pocket and felt the need to clarify her method of discovery. It was important that they understood what she was going through emotionally. But before she could explain, Megan was screaming at her.

"He's made a mockery of your whole fricken marriage, for Christ sake. How could you not suspect him of cheating?" Megan blustered, her eyes blazing with anger.

"I really don't know. Maybe, subconsciously I didn't want to. Maybe I loved him too much to care." Peggy answered her sister's question as honestly as she could.

Did she really not want to know? Peggy wrestled with that question sometime ago. She did suspect, but, in the end, Peggy's suspicions got her nowhere. When they were together, Jeff only focused on her, giving her all the love and attention she could possibly want.

All told, he was a very loving and considerate husband. Ask any of their friends. She could not have asked for a more perfect mate to spend a lifetime with. Now, it was plain that he had this one imperfection in his character...one with which she could not abide.

"Over the years, I've found snippets of things...you know, from the cleaners and doing laundry, but I never gave it much thought until lately." She took a sip of coffee.

"I don't quite understand," Janice questioned. "What gave him away finally?"

"Finding him in a motel room with another woman would do it every time," Megan interjected. "It doesn't get clearer than that."

Peggy ignored Megan's comment and answered Janice's question.

"I began to suspect Jeff of seeing other women months ago. The ticket date for the Shaw differs from Opal's second seating. So, Jeff was at Niagara on the Lake at least twice and maybe with two different women. But, then when Jeff was home, he was so wonderful to me. I erased all those ugly suspicions from my mind."

"I am truly shocked," Janice replied. "I had no idea this was going on. I am so sorry this happened to you."

"Why should you be shocked?" Megan addressed Janice. "She's been living with Dr. Jekyll for years. She finally met Mr. Hyde the other night."

"I just wanted both of you to understand why I can't stay with him," she dismissed her sister's harangue. "The trust has completely eroded, and the love that I once felt for the man has dwindled to nothing."

Peggy studied both women. They sat looking at her, waiting for her to speak.

"I can't explain it, my feelings, I mean. I guess, I thought because Jeff loved me so much, he would be unable to function when I went missing. Instead, he went outside our marriage to satisfy his own sexual perversions. I can't tell you how much that hurt me. How little, I must really mean to him." She wiped her eyes again.

Peggy began sipping her coffee slowly and picked up another train of thought. "What it all boils down to is this. Jeff Roberts loves himself more than he loves me," she explained. "I am not the first priority in his book of marriage. Second, I could never trust him to be faithful. That's who he is. If I stay with him, I have to accept his philandering, because I know it will happen again. No matter what he promises, I will always suspect him of playing around."

"No." She eyed the two women, explaining further. "I don't want that kind of marriage. I'd rather live alone, get a cat and shack up with the lawn boy when I want sex."

"The lawn boy!" Janice chirped.

Janice pictured the short, skinny, old man in khakis, who cut their grass, while Megan clapped her hands in glee. She was enjoying every minute of the conversation.

"I didn't mean that literally, for God's sake. I'm trying to explain how I can get my life back with some measure of respect."

"That's too bad," Megan opined. "I like the little old lawn boy, but I'm not sure he can fire up the innards!"

Megan caught Peggy's look, but said nothing further. The way things were going for her sister, sex wouldn't be the issue; the lack of it, would.

"Can you imagine what people will say when the news of our divorce gets out?" Peggy waited for their response.

"I can always tell them what a real shit he is," Megan replied.

"You don't want to do that," Janice interjected. "People tend to distort gossip and you don't want anything to mar Peggy's reputation."

"When someone asks either of you why we are getting divorced, just tell them I couldn't discuss anything on the advice of my attorney."

Peggy collected her thoughts momentarily and addressed the subject again.

"It is imperative that you do not, I repeat do not, ever mention Alice Beck concerning me or the divorce. Not under any circumstances. With divorce proceedings, you never can tell what will happen. I could lose everything. And I want the house."

Although Peggy spoke outwardly about real estate, she worried that John Beck would somehow learn of her knowing about him and his role in the kidnapping. Linking him to Mel would put her in real danger. Fighting in court for a house was a lot different than fighting for her life. She needed to keep as far away from John Beck as humanly possible. He would never hear about Alice from her.

"That's not going to happen, is it?" Megan eyed Janice. "You won't tell anyone."

"No. As a matter of fact, I won't. When Peggy's attorney gives her advice, that's the route she has to take. Otherwise, what's the point of having a lawyer? However, I do have a problem. What do I tell Fred?"

"Tell Fred about the kidnapping first," Peggy advised. "Then, tell him Jeff and I are getting divorced, but I am not allowed to go into any details. You know he's going to ask Jeff anyway."

"Will that affect you if he does?" Now, it was Megan's turn to ask the question.

"I don't think so. If Fred has to testify in court, then he can tell them his information came from Jeff."

"Oh, lord!" Janice exclaimed.

From her terse outcry, Peggy knew she had pulled it off. Fred would not be asking either of them questions. Janice would see to that. Her neighbor wanted no involvement in their divorce proceedings, and that was exactly what Peggy had in mind. No questions and no interference from anyone. Megan was another story. Peggy was determined to keep her sister away from Jeff and the fireplace poker.

"What about Ben?" Janice asked. "I know you aren't finished with the case yet. So, when do you see him again?"

"I don't know. I think he's still gathering information, talking to people. And, since I was blindfolded, I can't be asked to identify anyone he considers a suspect. Who knows? Maybe he will never solve it."

"And the man who saved you, I think you said his name was Seth."

"I was very lucky," Peggy offered. "I dread to think of the consequences if he hadn't come along."

Peggy did not want to linger on Seth's role in saving her. For all intents and purposes, she did not want to talk about him at all. There was no reason for Seth's name to be dragged into anything remotely connected to her divorce.

"But, isn't he still involved somehow?" Janice continued to question.

"Only to the extent of his missing brother. I think Burrows will meet with him when he gets more information about Judd. But, unless there are further developments, I think the case is at a standstill."

"Then, Ben better concentrate on finding whoever took you. He's very good at what he does." Janice stood up to leave. "Nothing rests unless he's satisfied."

"Don't worry about the store," she added, "I'll handle it. Amy's there now. If something happens, call me. You know I'm here for you."

Peggy hugged Janice and laughed. "You're not going to tell Fred I want to hump the lawn boy, are you?"

"No. I'll keep that our secret. Who knows, maybe short, skinny men are good in bed." She closed the front door and crossed the lawn.

***

Down the street, the sound of a mower roared in a neighbor's yard. Janice stood on the sidewalk fronting her house and studied the short, skinny old man cutting grass.

"I'll be damned. Speak of the devil," she muttered, as she walked up her driveway.

"What devil are you talking about?" Fred Sommers demanded, as he came out to greet her.

"I don't know. He's short, wears khaki pants and rides a lawn-mower."

"I thought something might go wrong next door, so I took the morning off," Fred told his wife. "Maybe I should take you to bed, your hands feel warm."

"That's exactly what I've been thinking." She led him inside the house. In a strange way, Fred reminded her of the lawn boy. Maybe, it was his khakis.

Chapter 19
Apartment

Seth slipped out of room three early Tuesday morning. He felt restless and couldn't determine exactly why he felt that way. He hadn't slept well and felt weary. Yet, there was no need to linger. The meeting with Burrows had already taken place. It had been long after midnight when the detective heard their stories: Peggy's, first; and then, his.

Except for the photographs, all the information Burrows required had been given. So their next meeting would only involve giving the detective pictures of Mel Travers and John Beck at Remmy's Tavern. Further testimony would not be needed, unless either of them came up with new evidence. And, that probability seemed unlikely.

Still, as of that moment, Seth had other considerations...things that concerned Judd and his apartment. The thought of sorting and boxing all of Judd's belongings bothered him greatly. It meant his brother would not be returning there. It also meant Seth had to accept the stark reality that Judd was dead. Even with the realization of his death, he could not afford the luxury of mourning for his murdered brother. Seth had to notify the management complex he was vacating Judd's apartment, which, no doubt, suggested breaking the lease and paying a penalty. The financial end didn't bother him; the finality of it all, did.

Seth wondered if Burrows should accompany him. If Ben searched the apartment, would the detective be able to find more definitive clues to the kidnapping and murder? Seth thought it might be a viable possibility.

Then, he thought of Clarisa. She would be so unhappy that he did not stay for breakfast. She wanted his company, along with all the information he fed Burrows. It was just that way with Clarisa. She had to know exactly what was going on every minute, and with whom.

But, Poag would take care of that. He would simply discuss Judd's murder with her and also the effect it had on Seth, particularly since he witnessed the shooting. Then, Clarisa would grow quiet and completely understand why Seth wanted to be alone. He needed time to realize the full measure of his brother's death. Seth needed time to grieve. She had witnessed it before.

Seth's thoughts flashed back to another black time in his life.

With Helen's death, Poag had to deal with mourning the loss of his own sister, while trying to comfort a broken Seth, who fervently loved the woman, but also felt responsible for her demise. Nothing, Poag could offer, assuaged Seth's guilt. Had he met her at the bank, instead of the restaurant, Helen would have been alive today. Seth lamented this belief over and over. He would go to his grave shouldering that ton of guilt.

In time, Seth became sullen. Then, he just grew silent. Only the passing years mellowed his outlook on life. Although he cared for his mother for many years, her passing away affected him differently than the death of Helen or Judd. Seth could equate age with death. It was part of life's continuous cycle. Not part of life's equation, however, was taking the life of someone so young, with so many unfulfilled dreams.

In many ways, Judd's murder affected him more adversely than Helen's accidental death. Seth needed more than justice, he wanted revenge. Seth yearned to inflict Mel with the kind of pain that he was currently suffering...one that turned your insides into one churning void of unrelenting sorrow.

Seth realized he should have done more. He should have taken better care of Judd. He should have insisted Judd stay with him at the house. Had Judd lived with Seth, it would have been less likely that someone would have taken advantage of his mentally challenged brother. But Judd wanted to live independently, so Seth helped him financially with a generous monthly check which covered more than just the rent. By doing this, Seth felt his brother could live comfortably and perhaps save the money he earned from his job as a mechanic.

And, while these thoughts ran through his mind, and although he was not aware of it, Seth was reliving the Helen tragedy all over again. Had he done this instead of that, the outcome would have been different. Between her death and that of his brother's, the parallel was the same.

Seth was still lost in thought as he and Gabriel walked toward his car. As soon as Seth unlocked the door, Gabriel jumped into the back seat, stretched out end-to-end and gave a grateful grunt. He knew they were headed home, a place he could roam freely. However, once they reached Seth's house, Gabriel refused to leave his side. He followed him up two flights of stairs to a multi-windowed loft where the flow of classical music usually blended with Seth's artistic endeavors.

Today, however, was different. Gabriel watched his master develop a few photographs before making a phone call. Then, trolling back down the stairs, Gabriel watched Seth place a packet of newly developed photographs into his camera case before making another phone call.

When the brief conversation ended, Seth and Gabriel went for a ride in the car. This time, they went toward Cheektowaga. When they reached their destination, Seth and Gabriel sat in the parked car and waited. Within minutes, another car drove up and pulled in beside Seth's.

"You must have really pushed the pedal to get here so fast," Ben Burrows greeted Seth.

"I let Gabriel drive today," Seth said, as he reached for the photographs inside his camera case. "I took some of Mel by himself and a few others with Mel and John Beck together. There are two shots of Nancy Travers with Mel."

"These will prove they knew each other but little else. I need some real evidence." Burrows pocketed the photographs and pointed to the building. "Shall we?"

Seth took the lead to Judd's apartment with Gabriel following behind both men. As soon as Seth opened the front door, he stepped back in shock. He could not believe his eyes.

The stacks of paper had been removed, the filthy dishes no longer sat on the kitchen table and all the scraps of food were gone. No longer were mismatched socks and dirty underwear scattered throughout the apartment and on an unkempt bed. The characteristic smell of disinfectant permeated the apartment but the scent seemed to intensify in the bathroom area.

"This can't be," Seth explained. "Peggy and I were here Sunday night, actually Monday morning, technically speaking. This place was a shit hole."

"You broke into Judd's apartment? That's breaking and entering." Their eyes met. "Shut the hell up. Don't say anything else. I don't want to know."

"I had a key." Seth flashed his credit card to the disgruntled detective. "We only took his phone bills and a book of matches. That's how we found Nancy Travers. Through her, we were able to locate Mel."

Then, Ben became silent for a moment, as if pondering a theory relevant to the case.

"In what way did you connect Nancy Travers to Mel?"

"I don't know what you mean?" Seth was confused.

"Look around. You said the apartment was a mess. So, who came in here and cleaned the place? Was there someone in Judd's life? Someone we don't know about?"

"I don't know. Really, Ben, Judd never talked to me about anyone special."

"Then, it's time we find out." Ben left Seth to begin a search of the entire apartment.

"What are we looking for?" Seth followed the detective while Gabriel trailed both of them.

"We need to identify the woman in Judd's life. Only a woman would clean this thoroughly. She will be back for something another time, memorabilia perhaps. If we're lucky we might even find a connection to Mel."

Ben eyed Seth and his dog. "Since he's old enough to drive, maybe he can dig up some clues."

"Funny," Seth said, dryly. "C'mon Gabriel, Uncle Ben wants us to sniff around."

Seth walked into Judd's bedroom and began searching the drawers of a very large chest and then, a small night stand. Finding nothing of interest, he took the freshly made bed apart and then looked between the mattress and box springs. Once again his search proved futile.

Finally, Seth went through all the pockets of Judd's clothes. Although it was a repeat of his prior visit, Seth feared there may have been something he overlooked. That was not the case. He found nothing. However, on the shelf above the closet rack, Seth found a box filled with memorabilia.

He studied a picture of two boys, one quite a bit younger than the other, standing near a wooden fence. Although Seth couldn't remember either of them being so young, he did recall Judd's toothy grin.

He continued to flip through the pictures but stopped abruptly when two photographs caught his attention. Finally, he could connect some of the dots to Judd's murder. While Seth continued to be mesmerized with the photographs, Gabriel was pushing his nose under the bed, emitting soft growls. Seth knelt quickly and found an earring.

"Good boy," Seth said, scratching Gabriel's ears.

"Ben," he called, just as the detective entered the room. "You might be interested in these pictures."

Ben studied the two photographs. The same woman appeared in both snapshots but with two different men.

Seth opened his hand. "Look at the photographs again. Her earrings match this one. It was under the bed."

Burrows let out a low whistle after making the comparison.

"This puts a whole different light on the case," he said, after reading the inscription on the back. "If they really are brother and sister, Mel might have had her talk Judd into the kidnapping."

"That doesn't make sense. Why would Judd do something like that? I know. You're going to say money."

"People do stupid things for money, sex or love. I've seen it all. Or have you already forgotten Peggy's kidnapping and Jeff's infidelity?"

"No. I haven't," Seth frowned, "but to trap someone of low intelligence pushes the notch below slime."

"You're forgetting that Judd was used before. That's how he landed in jail the first time."

"So, you think Mel used Judd to kidnap Alice and then killed him when the plan failed. He murdered Judd and would have killed me after I disposed of Peggy. Is that your theory too? No witnesses, no case."

"We know the motive for the abduction was revenge. Beck knew about Jeff and Alice, but we can't prove he planned the whole thing. The picture of him with Mel at Remmy's Tavern only means they knew each other. That's it."

He was quick to add a further assessment.

"I haven't found anything that's going to stand out here. I've gone through the apartment. The dishes have been washed. No fingerprints, but I did find a cigarette butt with lipstick on it."

"That could be Nancy's, if she cleaned up the place," Seth offered. "You said it would be a woman."

"That's probably right," Burrows agreed. "Now, what's on your mind?" He noticed Seth's frown.

"If you think it's okay, I want to terminate the lease after I box Judd's things."

"Not yet. In two weeks, maybe," Ben eyed his friend. "Did you find any keys?"

"No. But, I did search Judd's pockets. Why?"

"Obviously, someone has a key to this apartment. I need to know who it is."

"My money's on Nancy Travers," Seth concluded.

"I plan to interview her, now that we have a little more to go on. Meanwhile, call this man. He'll make a key for you." He scrawled a phone number on a slip of paper. "Don't say another word. I don't want to know."

He walked toward the door and exited the apartment.

Seth watched his departing friend. Ben Burrows always had a directive before leaving someone. Seth sat on the couch with Gabriel beside him and slowly dialed the number Ben had given him. He hoped the appointment could be made quickly. Seth had other things on his mind...things much more important than a key to Judd's apartment.

Chapter 20
The Note

Hours later, Seth and Gabriel strolled into a gift shop and greeted the young girl behind the counter arranging things on glass shelves.

"I'm looking for Peggy Roberts. Is she here?"

Why he came to the shop today was puzzling and Seth began to chastise himself. He did not expect her to be working so shortly after the abduction, particularly when she had other things to settle, primarily, her husband's infidelity.

"No." The girl replied. "She's off today. Is there something I can help you with?"

"It's very important that I contact her. Can you phone her for me?"

Seth wondered about Peggy's present circumstances. Was she at home with her husband or still staying with her sister, Megan? Although he had her cell number, Seth felt it was better not contacting her directly. He did not want their relationship, what little there was of it, to be misconstrued by Peggy's husband or anyone else for that matter.

The young woman stared at the man and his dog. She was curious about his strange request, but felt his sense of urgency and dialed a phone number. All they heard was the ringing sound of her home telephone. When she redialed the number again, the same ringing sound was repeated.

"I'm sorry," the young woman apologized. "I guess she went out today."

"I appreciate your doing this for me," he said. "If you have a sheet of paper, I'd like to leave her a note." He watched the woman scramble for a sheet of note paper hidden somewhere in the stack of drawers. "You must be new here."

"This is just temporary. I'm filling in for my mother. I'm Amy Sommers."

"You're Janice's daughter." Seth remembered the name of Peggy's partner.

"I'm Seth Stone, a friend of Peggy's."

"You know my mother?" Amy gave him the note paper, a pen and an envelope.

"Not really, but I've heard a lot of wonderful things about her. In fact, she's quite a remarkable woman," he said, finishing his short note, which he folded and placed inside the unsealed envelope. "Thank you again."

Amy watched the man and his dog leave the store and wondered why he had to contact Peggy Roberts. What was so important to him? She removed the letter from the envelope to examine its contents. His handwriting was small and the note was very neatly written. It read:

> *Peggy,*
> *You need to call me.*
> *Seth*

His whole message conveyed nothing. Had he planned it that way? How did he know that she would read the note after he left? This man, Seth, was very clever and also quite handsome. Amy read the note once more before placing it back into the envelope.

Amy would tell her mother about the note at dinner, since she would be closing the shop. She hadn't expected that, either. Her mother wasn't feeling well, according to her father's phone call. He put mother to bed and took the day off to care for her. Amy was not surprised. At their age, they had to start taking it easy.

Shortly after leaving the shop, Seth retraced his steps to the car and watched Gabriel do his end-to-end routine in the back seat. Seth checked a scrawled note inside his camera case for a particular address, and then drove through the streets of Amherst in search of it. Within ten minutes, Seth accomplished his mission and drove back to Lockport. Somewhere along the way he and Gabriel stopped for a hamburger. That was probably the best part of their day.

Chapter 21
A Further Betrayal

Later that evening, when Jeff found Peggy alone in the house, he joined her on the family room sofa and began the speech he had been rehearsing all day.

"We need to talk and I'd rather do it without our attorneys."

"I'm not sure my lawyer would approve," Peggy replied.

"That's only because he wants to earn his fee." Jeff explained quickly, studying her mood.

Something about his wife's demeanor seemed totally different from their morning exchange. She sat still, transfixed like some marble statue, with her hands neatly folded in her lap, like a museum piece waiting for the throngs of onlookers to pass by, unaware of her or her faceless expression. He could feel the air of resignation.

Jeff weighed the difference in mood. Approximately, eight hours had elapsed since their first encounter. In some strange way, he found the change encouraging.

Earlier that morning, although calm and focused, Peggy moved like she was on a mission, one with a quick, clear resolution. She acted decisively, pushing aside any of his demands. Now, she seemed quiet and sober. Had Peggy reconsidered her options? Did she think the marriage worth saving or was divorce still her primary goal? He would have to tread carefully when he executed his carefully prepared speech, feeling his way to determine which of his words had the greatest impact on her.

Historically, men had been in this marital quagmire many times over and still resolved their betrayal issues unscathed. He certainly had the mental acuity to play hopscotch in the connubial game and win. He just needed to pace himself.

When he moved to take her hand, she pulled away instantly, making him understand the real constraints of their being together.

Conversation was key, nothing else. Her deafening silence made him quickly realize the woman he faced would not bend easily to his wishes.

"I don't want to go through with the divorce," he began. "What can I do to save our marriage? I'm begging you," he pleaded. "How can I get you to forgive me?"

Her steady stare caused him some discomfort. Regardless of anything else, he had to sound sincere and unrehearsed. She would not be fooled by a mere collection of words, no matter how well they were put together.

"I know I've made a mess of things," he said, almost to himself, and then raised the volume of his voice. "It may not seem like it. Now, that I've screwed up royally. But, I've always loved you. You know that."

"Jeff, please don't."

He expected much more conversation than the negative response she gave his apology. He needed a reply he could build on, something he could use for persuasion purposes. How could he mend their marital fence, if she wouldn't talk to him?

"Peggy," he tried once more. "I know I hurt you deeply and I can't take away the pain I caused. I made a terrible mistake. But, if you can forgive me, it will never happen again. We can continue to have a strong marriage and go back to where we were."

"And, that's what you want?" she asked quietly.

"I'm asking you for another chance."

"I can't," she said.

"So, for one mistake, it's all over. One mistake in five years," he repeated, "and you won't forgive me."

"Jeff, please." She placed her hand to her forehead, as if easing a headache. "I don't want to talk about Alice. It doesn't matter now."

"It's over with her. It didn't mean anything." He spoke with reassurance.

"It did to me. And, I'm sure it would mean something to John... if he knew," she added.

"Who gives a shit about John Beck," he fumed instantly. "I'm talking about us. I want to continue our marriage. I'll do anything to save what we have."

Peggy turned toward him slowly and spoke evenly.

"We have nothing worth saving, Jeff. I don't need a confession of sins. I know about your Niagara on the Lake romps, so screwing Alice was just adding one more whore to your stable."

"But –"

"No." Peggy stopped him from challenging her response. "My turn. When I was kidnapped and thought I would die, my only regret was never being with you again. I loved you so much. Corny as it sounds, you were like my morning sun and my evening sunset. I'd wake up to you in the morning and go to bed with you at night. You were my life, all that I lived for, all that I ever wanted."

As she spoke, there was something wistful about her, as if she remembered a happier time, a better place.

"When I was finally free to come home, you stabbed my heart, killing me with pain because another woman had taken my place. The fact that I was missing had no relevance in your plans for betrayal. A love I thought was pure and perfect was really sullied and flawed."

"Peggy, I—"

"Don't," she said, raising her hand. "It would only get worse." She said nothing further.

Jeff eyed his wife. How could it possibly worsen? She knew about his philandering and never said anything until he was physically caught. He studied her more carefully. He hadn't noticed the puffiness around her eyes before. Had she been crying after he left her that morning? Had she been in tears all day? He had caused her pain; he was well aware of that. Now, he sought a remedy, something that could mend her emotionally, if that was at all possible.

He wasn't sure she wanted his help. At that point, Jeff felt powerless to do anything. Her silence worried him. In their five years of marriage, he had never seen her like this. Not that this was the time for animation. But, her state of melancholy and dejection was so unnerving, so out of character. She was so unapproachable.

"Please talk to me. We can't come together if there's no conversation between us. Please, Peggy."

"Tell me," she began, her words coming slowly. "Have you ever felt devastated or really beaten? I mean, to the point where everything you once held dear, everything you once felt sacred, everything you loved in life that felt so right, turned out to be nothing but a charade...an icy foundation to a slippery marriage."

Jeff could not understand the point she was making. Something told him there was a message somewhere in her response, but he could not decipher her meaning.

"Am I to understand that you think our marriage is a charade? Five years of marriage is a charade?"

"I spent the afternoon going through our papers and found this." Peggy pulled a slip from her pocket, which she slowly unfolded and gave to him. "I've been on the pill for five years, and you've been shooting blanks the last three. How could you have been so cruel? How could you take away my dreams of family?"

Tears spilled from her eyes. "You've betrayed our marriage on every possible level. The wound in my heart will never heal because you cast my love aside for other women. The scars will forever be there. Then, you compounded my pain by taking away my dreams of having children. How could you have done this to me? How could you do this, to someone you claim to love? This was the ultimate betrayal. Forgiveness is no longer an issue."

Peggy kept wiping the tears from the bottom of her tee shirt. Then, she could no longer speak. The raging storm within her had finally erupted. Peggy wept uncontrollably and would not allow him to touch or try to comfort her. Instead, she stepped to the bathroom near the family room, splashed water on her face and returned several minutes later with a handful of tissues.

In her absence, Jeff sat in quiet reflection and held the doctor's invoice in his hands. He could not overcome the initial shock of discovery, particularly when he thought the document had been shredded years earlier. He looked at it closely. It was not the original. Peggy had given him a copy.

Stunned by her knowledge of his duplicity, Jeff knew he was beaten. Now, she would never consider reconciling with him. He wondered how much more damaging information she had. Would Peggy use it during the divorce proceedings to get what she wanted? This silent stranger who had sat beside him seemed extremely capable of gathering information to justify her claim. He could not underestimate her.

As Jeff continued waiting for Peggy, he worried about his position at Pace. Would he be demoted? More to the point, would his license be terminated with the company? He could visualize being called into the head office and asked to look for employment at some other brokerage. They would not want someone with a sullied reputation working their respectably rich clientele. Word of his debauchery would spread and no respectable brokerage would want him. He would be forced to move to another city. Jeff would be compelled to start all over...at the bottom of the shark pool.

Then, there was John Beck. He would learn all about Jeff and Alice if the divorce went public. What would he do to Jeff? John couldn't castigate him to his co-workers without looking like the cuckolded husband. Would he divorce Alice? Knowing John, the man would probably forgive his wife. She was just too beautiful to let go. Aside from perfection, Alice had the intelligence to match. Her husband adored her, was proud of her. That was obvious during their conversations at work.

Jeff knew they could never be close again. What he had done to the man was unforgiveable. He had allowed his carnal desires to sever their strong bond of friendship. The icy relationship would continue until one of them left the brokerage. Would John stay at Pace if Jeff continued to work there? Jeff thought not.

During the entire time Jeff searched his thoughts, not once, did he consider the emotional damage Peggy suffered, first by the kidnapping and then, by his betrayal. Not once, did his wife's ordeal cross his mind. His ego wouldn't let him.

But, the agony Peggy suffered was not once, but many times over, with everyone involved. Of course, John Beck was already aware of his wife's deceit. He knew long before Peggy about the trysts between Alice and Jeff. But, that fact would remain forever hidden in Peggy's closet of secrets.

At last, he felt Peggy's presence beside him.

"I've lost you, haven't I?" Jeff said finally. He had betrayed the one person he most adored in life. Tears began to flood his cheeks. "It's my own fault. I did it all."

"Yes, you did." A wayward tear ran down the side of Peggy's nose. "When I was kidnapped, I felt so alone and frightened. I remember being so cold in the dark. Blindfolded and trussed like some animal, I was so afraid of being killed. Yet, all I could think about was you and the pain of never seeing you again."

Tears continued to spill down her face. "All I ever wanted in life was you and a family. I got neither! I got neither!" she gasped loudly, repeating herself. "Neither."

Her face sank into her tissue-filled hands and she wept loudly and uncontrollably, flinching from his outstretched arm, denying any offer of comfort.

Her repeated statements pounded his brain like a sledgehammer.

Jeff realized too late the callousness and grave duplicity of his actions: infidelity and denial of motherhood. Like some crazed animal, he was driven by his own wanton needs and desires. His conscience precluded his wife. She had been marginalized in his playpen of pleasures. Now, he was forfeit. He had to pay the ultimate price: the death of his marriage...the loss of his precious wife. A loss of everything meaningful in life, a gift he did not appreciate until it was taken away from him...by his own doing. He had been the sole instrument of his marriage's demise.

Peggy began to speak softly.

"I'm not interested in revenge, Jeff, or notoriety. I just want a little peace and quiet. Getting through this whole ordeal will be hard enough." She blew her nose. "I just want to settle the divorce like two civilized adults and get on with our lives."

Jeff was now convinced. The marriage could never be mended or even continued. Peggy always wanted a family and he ruined it for her. That final act severed their union completely. Now, he realized his cowardice and selfishness. Jeff should have told her the truth in the very beginning, long before their marriage took place. He never wanted a family, and it was time that he faced the consequences of his own undoing with complete honesty.

"You were the best thing that ever happened to me and I threw it away. What I did wasn't worth it," he said. "None of it was." As he stood up to leave, Peggy trailed behind him.

"Tell the attorney you can have the house and whatever else you want," he said. "We'll work it out."

After her husband left the house, Peggy leaned against the front door with one thought flooding her mind: she was celebrating her belated anniversary with a divorce. How many couples did that?

***

Bolting the door, Peggy took the stairs slowly to her bedroom, threw herself across the bed and began to sob uncontrollably. The life she had with the man she loved had come to an end. In two days, the world as she knew it had been taken away from her. It had been stolen.

Her head began to pound and Peggy found herself at the bathroom medicine cabinet hunting for aspirin. As she placed two tablets into the palm of her hand, Peggy eyed the birth control compact resting on the upper shelf. In a fit of rage, Peggy grabbed the packet and flung it across the length of the bathroom. Pills swirled through the air forming a hail storm, pelting both walls and ceiling. As they landed on the bathroom floor, Peggy began stomping the scattered pills, one by one, screaming a litany of profanity with each one smashed.

Megan would have been proud. It took only eighteen pills to crush Jeff's private parts.

With that thought in mind, Peggy rested comfortably until she could sleep no longer. Then, Peggy did what she always did when restless: Peggy washed clothes or more precisely, she did the laundry, all of it; her clothes and Jeff's.

Later, as Peggy placed the clean towels in the linen closet, her eyes fell upon the black lace sleepwear from Victoria's Secret. She held the camisole against her chest, as she stood examining the garment before the bathroom mirror. Absentmindedly, she placed the thong on her head, the inverted V portion standing up like a crown, the two hip flaps falling along the sides of her ears.

She studied the reflection of the ridiculous-looking queen and the image reminded her of the large, glossy truth mirror in Snow White. From out of the blue, Peggy began to chant the familiar refrain:

"Mirror. Mirror. On the wall.
Who's the dumbest one of all?"
A paused moment of regal silence passed.

"Speak to me, you stupid bitch!" A distraught Peggy screamed at the haughty figure.

In her emotional state, the discourse was very real.

The mirrored woman never moved; however, in Peggy's fragile mind, she was not silent.

"A five year mistake, you rectified.
Get on with your life, be satisfied."
The contemptuous queen added a scathing reminder.

"You had signals but did nothing," she sneered. *"Cowards never win."*

"You go to hell," Peggy fired back. "Try wearing my shoes for a while."

Peggy tore off the crown and, ripping the lacy set to shreds, raced to a back bedroom window and heaved the remnants over the garbage can. Peggy heard a soft thud hit the lid, as she slammed down the window with a huge bang. She didn't care about the time of the night or what her neighbors thought. She didn't give a good shit about anything anymore. Her life was totally screwed.

She grabbed the laundry basket with Jeff's folded underwear and placed them accordingly into his closet drawers. Without giving it much thought, Peggy noticed a shoebox on the top shelf that had not been there before. He must have bought another pair of black Amalfi's she thought to herself. Curious of his purchase, Peggy pulled the box down off the shelf and removed the lid. Within a cosmic second, her laughter shook the whole house.

***

Early next morning, Seth awakened to the incessant ringing of the telephone.

"I woke you up, didn't I?" Peggy quickly apologized.

"No. I'm glad you did. Call me," he corrected himself. "We needed to talk."

"Janice just dropped off your note and explained everything. Amy gave it to her last night, but she saw Jeff's car in the driveway and thought it best to see me this morning."

"Well, it worked out ok. No harm done." Seth reassured her.

"Wrong," Peggy corrected. "When you had Amy call me yesterday, I was home. Jeff turned off the phone, but I didn't know it. I guess he didn't want to be interrupted when we met."

Seth remained silent as she continued speaking. It wasn't long before Peggy sensed his uneasiness and changed the subject.

"You called me about the photographs didn't you?" she said finally. "You've developed them."

"Yes, but if Jeff's with you, I can destroy them just as easily."

"Jeff is not with me," she silenced him. "I do not want the photographs destroyed, as a precautionary measure, and I desperately need to talk with you."

"Are you or aren't you? Just give me a straight answer." Seth's voice was very cold.

"I am. We need to talk about that and the case. I need your help."

There was more than a hint of desperation in her voice. She was on the dangerous edge of an emotional meltdown.

"Seth, there isn't anyone else I can talk to. Someone I can trust. You were with me... when...," her voice trailed off.

"Miss me that much?" he said, kiddingly, trying to change her somber mood.

"I really do, although I hate to admit it."

"Call me after four. I'll set something up for tomorrow." Seth paused, as if to remember something he had forgotten. "Give me your cell again, just in case things get fouled up." After writing down the number, he said, "I can't do anything today. My dance program is filled with Gabriel."

"Am I going to be ok, really, ok?"

"You will be a lot stronger," Seth reassured her.

He could tell from the tone of Peggy's voice that something had triggered her mental state. It wouldn't take much for her to start crying. Yet, there was nothing he could do to assuage her current suffering. He could only give her reassurance.

He could not tell her that time was her only ally, nor could he speak of the scars she would carry for the rest of her life. While the kidnapping would forever be etched in her memory, Jeff's betrayal had the long reach of a smoldering volcano, swirling deep inside her, ready to erupt with a cross word or an ugly look. She would find it difficult to trust someone again.

"Promise?" She needed confirmation once more.

"I would not lie to you, Peggy. Now, have your coffee and call me later, young lady."

When Seth Stone hung up the phone a smile crossed his face. Peggy Roberts stood her ground. She was getting a divorce. That particular thought gave him a great deal of satisfaction.

***

Thirty minutes later, Seth Stone was eating breakfast while speaking to someone on the telephone. Gabriel lay curled on the floor at his master's feet, waiting for a piece of bagel to roll by. Sooner or later, something would drop. It always did. But the sermon would come first.

"I hope you can," Seth replied. "I need privacy without scrutiny. That would be perfect." Seth listened closely. "I need a specific time. You will make it your business to be there." He placed the phone back into the cradle.

"You win," he tossed a piece of bagel to the leering Gabriel. "But you're not getting cream cheese."

Gabriel sat up tall on his haunches, his ears erect. The beauty of his brown and black shaded fur coat, so full-bodied, seemed even richer in color with the sunlight streaming through the kitchen window. His large, dark eyes pierced his master's stare. As a piece of sculpture, Gabriel was perfection in stone.

However, once the bagel piece hit the floor, two large paws sprang outward to stop the roll and cover it completely. The man and his dog were silent for several seconds, each out-staring the other, each knowing the questionable objective. It was a game they played over and over.

"You're not going to win," Seth told Gabriel, "definitely not today." Gabriel ignored the bagel and continued to stare at Seth.

"Dr. Mike keeps wondering why your breath's so bad. Should I tell him you like cream cheese on your bagels but hate pickles on your burgers?"

As he continued to speak about his dog's unhealthy diet and the veterinarian's appointment, Gabriel disregarded Seth's whole discourse by looking away from him, totally bored. He had heard that same sermon before, many times. No question about it. The man needed new material.

"Oh. Hell." Seth grabbed the bagel and slapped cream cheese all over it.

Gabriel shot to Seth's side, wolfed down the bagel and nuzzled his nose against his master's knee.

"You're going to be the only dog in history on Lipitor," he said, scratching the back of Gabriel's neck tenderly. "Let's go."

Within two minutes, Gabriel stretched end-to-end in the back seat of Seth's car and was on his way to visit a man who was born with a long needle attached to his hand.

At precisely four o'clock that afternoon, Seth received a phone call to schedule an appointment for the following day.

Chapter 22
Police Station

"I was so surprised we'd be meeting at the police station," Peggy said, as she greeted Seth. He had arrived only minutes earlier and quickly ushered her into Ben Burrows' cramped, but windowed office. "Has something happened? Did they find Mel?"

"No, to both questions," Seth sat in one of the two scarred chairs, opposite the nameplate on Ben's paper piled desk. "Judd hasn't turned up either, but Burrows is working on it."

"I felt this place was a safer bet," he said.

Seth watched her take the other chair, knowing full well their meeting would be observed, maybe not constantly, but his fishing friend never missed a trick. He was always reeling something in, mentally.

"That's crazy. Why should we need a safe place to meet? Is there a problem?"

"I don't know the circumstances of your impending divorce," Seth replied, "but there are some things you should consider."

His piercing eyes locked on hers. It was important that he know everything up front about the planned divorce. The last thing he wanted was involvement.

"Would your husband have you followed in the hope of helping his own case?"

Peggy sat up straight in her chair. It was obvious from her body language that she had never considered the possibility.

"By meeting here," Seth continued, "there could be nothing untoward between us. The kidnapping case is still open and Ben is just outside in the bull pen."

"I never thought about it. After our conversation Tuesday night, I don't think he would go back on our settlement agreement. I get the house and we are to divide our assets equally. Jeff agreed to that."

She paused, remembering...

"Would he do this to me again? Could he be that cruel?" She spoke softly to herself.

"What is it?" Seth caught her strange expression. "I know something upset you yesterday. I felt it when we spoke."

He could feel the tension building by the expression on her face.

Seth remembered her Wednesday morning call. She seemed on edge then, but he didn't want to push the issue. Later that day, Peggy sounded more relaxed. Whatever bothered her that morning must have been resolved. At least, she gave that impression. Now, he wasn't so sure.

"I never expected my world to implode all at once. But it has." Peggy stared at him. "Would he try to take the house, after doing everything else to me? Could he be that spiteful?" She wondered out loud. "That would be the last straw to crush me completely."

"Slow down and take a deep breath," Seth advised. "Then, talk to me."

"It's not about Alice or any of his others." She gave him a folded slip of paper. "That's the original. I want it back."

His eyes scanned the invoice briefly, his brain fixed on the date. Seth raised his eyes again, and refolded the paper. He was silent for a moment. He could see the pain in her face.

"How long have you known?" he asked quietly.

" Since Tuesday afternoon. I was shuffling through his desk papers."

"So, for the last three years..."

"I didn't need birth control pills." She finished his sentence.

"I am so sorry, Peggy," he said regretfully. "I remember our conversation at Poag's. You spoke of family then."

"I know it sounds crazy, but this hurt a lot more than the infidelity. You can't sustain a marriage on cruel, selfish love, knowing your partner wants children. I feel so cheated all the way around. The whole marriage was nothing but a sham, a five-year pretense at love."

"I don't know what to say. I can't imagine having the procedure done without your consent."

Seth sat quietly thinking of some logical reason for doing this but soon gave up. "This man does not instill a great deal of trust. So, I would be very careful. Get the settlement resolved through your attorney as quickly as possible. Don't waste any time."

"What do you mean?"

"Look at his track record. I don't have to go through the litany. Sidewalk spittle can't begin to describe him."

"I have other issues. I guess I need advice."

Now, Seth was curious. Aside from the hidden vasectomy, what other information did she have to relate? Did she ever live a peaceful life like so many people he knew, or was her existence always in a state of flux?

She began speaking, drawing him away from his thoughts.

"After he left Tuesday night, I couldn't sleep so I did the laundry, all of it," Peggy said. "It calms me, somehow." She noticed Seth's frown. "Well, it does. The hum of the dryer is like music to me."

Seth arched both eyebrows. The woman really did need help.

"Anyhow, I wanted to get it done because Jeff's moving into an apartment this weekend. He's staying with a friend for now, probably a female."

"And, you found something in his clothing tying him to Alice." He pre-empted her discovery.

"I am so damn naïve," she bristled. "I've been taken in again by him." Peggy's expression was one of hesitation.

"How can I be so stupid?" She hastened to explain her discovery, while berating herself.

"When I put Jeff's clothes away, I noticed a shoebox on the top shelf of his closet. I never saw it before. He must have put it there Monday night. So I pulled it down to see his new shoes. There was fifty-six thousand dollars inside."

Almost whispering, to no one in particular, Peggy said, "A stack of ten one hundred dollar bills is less than a quarter of an inch high. Who would think that?"

"What?"

Shocked by the startling revelation, Seth repeated his one word question again.

Now, he understood. Emotionally, Peggy had hit the marital Trifecta: cheating, stitching and stashing. What a piece of work, this Jeff Roberts was.

"Did you ask him about it?"

"Why? He'd only lie to me. He probably thought I wouldn't find it," she fumed. "He thinks I'm a dumb blonde, remember?"

"Where's the money now? Did you leave it in his closet?"

"I wasn't going to let him get away with that, not after everything he's done to me," Peggy sneered. "God only knows what else he stashed away, but it's not at the house. I tore the place apart."

"If the money's not at the house, Peggy, where the hell is it?" All Seth wanted was a quick answer.

"Here, with me," she insisted, "where it's safe. I have it in the trunk of my car."

Her answer muted Seth's brain… at first…then, he exploded with uncontrolled laughter. Although he saw the total humor of it, Peggy was not on the same page.

"I came here for advice, Seth, not to be laughed at." She clenched her teeth in anger. Her angry reaction only made him laugh harder.

"Listen to yourself." He said, finally. "How safe is the money in the trunk of your car? You could have an accident or be picked up by the police."

"How ridiculous is that? I'm already in a police station, trying to get help from a friend who thinks I'm a running cartoon."

"C'mon, Peggy," Seth cajoled. "You know we'll figure out something, but you can't run around with a trunk full of money."

"I thought you could keep it for me."

Seth rolled his eyes in disbelief. "It doesn't work that way," he explained. "This is between the two of you. But, don't get the attorneys involved. They'll just muck it up."

"What would you do?"

Seth reached inside his coat pocket and gave Peggy an envelope containing the photographs. "I'd rent a safety deposit box and put the money and photographs inside. Do that today. Then, when you divide the assets, keep half of the money."

"He won't take this lying down. I expect a fight."

"That's a no brainer. He'll say the money isn't his, but don't believe him. Nothing he tells you will be true. Just be firm when he tries to convince you. Believe me, he has more somewhere else. What he's doing now is moving money, probably to combine it with his other stash, so he won't have to report it as part of your joint assets."

Seth found her hanging on to his every word. She obviously needed instruction from someone older and more experienced, someone she could trust.

"If Jeff threatens to stop the divorce, remind him of the consequences. Not only will you be fifty-six thousand dollars richer, but he will be out of a job when you send copies of the photographs to his bosses or show them in open court. What can he do? Go to the police? Whatever happens, don't ever tell him or anyone else about the safety deposit box."

"He's going to search the whole house. I know he will."

"Change the locks right after he moves out," Seth instructed. "If he takes a garage door opener, have someone enter a new code in yours." He studied her carefully, watching her body language to determine her belief in his guidance.

"You can't come to the bank with me, can you?"

"That would not be wise. I can't be involved in your divorce."

"That's the other thing, Seth. Should I go to Reno or the Dominican Republic?"

"Where did that come from? What are you talking about?"

Somewhere, the conversation suddenly changed course, but he missed the transition phase.

"The divorce. There's a waiting period before it becomes final in New York. If I go to Reno, I must establish residency, I think for six weeks, but in the Dominican Republic, I'm done in two days. It's final weeks later or when they finish the paperwork. I'm told getting divorced there is very fast."

"And, you don't want to wait."

"Think about it. What's the point? I'll never go back to him."

While she spoke, Seth remained silent.

"I want to move on with my life. Still, I can't leave Janice with the store for six weeks. Megan could fill in I guess. She would be thrilled to see our marriage dissolved so quickly."

"Why are you at such odds with your decision?" His question surprised her. "What's stopping you from doing what you really want?"

"How do you know me so well?"

"It's the butter pecan." He tried to make light of the situation.

"I remember that drive in. We did spend a lot of time together," she reminisced before changing the subject. "Then you think I should go that route?"

"Settle the estate first. If your lawyer coordinates both ends, the Dominican attorney will help you with the legal paperwork during your stay. But, you will need a passport."

"I miss you, Seth," she glowed. "As bad as it was, some good came out of it. We became friends."

"I might have to challenge that," he corrected her. "My kooky new friend drives around with trunk full of cash."

"I guess that is kinda strange."

"Kinda?" He posed the question loudly. "People who do that kind of thing are usually institutionalized," he cautioned, before taking a sober stance.

"I'm leaving," he said, quietly.

"I should go, too," Peggy agreed.

"In two weeks," Seth explained.

Peggy's expression changed. His news came on her so suddenly. Seth was going away.

He wouldn't be around when she needed him most. There was no one who could take his place, someone, who really understood her. A feeling of sadness swept through her. She would be lonely without her friend.

"Where?"

"West Coast."

"How long?"

"I'm not sure."

"You seeing someone?" Peggy blurted, without thinking.

Then, realizing her error, she quickly retracted the question. Where he went was none of her business. He had a private life of his own. And, if there was a special someone, she should be happy for him. Still, Peggy had come to depend on this man.

Inwardly, she didn't want to share him with anyone, no matter how special that person was to Seth. Peggy knew it wasn't fair. Seth deserved a measure of happiness too. But, she didn't care. Peggy needed him for herself, particularly now.

"I'll be driving out with Gabriel," he ignored the question. "We'll stop at some national parks on the way. He'll enjoy that."

"Sounds great," Peggy forced a smile. "Can I come?"

"No. You're headed south," he replied quickly. "But, right now you should go to the bank before it closes." Seth stood ready to leave Ben Burrows' office.

She followed his signal and stood up.

"I won't see you again, will I?" Her blue eyes glistened, as she faced the man whose steady brown eyes were fixed on hers. Their silence spoke volumes.

"That won't be possible," he said. "We're on two different paths now." Then Seth reminded her again. "Call my cell, if you need to talk."

"I'm going to miss you." A tear fell to her chin.

"Good friends are never far apart." Seth wiped the tear with his finger. "So, you shouldn't be sad."

As he left the room, Peggy watched Seth single out Ben Burrows, who stood talking with a group of uniformed police officers in the large outer office. After a quick exchange, Seth hurried to leave the building. As he walked toward his car, Seth wondered if Peggy knew that Ben Burrows had been watching them the entire time.

***

After Peggy left the police station, she took Seth's advice by opening a safety deposit box at another local bank. As she sat in the small solitary room facing the empty tin box, her thoughts were on Seth and how much he had helped her. She placed the box of money and packet of photographs inside and closed the lid. Peggy continued sitting in the dim solitary room, the safety deposit box, her only company. Seth would be gone now and she wouldn't see him anymore. She felt so lonely. Never could she remember crying so much at every little thing.

Even in the room where she had been held during the kidnapping, did she feel such melancholy. She feared for her life, feared that she would never see her loved ones again. But then...Seth came. Seth saved her. Now, somehow, her feelings were different. She felt hollow inside. There was a void that needed to be filled. She had hoped Seth would help her find it, but that dream had escaped. They were now going in different directions. Her friend was moving on with his life and he recommended she do the same. His message had been very clear. Even their platonic friendship had reached a different level. She would miss him and the advice he had wisely given her.

Peggy rested her arms on the safety deposit box and wept uncontrollably, a pathetic figure in a small dark room.

***

Ben Burrows entered his office and thought about the two people who had just met there. From their animated conversation, which he observed from a distance, it seemed they were resolving some issues that came up after her rescue. These, he assumed, were related to the husband perfidy and not the case itself. What case, he reminded himself. Without Judd's body, there was nothing but the word of a distraught man who reported his brother missing. He just had to wait...much like fishing. Still, it wasn't like fishing at all: he had no bait, not even a lure.

Although he didn't know Peggy Roberts well, he did know Seth Stone. The man may have saved the kidnapped woman, but he sure as hell wouldn't get sucked into her messy divorce. Their meeting at his office proved that. Seth Stone was a very smart man who happened to be leaving town at the right time.

The detective picked up the telephone and quickly dialed a number.

"I'm off tomorrow," he said, then waited for a reply. "Hell, yes. That's why I'm calling. If I don't catch something this time, I'm going to shoot a hole in your boat."

The reply Burrows heard tickled him as he hung up the phone. Poag could really come up with some doozies. He had to give the man credit. The man had a sense of humor, even if it was very dry.

Instead of facing Reese after the shooting, he would be confronting his toothy vampire sister, Clarisa!

Chapter 23
Gift Shop

Approximately four months after the kidnapping, in mid October, Megan breezed into her sister's gift shop with some exciting holiday news.

"Brad and I are having Thanksgiving at our house this year," she chortled. "Franklin Junior – really the second – and Rosalie decided to spend the holiday weekend on Long Island with her family. I think her father had a stroke, but she's not sharing any information. I'm sure Franklin told his parents all the details. Barbara would be pissed if she didn't know every little thing that goes on. Anyhow, Brad volunteered our services. Doesn't that just wilt your petunias?"

After the profound announcement, Megan continued her discourse in detail.

"Personally, I think the family is scared shitless about it. But, they couldn't say no. No one thinks I can cook, so they always pass us over for a holiday meal at our house. Maybe I should call Brad's mother and ask if she has a recipe for baking a turkey," Megan laughed wickedly.

"That's a terrible thing to even consider," Janice scolded. "Your mother-in-law may think you're serious." Then, catching herself, Janice challenged Megan squarely. "You do know how to roast a turkey, don't you?"

"Of course, I do," Megan scoffed. "But, she doesn't know that."

"So, you'll have Brad's parents and his sister's family. That's not bad." Peggy made a quick calculation. "You only have to cook for seven people."

"I count twelve," Megan corrected her, "with you, Janice and Fred, and two of my friends."

"No. No." Janice refused. "We're spending Thanksgiving with Amy. She wants us to meet a special someone in Ithaca," she winked. "I think it may be serious."

"A-ha...I'll bet her guy's a professor like Brad. He's either at Cornell or Ithaca College. Pick one." Megan offered. "Not bad. Not bad at all."

"I want you to stay over and help me with dinner," she said, turning to her sister. "I'm ordering a twenty pound turkey. Think that's enough for ten of us?"

"That's more than enough," Janice interjected. "You'll have tons of leftovers."

"I just don't want Barbara Croft to think we skimp on food. Her Christmas dinner has everything imaginable. It's really beautifully done, but she has tons of help."

"And, so will you," Peggy replied. "It will be a lovely affair, trust me."

"Wait a minute," Janice interrupted. "I'm confused. Who exactly is coming to your house for Thanksgiving?"

"I'm having Brad's parents, Barbara and Franklin, Senior; of course, Jennifer, with her husband, Robert Chambers; and their nine-year-old daughter, Susan. Those five are definitely coming." A second later, Megan began to calculate the number of guests she planned to invite.

"Then, I want to invite Ben Burrows and my librarian friend, Ann Quigley. Peggy will already be at the house helping me. That's why I'm so happy about having the dinner at our house. For the first time since our engagement, I can share Thanksgiving with my sister."

"Each of the Croft women has an assigned holiday," Megan explained to Janice. "Barbara has Christmas; Jennifer has Easter; and Rosalie, Thanksgiving. New Years Day is the Croft family's annual cocktail party. It's Barbara and Franklin's big hoopla. So, I never got a holiday. I told you before. They don't think I know my way around the kitchen."

"You better talk to Ben Burrows and your librarian friend before you order the turkey. They may have other plans. I know Ben has family here, so he may have already made a commitment for Thanksgiving. He usually spends the holidays with his sister, Clarisa. At least he did in the past."

"So, I'll have nine people at the table instead of ten. But, I know Ben will come when he hears my proposal. Ann Quigley's the big question mark. The woman is so independent and has a lot of friends. Who knows? She may have accepted an invitation already."

"Well, if you need more people at the table, I can always bring my service provider," Peggy volunteered.

"Who?" The two women sounded like a rehearsed chorus.

"The lawn boy, of course," Peggy smirked.

The unexpected quip caused them to explode with loud, resounding laughter. They were completely oblivious to the tall, dark-haired man with his dog, who listened to their conversation, while he examined gift boxes of very small stuffed animals. A small, brown fuzzy bear caught his attention, but he placed it back in its respective box when their laughter ceased.

He felt the piercing eyes of three women studying him, knowing somehow, he was not there as a customer shopping for a particular gift. His close-fitting shirt enhanced his noticeably muscular frame as he strode toward them, unaware his sculpted body was under scrutiny.

"Seth," Peggy greeted him, somewhat shocked. "Hello, Gabriel."

Having not seen, nor heard from him in months, Peggy felt somewhat surprised and awkward at their meeting in her gift shop, and she wondered what had possessed him to come.

"Sit," Seth commanded an obedient Gabriel.

"When did you get back?" She asked.

"It's been awhile," he said, leaving her question unanswered.

"I'm sorry." Peggy turned toward the women who had been watching them closely and then began making introductions.

Seth took Janice's hand and greeted her warmly. "I've heard a lot of nice things about you," he said. "Peggy considers you her very best friend."

Then, Seth approached the young woman standing near Peggy. "So, you're Megan," he said quietly. They studied each other, as if taking inventory, and then Seth broke into a wide grin. "Peggy worried more about you, than her own safety when she was kidnapped. I think she must be the kind of big sister everyone would like to have."

His clear unwavering eyes never left hers as he continued. "And, you must be the kid sister that everyone loves."

Between his steady stare and the gentleness of his remark, Megan was left speechless. This man...this stranger, whom she had been dying to meet, had completely beguiled her. Her tongue lay twisted somewhere deep down inside her throat. She could not think of a single reply.

Fortunately, Janice was quick enough with a response.

"We heard how kind you were to Peggy when she was taken. I know we can never thank you enough," Janice said with a great deal of sincerity. The woman was more than her partner at the gift shop. Peggy had always been like a daughter to her.

Seth acknowledged her comment with an appreciative nod and then approached Peggy.

"I brought you something." Seth walked toward the animal display where a large thin package rested against the table leg.

"What is it?" Wild with excitement, Peggy tore into his present hurriedly.

"Oh. Seth!" She screamed with delight.

"You said you wanted me to paint your house."

"When? How?" She propped the painting against a stand on the counter. "It's beautiful."

The three women gathered quickly to appreciate the painting and unwittingly blocked his view, causing him to smile at their enthusiastic response.

"How did you do that?" Megan asked.

"That was my question," Peggy interrupted, as she waited for his answer.

"After missing you at the shop on that famous Tuesday, I drove by your house and took pictures," he shrugged. "It saved me a trip from Lockport since I was already in the area."

"That's the day my ex turned off the phone," she remembered. "In fact, the three of us might have been drinking coffee in the kitchen while you were outside."

She remembered it well. That particular day would be forever etched in her mind.

On that very morning, a screaming Megan freaked out totally when learning of Jeff's multiple philandering romps, while, on that same afternoon, a heart-broken Peggy wept uncontrollably upon finding the vasectomy invoice. All in all, it was one big discovery day for the two Burke sisters.

"I'm so sorry Seth." She quickly added.

"It's not your fault. Things happen," he understood. "When did you get divorced? You are, aren't you?" He waited silently for confirmation.

Before Peggy could explain, Megan interrupted.

"It would have been the middle of August, but her stupid attorney misspelled her name," Megan exploded. "Instead of spelling Margaret with a garet, he wrote geret. But, she's legally divorced now from that asshole."

Realizing how coarse she sounded, Megan quickly covered her mouth, totally ashamed.

"Don't sweat the small stuff," Seth laughed. "I've heard that same usage before. I think that word description must run in the family."

"Speaking of family, would you like to have Thanksgiving dinner with us at my house?"

Her impulsive invitation came as no surprise to Peggy. Her sister thought nothing of inviting the man she dreamed of meeting, so many months earlier, to her dinner table. Essentially, she was giving him her stamp of approval.

"I'm cooking this year," she explained. "Actually, Miss Margaret is," she teased. Then Megan became serious. "Peggy's a fantastic cook and I really need to impress my in-laws."

Seth chortled. He found the young woman's honesty rather refreshing. "I'm sorry, but I have another commitment," he said, politely. "But, thank you, anyway."

Then, exchanging all the niceties after being introduced, Seth turned to leave. Peggy hesitated…but only momentarily, and then followed him.

***

Peggy stood on the sidewalk near the gift shop door with Seth, while his dog rested comfortably at his feet. Gabriel stretched out lazily. He knew they would be there awhile. The woman from the gift shop never stopped talking. When it came right down to it, what did she have to talk about that was so important? If they wanted to chit-chat, why didn't Seth just call her on the telephone? That way, both of them could be relaxing at home right now, instead of him standing like some wooden door frame shielding her from the wind, while Gabriel's own body hairs were growing more and more chilled from lying on the cold concrete sidewalk. Why couldn't his master see that? Sometimes, Seth could be so dumb. Gabriel rested his head while they continued to talk.

"I didn't want to tell you in front of the girls," he said. "I've been home since August."

"August? Why didn't you call me?" she demanded, her question slightly laced with anger.

Seth could tell she was clearly displeased, but didn't know why. He had done nothing to upset her, at least not knowingly. Had something happened he was unaware of?

"I couldn't under the circumstances, Peggy. I thought you were still married and would call me when..." Seth left his thought unfinished.

His being detached from her marital quagmire was necessary. Surely, she could see that. If not, she wasn't thinking clearly. Essentially, by not making the phone call, he was protecting her. What part of his conversation could she not understand?

"I thought we were friends," Peggy persisted. Her curt manner waved all logic aside. She wasn't interested in the reasons he gave for not calling her. She simply wanted an answer...why didn't he call her?

That did it for him. Seth's lips tightened, a hard line furrowing across his noticeably frowned face. He could feel the anger beginning to surge inside him. If he were a violent man, he would have shaken some sense into her. That probably would have had no effect either. Not in her present frame of mind. She was too hell-bent on a missed phone call. How stupid!

They stood glaring at each other in silence, each annoyed with the other, each sharing a demeanor of repressed hostility. After all they had been through together, was this to be the totality of their relationship? A hit and miss friendship? At this point, pen pals were closer than they were.

Seth was clearly provoked by her denial of something so glaringly obvious.

"We are friends, but my very good friend didn't call me if she needed help, did she?" His sarcastic reply forced the blame game back into her court. "As it is, I'm faced with a dilemma of my own." He then went on to explain.

"Ben called me three weeks ago to meet him at the morgue. After all this time, they found my brother's body in a wooded area off Route 79. It was tough identifying him. I didn't think I could do it. He didn't look anything like...Judd."

"Oh. Seth. I'm so sorry." Peggy embraced him briefly, regretting her harshness with him. "Is there anything I can do?" When he shook his head, she asked another question. "What about Ben?"

"You know how determined he is. After Judd's body vanished, Ben learned of his intimate relationship with Nancy Travers and questioned her about his disappearance. He used me as an excuse."

He paused, finding it difficult to discuss his half-brother.

"She told him about their wedding plans and the lucrative job offer Mel gave Judd. Although he never discussed the details, Judd did tell her they could afford to get married sooner than planned. But, she never saw him again."

"How did Ben react to that? Did he believe her?"

"He said she was really broken up about Judd's disappearance. The only thing Ben could tell her then was that he suspected foul play, since neither she, nor I heard from him."

"What about Mel?"

"Mel told Nancy that he and Judd would be back in a few days. After leaving Remmy's Tavern the afternoon we saw them, they went to her house for his clothes. Mel used her extra room sometimes. Then, Nancy drove him to a restaurant on Transit Road. That was the last time she saw her brother. His cell wasn't working either. But, that's not surprising."

"So, Mel could be anywhere."

"True," he nodded. "The police are still looking for him, especially now, with Judd's..."

"So, Nancy knows about Judd...now that they found his body?"

"Ben told her. He had already searched her house earlier... before Judd was...," his voice trailed off. "That was months ago, when he thought there might be something left behind to help him locate Mel. But the search turned up zero. They never found Judd's truck either."

The furrow lines of his forehead deepened as he spoke, and his facial expression reminded her of their time together, when they were investigating Mel Travers and John Beck. As if jarred by sudden traffic noise, her thoughts returned to their conversation.

"But, nothing adds up," he added. "The hollow points I gave Ben weren't used to kill Judd. Mel must have kept other bullets at the house, or he used another gun to shoot my brother. I don't have the answers. Ben couldn't talk. One of the detectives came by his office, so I left."

"One question," A frown crossed Peggy's face. "Does Nancy know her brother killed the man she wanted to marry?"

"Ben wouldn't tell her that," Seth shrugged. "He doesn't have enough evidence to convict Mel. After Judd's body was found, Nancy had to learn of the shooting. She didn't know about the kidnapping until Ben told her. Nancy thinks someone behind it killed Judd, but she doesn't suspect her brother of his murder. She did mention getting a strange phone call at the time."

"The one you made?" Peggy caught Seth's nod. "Then, she is cooperating with Ben."

"Absolutely. She wants to know what happened. On the night of the kidnapping, in addition to working from eleven to seven at Connie's restaurant, she worked a double shift. Nancy left the house at four o'clock to relieve another waitress who attended a graduation party. The next morning, she thought Judd's job might be over and kept phoning him."

"Then your call told her their operation was illegal," Peggy reminded Seth.

"Exactly, and that's the reason she phoned Mel and met him at Remmy's."

"Don't forget John Beck," she added.

"How could I? That's how this whole mess got started in the first place. Because John wanted his wife dead, Mel killed my brother when the plan failed."

"What can I do to help?" Peggy made another offer.

"Nancy's taken care of everything. We're having a memorial service for Judd in Clarence on Saturday at eleven. I didn't know he belonged to the Methodist church until she told me. The woman was a good influence on him. He would have been happy with her."

"I think he would have," she agreed. "Unfortunately, we have two people responsible for wrecking their lives."

"Burrows won't let them off the hook. I know him well."

Then seeing that Peggy was getting cold, Seth shielded her body more by moving in closer. "Regardless of what happens now, I wanted you to have the painting," he said.

"Why didn't you tell me you were a painter?"

"I did tell you."

"No. I mean your work as an artist," she explained.

"I don't like talking about myself, but I would have told you my specialty." He looked away from her. "In a way, I was glad you never asked."

"I never did ask about your work, did I?" she reflected. "I was too busy prattling about Jeff. It was all about me." She chastised herself. "I'm so sorry, Seth. I've been so selfish."

"We had different priorities then. I understand," he reassured her. "Someday, I'll tell you about my father."

"Your father was a painter?"

"He was a math teacher and taught painting on the side. He was very good. That's how I got hooked. In some strange way, he opened my eyes to another world." He stopped speaking suddenly and brushed a stray hair from her face. "I have to go."

"Are you going away again?" Peggy asked.

"I'm leaving town after the service, but I'll be back for the holidays."

"Can I call you if something comes up?"

"Don't we always try to help each other?" Seth ran the back of his hand along the side of her face, as she turned to leave. He knew exactly how to play the game.

"Margaret," his resonant voice echoed back to her.

Seth deliberately stepped closer to her and looked down into her eyes. They were inches apart.

"Tell me," he whispered, tilting her face gently, and nearly brushing her lips with his. "Just how old is your service provider?"

Peggy started to laugh as she inched away from him, banging her body into the gift shop door. Seth had this uncanny way about him...always the unexpected remark.

"He's gotta be on Medicare. I'm sure of that. This time around I'm only going after old men."

"I'll keep that in mind." Seth tweaked her chin, and then spoke to Gabriel who waited impatiently for his master.

***

From the gift shop window, Peggy watched Seth saunter down the street to his parked car. When the car door opened, Gabriel leaped into the back seat and suddenly disappeared. Moments later, Seth's car sped away.

After watching him leave, Peggy turned abruptly and felt her head spinning. She probably needed something to eat. Had she skipped lunch? She couldn't remember. In fact, she couldn't remember anything other than the feel of him...of his breath...of his lips so close to hers.

Why was she having these thoughts? Was she that incapable of joking about her service provider, or just hard-up for a man? Peggy knew she was lonely. But, that lonely? Taking Seth's remark out of context and construing it for something else was just plain sick.

His cryptic explanation months ago told her there was nothing but friendship between them. Yet, today, he implied something different. Could she have mistaken his inference? If Seth wanted something more than a platonic relationship, why didn't he just tell her?

"He doesn't want that with me." Peggy weighed every possibility. He would have told her. Seth was not shy about things like that. No! She was jumping the gun. If she wasn't careful, Peggy would shoot herself in the foot and end the friendship with a wonderful man.

***

"He's gone now. You can come back to us," Megan scowled. "You could have warned us, you know. The man's a hunk. And his eyes! His voice! He could talk his way into my bedroom anytime."

"Amy said he was nice looking," Janice remembered.

"Nice looking! If I had to be saved, I'd want him." Megan gave a thumbs-up. "He's not cutesy-gorgeous like Jeff. He's manly-handsome like the old cigarette ads with a man riding the open range on his horse. But, he sure as hell doesn't look like an artist. I mean, he's not affected like some of them are with scarves and hats."

"That's stereotyping," Peggy interrupted.

"I know you're right," Megan agreed. "But, if you go to some of those art shops in East Aurora, you'll see what I mean."

"That's a come-on to sell paintings. Seth doesn't need that." Peggy scolded.

"He needs to come to my house for Thanksgiving. That's what he needs. Make him come."

"He's not thinking about Thanksgiving right now. He's more concerned about the memorial service this Saturday for his brother. The police found Judd's body three weeks ago."

"Oh. Peggy. I am so sorry. Surely, you're going to the memorial service," Janice insisted. "You owe him that."

"I guess I do," she replied.

"I'm with Janice. You have an obligation to go. But, do me one favor. Go out and buy a new dress."

"It's a memorial service not a fashion show," Peggy reminded her sister.

"It's a service of the living remembering the dead," Megan corrected, "not of the dying going along with the corpse. You need a simple black dress with good-looking jewelry. Something really chic. We'll shop tomorrow. Right now, I have to meet Brad."

Peggy and Janice watched Megan leave the shop and heaved a sigh of relief.

"She's tough." Janice sighed again.

"But, is she right?" Peggy questioned. "Should I buy something new for the service?"

Ever the diplomat, Janice eyed her partner and, with great wisdom, offered her the advice only a mother would give her loving daughter.

"It wouldn't hurt if you bought something new. It's an uplifting kind of thing women do. But, I wouldn't wait for Megan. Go to the mall now. I'll close up."

After Peggy had gone, Janice noticed the painting that was left behind on the counter.

She studied it more closely. The work had to be painstakingly slow. Her fingers gently traced the signature of Seth Stone. Peggy was a very lucky woman to have such a good man save her.

Chapter 24
Memorial

The following Saturday evening, Peggy sat quietly on her living room sofa. She no longer felt smug. In fact, she felt very much alone and miserable.

She scanned the all-too-familiar rooms briefly. Blue, blue, everything blue. From the living room to the dining room, a flood of blue silk flowed from one room to the other, a perfect blend of formality for the L-shaped floor plan.

The house décor had always impressed her dinner guests. The formality of the two blue rooms was in sharp contrast with the informal family room of brown, green and gold earth tones. Sincere or not, someone always offered a compliment. At least, that's how it seemed.

Blue captured her mood completely, as she lingered on the French provincial sofa fingering the small pink and blue flower patterns. "Yes," her eyes swept the room. "The blue draperies did tie the room together." They highlighted the two upholstered chairs and four mahogany tables, which rested on an Oriental rug, whose central design was bordered in a companion blue. To Peggy, the living room always imbued the formal air of royalty.

Did she feel like a blue blood? Is that why she sat in the cold formal living room rather than the warm comfortable family room, so much more in keeping with her lifestyle? It was a beautifully decorated room. No one could doubt that. But, was it really her or the person she was becoming? Or was it just the way Peggy Roberts lived during her five year marriage?

Sitting in the living room suited her perfectly. She knew now why she elected to sit there. There was a growing sense of detachment within her, and that was exactly what the stiff room portrayed. She was no longer a part of a union…no longer, a two. She was a one, now: cold, alone and detached.

Her eyes rested on the solitary glass of wine perched on the mahogany end table. Her life was not supposed to go this way. She fully expected to be happily married and living a wonderful life with the man she loved. Instead, she was single and miserable. Was she feeling post-depression after the divorce? After all these months? Was that possible? Nothing seemed to make sense anymore.

Would she have been better off staying with Jeff?

No, a voice somewhere in her head answered. That part of her life was over, more than over. He was out of her life completely now.

It started with his phone call and ended with a final goodbye. It was important that she knew he still loved her, in spite of the pain he caused. Jeff was going back to the city he loved, and perhaps, he would find a measure of happiness there. That was late August. The divorce had become final a few days earlier.

But Peggy was too smart to believe his affirmations of enduring love. In fact, her conversation with Megan enlightened her even further.

"What do you mean Jeff called to say he still loved you?" Megan began the interrogation. "He had to be drunk."

"I think I can recognize passion in my ex-husband's voice," Peggy objected.

"Well, if he still loves you so much, what the hell was he doing with the sweet young thing at the Lancaster Opera House? He was all over her."

It took Peggy a moment to respond, "When?"

"Last Saturday."

"Why didn't you mention it?"

"Because you're divorced!" she reminded her. "At this point, I didn't think it mattered. But I've seen them together before, at the airport. I think she's a flight attendant. And yes, she's beautiful, but also very dumb to link up with him." Megan ridiculed the woman's intellect.

"Jeff said he was leaving town."

"When? Where?" She pressed her sister. "What can you tell me? I want to know."

"To the city he loves," Peggy shrugged. "Pittsburgh, I guess."

"I don't believe it," Megan answered quickly. "He always lies to get what he wants. Do you have any idea what it could be? What he's up to?"

What Jeff wanted was in the safety deposit box, but Peggy couldn't tell Megan about that. Seth had given her explicit instructions. She was to tell no one. Up to now, she had been smart. She had followed Seth's directive.

"I guess we'll just have to wait and see," Peggy answered.

"He's given you enough grief," Megan reminded her. "I'll call his office next week to see if he's still there. If he's gone, we'll go out and celebrate."

But, Peggy didn't wait for Megan's report. She called Jeff's office the next day to arrange a final meeting. Once he received his share of the money, Jeff would be out of her life completely.

As she recalled, it took all of five minutes. A meeting at Starbucks and it was over. He took the box and she grabbed a frappe.

So much for enduring love…and half of the money.

Later, Megan told Peggy Jeff was moving to Savannah. However, she was uncertain whether it was a lateral move, a promotion or a new company entirely. When all was said and done, Megan really didn't give a shit on which pile Jeff landed.

Peggy sipped her wine slowly, her thoughts shifting to the memorial service she attended that morning. It really was a beautiful tribute to Seth's dead half-brother. Nancy Travers had planned it well. She left nothing to chance.

The photograph of Judd Thorne that was placed on the chapel altar flashed through her mind. There was not a hint of resemblance between the half-brothers. Then she thought about the easel in the party room. Several pictures of the Thorne family and a few with Nancy Travers framed the centered photograph of Judd.

Peggy remembered studying them closely and observed the distinction between the two men. Judd looked more like his father, while Seth definitely had his mother's high cheekbones. She recalled Seth telling her of his mother's second marriage after his father's death. When Judd was born, Seth's mother kept a close watch on her cohesive family. She caught Judd's slow mentality long before anyone noticed and took extra measures by giving him the extra care he needed. It made little difference now. They were all dead.

The memorial service that was held in the chapel seemed somewhat strange to her. There were so few in attendance. Aside from Seth and Nancy, only eight people came to pay tribute to Judd Thorne's existence. Two garage workers hurriedly approached Seth with their condolences and left before the service began. However, two waitresses from Connie's restaurant stayed the entire time and took Nancy Travers home after the menu of tea sandwiches, cookies and punch had been consumed. Much of the food that was served in the party room was packaged and divided among those who remained after the service.

So, if Peggy paced her weekend correctly, she wouldn't have to cook. Of course, by tomorrow , the soggy tea sandwiches would taste like her elementary school's third grade paste. She remembered sampling the white gluey stuff from the school's wide mouth gallon jug. Her pencil box ruler served as a very handy spoon as she recalled.

The thought of eating pasty leftovers repulsed her now and she opted for a real cooked meal. She needed to feed the garbage disposal after neglecting it for so long anyhow. The tea sandwiches would do nicely. Within minutes, she dismissed the sandwiches from her mind and concentrated on Judd's funeral.

The solemnity of the service hit an especially somber note when Seth spoke of his half-brother to the gathering of his friends. He talked lovingly of their formative years and the dreams they shared as they got older. There were moments of tenderness and of sadness. But most of all, he expressed the grief of losing a loved one so young and so filled with the promise of a coming marriage.

Neither Seth's speech, nor the homage he paid Judd surprised her. During their time together, Peggy found him extremely articulate, particularly when he had interrogated her. And, after so much concentrated time with him, Peggy soon realized she was in the company of a very smart man.

Seth seemed genuinely pleased to see her at the service, although he was initially surprised by her presence. After she expressed her condolences, he took her hand and introduced her to

Nancy Travers, a small, attractive blonde, who stood glued to Seth's side the entire time and held his arm for support and comfort, blocking any possibility of her intervention.

Peggy never found an opportunity for conversation with him. His attention to the woman, who cried continuously during the service and in the party room, never ceased. Perhaps, the displayed pictures had more of an impact on the woman than Peggy previously thought.

"No." Peggy told herself. It was the service that exacerbated the acceptance of Judd's death. The realization had finally set in. Her life with Judd was over. Now, Nancy Travers had to move on with her own life.

Still, Peggy was not left unattended. After the service, Clarisa snagged her in the party room while Poag and Ben Burrows recaptured the memories of their last fishing expedition.

"It's good you came," Clarisa told her. "Seth needs all the support he can get. He's all alone now. Not that Judd was ever there for him these last few years. After jail, he kinda went his own way, although Seth never gave up. That's how it was."

Clarisa spoke about Seth's brother with a great deal of authority. The woman assumed Peggy knew more about Judd than she really did. So, Peggy did the only sensible thing: she remained silent and very attentive.

"It's sad, and yet, maybe a blessing with the miscarriage," Clarisa rattled on. "How could she raise a kid with the kind of money a waitress makes?"

Before Peggy could respond, Clarisa answered the question herself.

"She'd be looking to Seth for help. So, who are we kidding? I'm sure Nancy loved his brother. But, I think with a baby coming, she expected more than what Judd could give her."

"Do you think he was aware of her financial expectations?" Peggy asked, referring to Seth.

"He's a quiet one. Keeps his thoughts close to the chest and his mouth shut, if you know what I mean," she offered, "keeps it all to himself."

"So, you're saying he knew her expectations?"

"I just told you that," Clarisa scoffed. "He's quick."

Peggy nodded in agreement. Seth read people well.

"She knew her brother wouldn't help. He didn't know about Judd until she got in a family way. The brother wanted her to abort the baby. That's because of Judd, up here," she pointed to her head, indicating the man's mentality. "The one over there," she nodded, directing Peggy's attention to one of Nancy Travers' helpers, "told me the whole story today."

"But, you said she had a miscarriage," Peggy interrupted.

"Three or four weeks after Judd disappeared, probably from stress. Being alone and all. According to Ben, no one's seen the brother. Everyone thinks he left the state."

"That's been months ago," Peggy reminded her.

"You know, he's leaving town again," Clarisa dismissed Peggy's comment and watched Seth deep in conversation with the minister. "He's got so much on his plate these days, what with the brother, his work and Blarney Stone, we don't get to see him as often as we used to. Poag was hoping he would stop over later tonight."

"Blarney Stone," Peggy questioned. "What's Blarney Stone?"

"It was his uncle's restaurant on Niagara Street, the one facing the river. It was known for scampi. Seth ate there almost every Sunday. The partner took it over when Barthalemew Stone died a year or so back. Seth inherited the uncle's estate, plus his big old rambling house that sits way back in the trees on North Forest Road. Living in Amherst, you must have passed the red brick house millions of times. Seth's been working on it since last year. Poag calls the place, Blarney Stone Two, or just TWO, so we don't confuse it with his house in Lockport."

"I didn't think Seth had any relatives." Peggy expressed surprise. "Is he going to sell it?"

"He was the last, I think. His father and Barthalemew were brothers. Seth and the uncle were close, but he never discusses his relationships with people. Don't get me wrong. Seth's friendly with everyone. He just never talks about himself. It's hard getting inside his head. I think Poag is closest to him, but he doesn't talk either. So, I'm faced with two mutes."

Then, thinking of Peggy's second question, Clarisa explained further. "I know he won't sell the house. There's a huge windowed loft on the third floor where he spreads out his work. He has a lot of projects scheduled this year, so he needs the room. At least, that what he told us. I think he sleeps there sometimes. The place is completely furnished…with his uncle's stuff."

"I don't really know what's going on with him anymore," she sighed. "He seems more preoccupied with Judd's death these days. Now that they found the body, Seth has to accept the reality of his death and I'm not sure he has."

Clarisa moved her eyes away from Seth to Peggy.

"So, where's your husband today?" Clarisa changed the subject. "I was hoping to meet him sometime."

At that point, Peggy gave Clarisa the short version of the divorce, as it related to the kidnapping. Obviously, Seth never told her about Jeff's illicit affair with her good friend, Alice.

Still, Clarisa was not surprised. "Seth's not one to gossip." She told Peggy.

That meant Seth never told Poag either. Clarisa was right. Seth kept secrets.

"What did I say the night you were waiting for Ben?" she admonished. "Didn't I tell you men were a bunch of shits?"

"Yeah, I think you did," Peggy said, amused.

"So, flush the turd and get on with your life," she advised.

"I've never heard divorce portrayed quite that way before, but it's good advice." Peggy laughed, as she watched Clarisa walk toward her beckoning husband.

"Keep in touch with me, honey. You know where I live," she bellowed, as Poag coaxed her toward an open door, where Ben Burrows stood waiting for his talkative sister.

At that point Peggy couldn't help thinking of the commonality between Megan and Clarisa.

They certainly spoke the same language.

Following their lead, Peggy said goodbye to Nancy Travers and her two remaining friends, before approaching Seth once more. She repeated her condolences again and hurriedly left the church party room.

Now, she was home and totally alone. Peggy eyed her wine glass again. Is this what she had to look forward to? Would all her

Saturday nights be like this? Peggy had to face facts. She was lonely. Peggy drained her wine glass, took it into the kitchen and prepared for a night of television in the family room. The couch was so much softer there, and she could prop up the pillows to a comfortable position for watching her programs.

Within the hour, she was fast asleep.

Somewhere in the distance, a ringing jarred her awake. Peggy couldn't comprehend the direction of the noise. Did it come from the television, which was unusually loud for some reason, or from the telephone? When the ringing continued, the television remote drifted off her lap and fell to the floor as she ran to answer the phone.

"What?" She growled, unable to hear anything with the television blaring in the background.

"Turn off your TV." A voice shouted back.

"I can't hear you. Wait til I turn off the TV." She yelled in return.

"Hello," Peggy answered. "For some reason the television was on louder than usual."

"Peggy. It's Seth. You must have pressed the volume button when you fell asleep on the couch."

"How do you know that?"

"Everybody does it, at some time or another." His response was simple.

"He did it again," she thought. Nothing seemed to slip by him.

"I guess so," Peggy answered, not knowing how to reply.

"I didn't call to discuss television. I wanted to thank you for coming to the memorial service. Your being there meant a lot to me. We were together when it all came down with Judd…," he faltered. "Now that it's final, I'm finding it hard to accept."

Peggy sensed the sadness in his voice. How could she respond? What could she say that would be comforting? How could she lessen the pain he was suffering with today's reminder?

"Yes, we were together," she said, quietly. "I'm glad I came today. Your tribute to Judd was beautiful. You will always cherish those memories of growing up together. I think everyone there appreciated your sharing them with us."

"You think so?"

"I know it. The warmth and love of your being together was genuinely felt by everyone. It was heart rendering."

"I'm glad I called," he said, "although I am sorry I woke you up."

"Don't be. We didn't get a chance to talk at the service, so I'm glad we have this opportunity."

"It had to be tonight. My flight leaves at seven tomorrow morning. I left Gabriel with Poag and Reese. But, it feels strange without him."

"Will you be gone long this time?"

"A few days: A week, max. Are you going to miss me? Is that what this is all about?"

His questions always seemed to surprise her, but she did miss him when he went away during the summer. He was the only one she could talk openly with, about her private life. Was that because they shared so much grief together during her kidnapping? Or was it because he proved to be the only trustworthy man she knew?

"I always miss you, Seth. You are the best thing that happened to me throughout this whole ordeal. I couldn't have asked for a better or truer friend," her voice cracked. "You've helped me with everything."

From the tenor of her voice Seth could tell she was still in pain… how fragile she really was. She had reached that familiar edge again. What could he say to prevent the dam of tears from bursting? He knew she was alone and very, very lonely.

"I think we developed this closeness, because we were thrown into a situation that could have ended very badly for both of us," he said. "I will always be here for you. You do know that, don't you?"

"Yes, Seth. I do."

"Call me if something comes up."

"Before you hang up, I want to thank you again for the painting. I have it on display in the foyer. Megan wanted me to put a spotlight on it," she laughed.

"Your sister's a lovely young woman. I like her."

"It's mutual, believe me," she said, and then changed the subject. "When are you going to tell me about painting with your father?"

"I'd have to know you better before talking about things in my personal life," Seth stopped suddenly.

As he spoke, Peggy detected a slight edge in his voice.

"It's just the way I am," he offered.

"How could I possibly know you any better than I do now?" It was a simple question.

"Think about it, Margaret." Seth called Peggy by her given name. Then, after a moment's hesitation, he made a quiet statement. "You looked beautiful at the service today."

Then Seth pressed the end button.

Peggy eyed her phone briefly, and realized what had just happened. It was strange that he would terminate the phone call that way, although it ended with a compliment. But, Peggy understood. It was his quiet way of thanking her for coming to the service. He was not a gushy-type guy. Still, his cryptic statement concerning his father puzzled her.

How could she get to know him any better than she already did? Did he expect an invitation to dinner? No. That couldn't be right. Peggy couldn't invite Seth over for the purpose of grilling him about his work and his father's influence on him. No. Peggy concluded. That was not what Seth meant. Then what other scenario existed?

"*Think about it, Margaret.*" His words echoed her thoughts.

It couldn't possibly be sex. Seth stayed within the marital boundary when he had every opportunity for wanton lust after Jeff's betrayal. Taking advantage of a bad situation wouldn't be like him, either. Rather than stew about it, Peggy would ask him directly the next time they met.

"*What exactly would you say, Margaret?*" Peggy asked herself.

"*I'd ask him if he wanted dinner or sex in exchange for information about his private life,*" Margaret replied, without a second thought.

Then, slowly, Peggy came to reconsider the conversation she just held with herself.

"Jesus, Margaret, we are two sick people," Peggy said aloud. "Schizophrenic: maybe, but very, very sick."

Nevertheless, she was pleased that Seth called. Peggy was even more pleased that she went shopping for a dress. Maybe Megan was right. She needed a new wardrobe.

Chapter 25
Thanksgiving

A month passed by without any communication from Seth. Not that Peggy expected to hear from him. Of course, he might have been waiting for her call, too. Friends were like that. They could depend on each other. But, what kind of friendship did they have, when neither one kept in touch with the other? Maybe he would call and wish her a Happy Thanksgiving.

That did not happen. Nor, did she send him a birthday card. He would turn forty without hearing from her. Not that it made a big difference. He never mentioned the November date.

Nevertheless, this particular Thanksgiving was very important to Peggy because it would never be repeated. She would be able to spend the holiday with Megan, according to the strict Croft schedule, and that made it very special.

No doubt, Rosalie would retake the mantle and host the November holiday at her home the following year. The woman would never think of Megan as competition. Brad's wife was of no consequence, none whatsoever.

If the Thanksgiving dinner turned into a terrific party, that would have made Rosalie a totally enraged woman. She would be told how thoroughly the family enjoyed themselves, overstaying at the dinner table, unwilling to end an evening of lively conversation.

However, long before all the pleasantries took place, a great deal of planning and effort were expended by Megan, Peggy, and Brad. Peggy, the list person of the trio, broke down all the things necessary for a successful party and, as a result, the affair flowed flawlessly. By far, it was the best of all Croft dinner parties and the most enjoyable.

After all the guests had gone home Thanksgiving night, Brad, Megan and Peggy sat around the kitchen table discussing Megan's success as a hostess.

"The meal was wonderful," Peggy complimented her sister, "and you did a beautiful job decorating the house. You should be very proud of yourself."

"I couldn't have done it without your help," Megan said, returning the praise. "You got everything organized."

"Don't sell yourself short, Meg. You put in a lot of time for this dinner and it showed."

"I couldn't believe how taken the women were with Ben Burrows, especially, Barbara," Megan reflected. "She hung on his every word. He was so charming. You'd never know how grisly his work can be, listening to the table conversation."

"I liked his fishing story with the rented boat in the Thousand Islands. Can you picture him and his buddy stuck in the middle of nowhere with a propeller full of seaweed? Then, to add to their problems, didn't he say the horn went off as they made their way back to shore? Burrows may have been ticked at the time," Brad laughed. "But it was funny the way he told it."

Brad continued to review the success of their dinner party.

"I think Dad and Robert really enjoyed Ben. The man was a breath of fresh air to our very stale family. I wish we could see more of him."

"I noticed that Ann didn't say much at the table," Peggy pointed out.

"She is a rather quiet person, but I could tell she enjoyed herself," Megan said. "When you think about it, everybody was talking and laughing throughout the whole meal. There was never any kind of pause."

"I give Megan a lot of credit." Brad patted her hand. He was so proud of his wife. "It's been a long time since our family actually enjoyed a holiday dinner. I attribute that to Megan's foresight by inviting Ben. He gave a measure of attention to everyone at the table. Did you notice? He even encouraged a conversation with Susan when he did hand tricks before dinner."

"Personally, I think she just wanted the quarter," Megan corrected, playfully.

"Regardless, it went well," Peggy concluded. She watched her sister take three flute glasses from her cupboard, while Brad cracked open a cold bottle of champagne and began filling them.

Megan disappeared momentarily. Then, she reappeared with an envelope which she placed on the table in front of Peggy.

Megan and Brad reached for their champagne glasses and waited for Peggy to follow suit.

"Merry Christmas, Peggy!" they toasted.

"Open it," Megan prodded.

Peggy's eyes rested on the envelope. She felt somewhat awkward without having something to offer in return. Bringing Christmas presents to their house on Thanksgiving never entered her mind. She would remember next time, if ever there was a repeat of this one.

"This is a special night for us. Brad and I spend Christmas with his parents, so we wanted to do this tonight. That's why we wanted you to stay over."

Peggy opened the envelope and found a bank passbook listing her name first and Megan's name second on the joint account.

"I don't understand. What is this?"

"It's all your money," Megan replied. "At least seven thousand is."

Although Peggy was confused by the dollar amount listed, Megan hurriedly explained the details of saving her sister's money while she pretended to be constantly short of funds.

"Why? What made you think I would need it?"

"Because I never trusted Jeff. I thought if that asshole ever took off, you'd be able to get some of his money. That's the least I could have done for you."

Suddenly, Peggy burst into a fit of laughter.

Megan couldn't understand what was so funny. Brad thought Peggy was amused by his wife's cleverness. But, neither Megan nor Brad knew Peggy *already had* some of Jeff's money.

When Peggy stopped laughing, she pointed to the two entries in the savings account that totaled over seventeen thousand dollars.

"Can you explain these to me?"

"The ten thousand is a Christmas present from Megan," Brad replied hurriedly, hiding his own contribution. "You can't refuse it."

"But, it's too much," she insisted.

"This is a one-time thing, but it's nothing compared to what you've given me, Peg. Besides, now you can take a trip. Go to Europe.

Meet some Italian ass-pincher in Rome. Have a blast while you're still young and beautiful."

"Does that mean six weeks from now my face will wrinkle and my body will sag?"

"What's in six weeks?"

"Hopefully, a trip to Paris. I have a bunch of brochures, but no arrangements. I know Janice will watch the shop after the Christmas rush. She's been after me to get away for a long time. Think my body will hold up until then?" Peggy laughed.

"It will. Provided you come back refreshed and with something other than a cat." Then Megan's eyes widened. "Did you notice Ann Quiqley?"

"How she was dressed," she added. "Did you notice?"

"Megan lost me," Peggy told Brad. "Do you know what she's talking about, felines or clothes?"

"Maybe the woman got a new dress for the occasion," her handsome brother-in-law suggested. "I think that's what Megan meant."

"She did," Megan smiled. Not *only that*, she thought to herself. *Ann also bought a new brassiere. Well, it looked that way anyhow. Her boobs were on full alert and not resting anywhere.*

"You are a good influence on everyone," Peggy concluded. "And you throw a great party."

Peggy finished her flute of champagne and rose to kiss them. She placed the bank book in an old handbag that rested on a nearby chair.

"Thank you for a wonderful Thanksgiving and an early Christmas. I love you both," she said. "Now, I'm going to bed. We have to get up early tomorrow. You're helping me at the shop, aren't you?" she asked, reminding Megan of Black Friday. "Janice and Fred are still in Ithaca."

"That's right," Megan remembered. "They're meeting Amy's new boyfriend."

They watched Peggy cross the hall and go upstairs.

She's lonely," Megan whispered.

"Yeah, I guess she is," Brad agreed. "Sometimes, things work out better this way."

A quizzical look crossed Megan's face as she thought to herself. "What the hell is he talking about?" The only good thing, about her sister's being alone, was that she no longer had to put up with JAR, or Jeffrey Alan Roberts. In Megan's mind, the A really stood for Asshole.

Is that what Brad meant? She knew not to press it. Sometimes, Brad was off in his own little world where everything worked out for the best. He was such an optimist. But, Megan knew better than her hazel-eyed husband. The world was filled with a bunch of agenda promoting shits.

Brad placed the flute glasses on the sink, indicating that it was time for bed. Before going upstairs to her bedroom, Megan slipped into the dining room and pictured everyone at the dinner table hours earlier. She recalled the chatter and laughter over the passing of food. The memory filled her with a great deal of satisfaction.

Everyone loved her Frog Prince

***

Peggy tossed and turned trying to get to sleep. Nothing seemed to work these days. What had she to look forward to? The same routine repeated over and over...work, dinner, bed. Why did life have to be this way? She wasn't meant to be alone. Obviously, she had made the wrong choice in a mate. But, how was she supposed to know it would turn out like this? Jeff met all the criteria necessary for marriage.

Right, she thought to herself. He was male, gorgeous and available. *Face it*, she admonished herself again. *He was loaded with personality. He had it all. Still has.* Now, he's giving it all to someone else... some beautiful flight attendant. Without even knowing the woman, Peggy hated her. With that thought in mind, her attention shifted to Alice.

She wondered what really happened between them after Peggy's confrontation at the motel. The night he came by the house and agreed to her divorce terms, Jeff told her then that it was over with Alice. Perhaps it was. She would never know.

But, there still had to be some connection between Alice and John Beck since Megan saw them recently at the mall parking lot.

Could they both be living a lie together, each thinking the other was unaware of Jeff's betrayal? What of Alice's role in the wanton affair?

Neither Jeff nor Peggy mentioned her in the divorce papers. Irreconcilable differences covered a lot of territory. Of course, it was blackmail justly served. But Jeff agreed to everything so he could keep his current job or go elsewhere. He may not have been able to face John Beck squarely, but neither Jeff nor Peggy said anything to the man about his wife.

That was totally unnecessary, since John Beck already knew of their affair; but both, Jeff and Alice, were oblivious to that fact. So if Peggy kept her mouth shut, Alice could go on living with John as if nothing untoward happened.

Is this how life really is? The thought swirled around her head.

Alice screws around and ends up with her husband as if nothing ever happened. Jeff's disloyalty grants him the arms of another gorgeous woman, while Peggy sits at home alone. How fair was that?

Maybe she should go to Paris. Could she possibly meet someone to her liking? How could she meet an eligible Frenchman? Surely, Paris had a dating service. Why would she want that in the first place? She didn't even speak the language.

A smile crossed her face in the darkened bedroom. "How desperate can I be when I'm thinking of crossing an ocean for companionship? Go to sleep," Peggy told herself. "Although things will still look the same in the morning, you'll feel rested."

***

While Peggy was having a fretful time trying to sleep, in another bedroom down the hall, Megan was listening to Brad's snoring. On the count of three, she heard soft, intermittent whistles in his breathing. In a strange way, she found it rather soothing. It was like the background music of a dinner opera with Ben Burrows.

Her thoughts shifted back to the month of October when Peggy agreed to help her with Thanksgiving dinner. That was precisely the same day she met Seth Stone at the gift shop.

Several days later she was in Ben Burrows' office on a mission of mercy. Of course, he was very surprised to see her, but the poor man had no idea that Megan called the station days earlier for his schedule, saying he wanted to see her, so she could know when to pop in.

"What are you doing here?" he asked from the doorway of his office.

"I need your help," she pleaded. "You brought back my sister, now you have to save me."

"You want what?" his voice resounded when she extended the dinner invitation. "Why would you need me?"

"I've never had Brad's family for a holiday. Never, ever. It's got to be special. They have to think I know what I'm doing, and I don't know shit about entertaining those people. Sure, I know what fork and knife to use, but Barbara knows etiquette so well, and I'm such a klutz."

"I'm sure you're exaggerating," he said, trying to calm her.

"No. No. I have a plan. I got Peggy for food and decorations and I want you for entertainment."

Ben Burrows stared at Megan with his mouth wide open. The man was positively speechless. "You sound like a wedding planner. Who'd you get for music?"

"You think I need music? Who could I get?" Megan became frantic.

"I was being sarcastic. You don't need music."

"Then, why the hell would you say that?" she turned on him. "You've got a desperate woman in front of you who needs help."

Ben Burrows never responded to her statement, choosing, instead to listen to her rattle on.

"I have the literary angle covered, if Ann Quigley comes. She's the one who works at the university library."

"You mean the one with..." His hands went below the nipples on his chest.

"That's the one," she acknowledged his gesture, and then switched back to her original thought.

"The family's a bunch of readers, so she can handle that end. Plus, she is very nice."

"Now, I get it." His eyes locked on hers. "You want to fix me up with your librarian. That's what this is all about, isn't it?"

"No, I am not interested in fixing you up with Ann Quigley. I have a group of women in mind for you, not just one," she corrected. "It will be a virtual smorgasbord."

"Go home, Megan. I'm getting a headache."

"Are you willing to take a bet?" she challenged.

"It has to be good."

"My house: Thanksgiving. If I'm right, you'll charm Barbara Croft right out of her bloomers. She'll invite you to her New Year's Day party and all the single women there will want a piece of you. You probably know most of the men already."

"So, if I pass the charm test and get an invitation, I lose the bet." He was testy.

"Right," she agreed.

"No. Megan. I don't like it."

"Then you have to help me without the bet. You know damn well I'm going to screw up somewhere. I can't keep a conversation going without some profanity slipping out. If you come, all I have to do is pass food and smile."

Burrows eyed the pathetic young woman. Her life experiences were so difficult and she was so vulnerable. She really wanted to make a good impression on her husband's wealthy family and felt he could help her make the difference. So, he would be the family entertainment while Peggy, with the aid of Megan, did the cooking and decorating. These duties, of course, would be understood, but never discussed openly.

"Is my being there really that important to you?" His bulging eyes met hers.

"It is. I really need you," she pleaded.

"What time am I scheduled to perform?" A smile crossed his face.

"Cocktails at four: dinner at five." She threw her arms around him and nearly knocked him off his footing by rocking his body back and forth. "I'm so happy. I'm so happy!" she shouted, kissing him repeatedly all over his face.

"Calm down, woman! Now, go home," he blustered. "I'll see you on Thanksgiving."

"Wait. Wait," she shouted. "Is there anything you can tell me...?"

But, before she could continue, Ben quickly interrupted her, and placing his finger on his nose, hushed her completely.

"I have not forgotten," he said quietly. "Now, go home."

At that moment, she knew he would not fail her. At some point in time, Ben Burrows would find her father, providing he was still alive.

Megan left him thinking all sorts of wonderful things.

He was the best Frog Prince on the lily pad.

She rested her head on the pillow and fell asleep.

Chapter 26
The Mall

On the day after Thanksgiving, known everywhere as Black Friday, or the day people shop for Christmas bargains at the most ungodly hours, Peggy rose at five-thirty and reminded Megan of the early morning shopping rush. By seven o'clock, Peggy and Megan were at the gift shop and ready for an onslaught of customers.

At nine o'clock, their first customer entered the shop to buy a knitted throw she had seen days earlier, now on sale. From then on, a steady stream of customers browsed through the shop to make Christmas purchases and wrist-spray every test bottle of perfume in the store.

At day's end, they were both exhausted, but very satisfied with the day's receipts. Fortunately, the Saturday hours were somewhat later, so both of them were glad for the extra hours of sleep.

"What's the matter?" Megan questioned her sister, as they were closing the gift shop.

"It's the clasp. It doesn't snap closed," she muttered, as she fiddled with her purse. "Maybe the shoemaker can fix it."

"You need a new handbag." Megan inspected it closely. "The leather looks worn."

"I never noticed." Peggy examined the purse. "You're right. It does look tacky."

"Check Coach or Dooney and Bourke at the mall. They're smashing."

"I am not paying three hundred dollars for a handbag. Forget it." Peggy reacted.

"They're on sale! It's Christmas." Megan was quick to remind her.

"Can you spell me for a couple of hours when Janice gets back next week?"

"Don't you want me here tomorrow?"

"Of course, I do," Peggy replied, puzzled by her question. "I was thinking of shopping for a handbag next week. That's what I meant. This one's beyond repair."

"I can work whenever you need me," she offered. "Barbara's doing the holidays, so all I have to do is buy presents."

"What's wrong, Megan? What's on your mind?" Her sister was visually upset.

Megan blinked several times, clearing her eyes. A lump in her throat stopped her from speaking immediately. Thoughts coursing through her mind saddened her.

"It's not fair. You work your ass off and then spend Christmas alone. At least last year, you were with Jeff, asshole that he is, but you weren't alone."

"Is that what's bugging you? Good grief. I'm looking forward to a day of peace and quiet. Really, Meg, don't feel sorry for me. I'm ok. Frankly, I could use a day off."

"Are you sure? I have to be with Brad at Barbara's house. Christmas is always her turn to be the dinner hostess. But, she does set a beautiful table. Sometimes, I hate her for being so ... what's the word? Knowledgeable. Knowing what to do all the time. It makes me sick."

"She has nothing on you. Your party was absolutely wonderful. Aside from being festive, it was fun. You know it, Brad knows it, and more important, the family knows it. Rosalie, well? She's another story. We both know she'll try to outdo your Thanksgiving dinner next year. But, the family will make a comparison privately. You know Franklin Senior and Barbara will."

Peggy set the burglar alarm, turned out the lights and locked the door of the shop. The two sisters walked arm in arm to their respective cars before heading home for the night.

Megan turned to her sister, suddenly. "I am so glad you're safe. I don't know what I would do without you." She kissed her sister's cheek.

"I love my kid sister." Peggy hugged Megan and kissed her goodnight.

A tear slid down the side of her face, as she watched Megan drive slowly away into the night.

"She knows," Peggy said to herself. "But, I am getting accustomed to cooking for one. It does something to the body mass, like losing ten pounds."

Within minutes, Peggy was home and in bed for the night.

***

A week later when Peggy was sitting in the mall food court sipping a cup of coffee, she felt a hand touch her shoulder.

"You Christmas shopping too?" Clarisa's voice surprised her.

"I almost wish. My handbag's shot. So I'm shopping for a new one, how about you?"

"Did you go to Coach?" the woman asked. "I know some of their purses cost an arm and a leg, but I saw a gorgeous black one for seventy dollars. I always stop there when I'm at the mall. Christ knows why, I never buy anything."

"I haven't made the circle yet, but I will. Thanks for the seventy dollar tip," Peggy said, appreciatively. That figure was much more in line with what she wanted to spend for a purse, particularly one for work.

"I need to get something for Poag and Ben, but haven't any idea what to buy them. They have everything." Clarisa slid into a chair opposite her.

"How about fishing gear," Peggy suggested, "something that might be new on the market?"

"I don't know," Clarisa mused. "They're kinda picky about fishing stuff. But, I'm tired of buying them shirts and ties."

Suddenly, Peggy became enthusiastic. "I got an idea. It's a pip. Call Seth and ask him where they might like to go for a weekend fishing trip. Then make a reservation. It doesn't have to be that far away, and they can always change the date if something comes up. What I'd do," Peggy continued, "is get some returnable lures and place the reservation on top of each gift."

"I think Seth could help me with that," Clarisa agreed enthusiastically, relishing the idea. "They'll be so surprised. Not that Ben deserves it," she paused and groused aloud. "He went somewhere else for Thanksgiving this year. I think he has a girlfriend and won't tell us. He was very secretive about his plans. He wouldn't say one word and just changed the subject when I asked. I'm sure it's a woman."

While Clarisa continued to be upset with her brother's sneaky behavior, and verbalized her feelings in great detail, Peggy couldn't contain her thoughts any longer.

"No, Clarisa. He wasn't with a girlfriend. Ben spent Thanksgiving at Megan's house. From what I understand, my sister begged him to come."

Peggy then explained the circumstances surrounding the importance of Thanksgiving with the Croft family as Megan's guests, and the support she desperately needed from Peggy and Ben to help make her first experience at entertaining a success.

"I thought your sister came on like a Mack Truck," Clarisa interrupted.

"Megan does. Her street smarts allowed her to survive, but she's fragile inside. Part of it was my fault for not being around her more. Our mother was not the best parent on the block, if you know what I mean. Going to school was the only way out for both of us."

"Now, I understand," she said. "Ben wouldn't talk about it, so I thought...well you know what I thought."

"He was wonderful, Clarisa. He made her feel so comfortable. Megan was so scared she'd make a mistake or say something wrong. It was a one-time thing so she won't have to worry about doing it again."

"You mean they won't let her?" Clarisa looked puzzled. "I don't understand."

"Each of the Croft women, except Megan, hosts the same holiday every year with drinks and dinner. So, when Rosalie Croft, the one who has Thanksgiving, went upstate for reasons unknown, Megan and Brad filled in. But, don't worry. The regular schedule will be in effect next year, and Ben will be eating at your table."

"So, she never gets to entertain. Is that what you mean?"

"Exactly, that's why this Thanksgiving was so important. Normally, she and Brad merely attend the holiday dinners like two invited guests. Barbara and Franklin Senior host Christmas every year and I understand it's quite beautiful...the dinner, the drinks and the decorations."

"But, you're never invited to these gatherings."

"It's strictly family," she said, shaking her head. "But, since Brad and Megan were hosting Thanksgiving this year, they invited us to celebrate with them. It was a smart way of making certain everything fell into place. It had to be perfect and it was."

"So, I'm to understand that you and Ben helped her with everything."

"We were there for her," Peggy repeated, "a real support team."

"You would have been so proud of your brother, Clarisa. He was so charming. The entire Croft family enjoyed his fishing stories. Barbara, the queen of the clan, was completely taken by him. She smiled so much that night I was waiting for her face to crack."

Peggy stopped talking. A sudden thought alarmed her.

"Please don't say anything to Ben. If he wants you to know he spent Thanksgiving with Megan, let him tell you first. I don't want your brother to think I'd betray his secrets."

"Hold on," Clarisa interrupted her. "I'm not thinking about Ben right now. That won't be an issue. So, if you're not going to be with your sister on Christmas, where will you be eating dinner?"

"I plan to spend a lazy day with steak, salad and old movies."

"Sounds terrible. Come to the motel for Christmas. We'll eat around the kitchen table like we always do. Nothing fancy. Poag will cook something good. I know Ben's coming for sure, but I don't know about Seth. He's still grieving, I think. If that's not it, then I don't know what's on his mind. Something's bothering him. I can feel it. He just doesn't open up...but then he never did." She shook her head. "Anyhow, I need a woman to offset whoever does show up."

"Are you sure, Clarisa? I don't want to put you out."

"Hell, yes, I'm sure. Just don't bring any food. The man I live with likes to be King of the Kitchen. We'll eat around five, so swing by around four or four-thirty." Clarisa stood up to leave. "Don't disappoint me on Christmas," she said.

"If I do, check the hospitals or funeral homes for visitation hours," Peggy chuckled.

"Now, that's a mouthful," Clarisa laughed and walked away.

***

Peggy sipped her coffee slowly and thought about spending Christmas with Clarisa and Poag. She would enjoy listening to their banter again. In a strange way, the game they played was a declaration of love...Poag inviting her to room five, the unit with the king-size bed and Jacuzzi, to prove his superior manhood, while Clarisa continued to resist his advances.

An outsider, listening to their extended harangue, would naturally assume that they were married to other people. Peggy did, until Seth explained their marital game by directing Peggy's attention to his ring finger. The way he did it was so slick, so silent and so sneaky... just an unaware point like someone scratching his hand.

She would enjoy seeing Ben again. He had been so helpful with Megan's dinner at Thanksgiving. Helpful. No. He carried the entire dinner conversation along. Ben was the one responsible for the flow; he made certain everyone joined in. He was Megan's ringer.

According to Megan, it was the first time she ever heard the Croft family laugh as much as they did exchanging fishing stories with Ben. It was too bad they would not be able to repeat the dinner again next year. But the schedule had to be kept. Rosalie would see to it, when she heard how pleasant Megan's dinner party turned out. Pleasant. That's how intuitive Barbara Croft would describe the holiday to keep peace in the family with the snobby daughter-in-law. But, that description would be enough for Rosalie to start thinking of ways she could make her Thanksgiving dinner more spectacular. Unfortunately, it would never equal Megan's effort. She didn't have Megan's street smarts, nor did she have Ben, Ann and Peggy as the background chorus orchestrating the entire evening. Rosalie would have to stay within the confines of the Croft family. No doubt, it would be a beautiful but very staid affair.

Peggy would ask Ben about Mel, if the opportunity arose. His being out there somewhere made her apprehensive. The man would recognize Peggy if he saw her around town. In turn, she, too, could recognize him. But, he wouldn't know that. Still, that fact was of little comfort to her. She only wished the man would be found...soon.

Peggy wondered if Seth would be at Clarisa's for Christmas. She had not heard from him.

In fact, they had not seen each other since the memorial service. Nor had they talked on the phone since then. She could not call him. Peggy had no reason to have a conversation with the man. Still, she thought about Seth every day. Why hadn't he called her? Clarisa said she thought that he was still in mourning. Either that or something else was on his mind.

A wild thought suddenly occurred to her. Had he taken up with Nancy Travers? Peggy couldn't picture the two of them together. It couldn't be. Could it? They had nothing in common. If he came to Poag's house for Christmas, would Clarisa mention his involvement with the woman? Would she make the announcement to everyone there? More revolting was the thought of Nancy Travers actually spending Christmas at Clarisa's house...with Peggy there.

On the other hand, Seth could still be mourning the loss of his brother. It would not surprise her. The man did suffer feelings of guilt. Seth always felt he should have done more for Judd. He explained this fully during their time together.

Once reality surfaced, Peggy realized she had the same problem all women face at some point in time. Her wardrobe held nothing extraordinary for Clarisa's dinner party. She had nothing that stood out or was drop dead gorgeous. *"Face it,"* she told herself. *"You need new clothes."*

Peggy drained her coffee cup quickly. She had an errand to run. She was determined to break her piggy bank and buy something sensational to wear on Christmas. Cost was not going to be a factor. She needed something really chic. She'd even model it for Megan's approval. Her sister would be glad that she was not spending Christmas at home...alone.

Chapter 27
Christmas

On a very cold and wet Christmas afternoon, Peggy stood huddled by the motel office in Clarence, her purse in one hand and a shopping bag in the other. It was an undeniable fact. Peggy was shivering. Her black winter coat wasn't warm enough for the freezing weather, nor was the top button closure high enough to clasp around her throat. The knit pull on cap added little warmth to her head, and the only saving grace seemed to be the wool knit gloves on her hands.

Peggy's feet felt the cold, as she stepped from her car onto the snow laden sidewalk, and she treaded slowly to the motel office in her skinny high-heels, fearful of falling. Her boots lay idly on a rubber mat in Megan's laundry room since Thanksgiving, neither sister giving them a thought. They weren't really needed until today.

"When it started snowing, I was afraid you were going to cancel on me," Clarisa said, taking Peggy's coat when she entered the motel office. Then, Clarisa ushered Peggy behind a party wall into the living room.

"If it starts to accumulate, I might have to leave early," Peggy answered quickly.

"You'll do no such thing," Clarisa replied. "Your shop's closed tomorrow. You can stay here tonight. I'll even throw in Poag's favorite room. Hell. You can have any room you want. They're all available."

"You mean I can have room five," Peggy teased, "the one with the Jacuzzi and the king-size bed? Wow! That is tempting."

"Why not, it's Christmas? We'll even feed you breakfast in the morning."

When Peggy entered the living room, she soon realized two of the men who greeted her from the couch, and the third one sitting in an overstuffed chair, had overheard her entire conversation with Clarisa. She eyed all three briefly and understood why the two men sitting on the couch had no love for sleeping there. Although he was about six inches shorter than Seth's six foot frame, Ben Burrows looked taller than the man sitting beside him on a couch pillow, whose resilient springs died some time ago. For some inexplicable reason, Peggy pictured a lopsided seesaw in her mind.

Their mood brightened with animated conversation, when she greeted them laughingly about reserving the notorious room with the Jacuzzi and king-size bed.

"I guess Clarisa's going home to her husband tonight." Poag focused on the two men.

"You should have reserved room five earlier," Ben told his brother-in-law.

"He was too busy cooking dinner," Seth reminded him.

"Maybe the meal will tempt her to stay," Ben suggested.

"Don't count on it," Clarisa scoffed. "He has to come up with something a lot more original than that."

"Maybe I will," Poag met her stare. Then, he turned quickly to Peggy. "Glad you could make it. I need all the help I can get."

Peggy acknowledged his comment and reached into her shopping bag that contained two boxes. She gave the first one to Poag who let out a long low whistle at the pricey 2007 Clos du Bois Briarcrest Alexander Valley label.

"Now, this is what I call a good Cabernet," he said, as he examined her present. Poag was obviously pleased by her thoughtfulness. "We're cracking this baby open at dinner."

"So, what are you offering her now?" Clarisa asked Poag, as he stood caressing his wine bottle.

"Don't worry about me," Peggy interrupted, "I'll have whatever Ben and Seth are drinking. Please, Clarisa, it's your turn to open the box."

While Poag was pouring her drink, Peggy felt someone kissing her cheek.

"Good God, you don't forget a thing," Clarisa said, showing off a black Coach handbag. "This is the one I mentioned at the mall."

She shook her head. "I can't believe you did this. You spent too much money."

"You and Poag have been so good to me. I just wanted to show my appreciation. There should be a gift voucher in the box, in case you want to return it."

"I'm keeping it." Clarisa busily removed the gray paper inside the handbag and rolled it into a ball. "You still spent too much money on us."

"Well, I came into a little extra money," she winked at Seth and sat in the chair Poag vacated. "Anyhow, I wanted this to be a special Christmas with my very special friends."

"Let's see how she feels when we have her do dishes," Poag chuckled.

"Being stuck in the kitchen won't be anything new to her," Ben informed them. "She works fast and cooks a great meal."

"How would you know that?" Clarisa demanded. "Did you have dinner at her house?"

Ben eyed Peggy briefly and realized his error. Clarisa had been so upset when he refused her Thanksgiving invitation and gave no explanation for his absence.

"No. I spent Thanksgiving with Peggy at her sister's house. Megan was entertaining her husband's family and wanted us to help her."

"She needed our support." Peggy told everyone in the room, knowing Clarisa would play along. "It was the first time she had the Croft family as dinner guests and she was very nervous. For some reason, Ben has a very calming effect on Megan." Peggy clarified his position.

"Does that mean Ben will be spending Thanksgiving with your sister instead of us?" Clarisa continued the charade.

"No." Peggy replied. "This was a once only." Then, Peggy went on to detail the Croft yearly schedule. "Each of the Croft women has a particular holiday to host dinner for the family. Brad and Megan were the Thanksgiving substitutes for Rosalie this year. But, I'm sure the five members who attended Megan's party won't have as much fun next year as they did this one with Ben."

"Your sister is married to Brad Croft?" Seth asked.

"Yes. Why?" His question surprised her.

"You also mentioned a Rosalie," he shrugged, leaving her somewhat confused.

"Where was he in all of this?" Poag asked suddenly, puzzled by the man's omission on their duty roster.

"He had to make drinks and be a charming host," Burrows answered. "He did a great job."

"But, it was Ben's job to carry the conversation along and make certain everyone was having a good time." Peggy precluded Poag's next question. "Megan's was so afraid of making a mistake; she relied on Ben to charm everyone."

"Where were you in all of this?" It was Seth's turn to question. "What was your chief function?"

"Hiding in the kitchen, mostly, preparing the meal and doing dishes," Ben chortled before Peggy could reply.

"Maybe so, but without you, it would have been a bust." Peggy continued to praise him.

"Speaking of bust, Clarisa come out and help me in the kitchen." Poag took her arm. "I need your help," he winked. "Let's leave them alone."

As soon as they left the room, Ben clarified the awkward situation with Clarisa.

"My sister thought I had a girlfriend and was spending the holiday with her. So, I let her run away with her suspicions. It was fun to watch her. She was so ticked." He was amused by it all.

"But, now she knows the truth," Seth assessed Ben's situation.

"I'm not so sure about that," Ben said, his voice dropping to a whisper. "If Megan has her way, I'll be meeting a host of eligible women. Her word, I think, was smorgasbord."

"Oh. My God! You got an invitation!" Peggy became excited. "You're going to Barbara's New Year's Day party."

Her excitement made Seth curious. "And this is great because..."

"The Crofts have a huge cocktail party at their big home on Lebrun every New Year's Day." She caught Seth's, so what, expression. "They have his huge house in Snyder. All of the properties are big on

Lebrun. What would you say, Ben, ten minutes west of Williamsville? Snyder, I mean."

Peggy caught Ben's nod then went on to explain. "A lot of women attending the affair are single or widowed and Megan wanted Ben to meet some of her friends."

"So, how did the old codger get invited? Megan didn't send out the invitations." Seth chuckled when he thought of Ben, the dashing Romeo romancing the ladies. The role didn't seem to fit the fishing friend he pictured with a rod, a reel, and hip boots.

"No. Barbara Croft did. Ben charmed his way into her heart at Thanksgiving." Peggy's remark made Seth chuckle even more. "He was the quintessential silver-tongued fox. Go ahead and laugh," Peggy sneered. "How is Ben going to explain his absence for New Years? Clarisa is going to be furious."

"No. no," Ben reassured her. "I never come here after Christmas. They have their hands full with the New Year's Eve crowd. Everyone's throwing up on New Year's. Poag doesn't even bother to cook."

"So you're off the hook, Romeo," Seth snickered.

"I might be better off staying home."

"Megan would be very disappointed if you did that," Peggy frowned.

"And very pissed," Ben added. "She'd probably come and get me."

"It's settled then. You're going." There was a definite finality in Peggy's voice. The subject was closed. She had another one to pursue. "I know it's only been three weeks since I asked," she began.

Ben knew exactly what was on Peggy's mind before she started to question him.

"We still have no leads on Mel. He seems to have totally disappeared," he said. "We've watched his sister's house and the places he frequented. But, we've come up with nothing."

"I was hoping for a break. It's been six months and I'm still apprehensive," Peggy complained. "Being alone..." She never finished the thought. The anxiety the woman felt was glaringly obvious to both men.

In trying to allay her feelings of insecurity, Ben gave her some additional information that he added to the case file recently. "I have followed John Beck's movements, hoping to find Mel. But, all I can tell you is that he and his wife are still together. They just moved into another house two weeks ago."

"Is it in Wellington Woods?" Peggy remembered her conversation with Seth regarding the area.

"I believe so." Burrows recalled the subdivision.

"How nice for Alice," she said sarcastically. "Two people involved know the whole story, four lives are ruined and the guilty live happily ever after."

"Is that how you really feel?" The harshness of Seth's sudden question unnerved her completely.

"What I really feel is scared." She challenged his remark. "I'm frightened that Mel may come after me. Why I feel this way, I don't know. I think John Beck should be in jail for having me kidnapped. And as for Jeff, I'm glad it's over."

"Why didn't you tell me you were frightened?" The strident tone of Seth's voice told Peggy he was upset with her. A frown furrowed his forehead. Outwardly he was annoyed. She should have shared those fears with him. He knew she was lonely when they spoke on the phone, but was she also afraid? Living alone all those months? It was his turn to be angry. Peggy should have called him…this time.

"You can't keep looking after me, Seth," she bristled. "You have a life of your own. Plans you want to pursue. Anyhow, I'm not your responsibility." She emphasized coldly.

The growing divide between them was blatantly obvious.

"Am I interrupting something here?" Ben asked.

"No!" They barked, simultaneously.

But, Ben Burrows was a very smart man. He knew better. He had made his mark as one of the best detectives in the county and this was a no-brainer. Something was going on between them and Ben was not going down that road. It was none of his business. His memory of their past history served him well.

Although Seth seldom spoke of Peggy during their subsequent conversations, when he did, it was always in complimentary terms. However, during their time together at Thanksgiving, Peggy never mentioned Seth at all. Ben decided that the motto from Las Vegas was the best approach. What happened between them, he didn't want to know. It wasn't exactly the Vegas motto, but the drift of it was still the same. Ben really didn't want to know about any of it. His thoughts were interrupted at the exact right time...before another exchange occurred.

"Come to the table." A man's voice shouted from the next room.

***

Seth and Peggy followed Ben silently into the kitchen where a mountain of food graced the festive looking table.

"Peggy, you and Ben sit over there," Clarisa pointed to a designated area.

"Seth, you sit here," she directed, pulling out a chair. "Gabriel's been chewing at the bit for your company. I think you should have him checked. His breath is really bad."

At the mention of his name, Gabriel stood up and stepped away from Reese to catch Seth's attention. Seth turned to his dog. With a slight turn of his head, he signaled Gabriel to lie back down again. Although Seth's command was not to Gabriel's liking, the dog placed his long body on the floor and, with his head on his front paws, studied his master with disgust.

Seth would be eating all that wonderful table food, while Gabriel and Reese would be resigned to eating dried kibble that tasted like wood chips. Gabriel tasted wood chips once and didn't like them. He strongly preferred bagels with cream cheese, that is, if the table meat scraps weren't available. He would pass on those mushy potatoes and the little green tree shrubs everyone raved about. He'd wait for the dessert. Clarisa had a sweet tooth and always gave Reese and Gabriel a taste of cake or pie. Of course, Poag never knew the dogs feasted on dessert more often than table scraps. But, then, who was around to tell the man their dirty little secret?

Still, there was no telling about these people around the table. They talked too much instead of concentrating on food. So, as was his role, Gabriel watched for dropped morsels and listened to the banality of their conversation.

"This is so good, Poag," Peggy said of the succulent prime rib. "I think I taste a hint of...garlic. Did you use it to season the meat?"

"I told you she could cook," Ben responded to Poag's nod.

"I've never used it in prime rib but I will now, if I ever get the chance to make it again," Peggy replied.

"Just make sure you have the same wine on hand," Poag advised. "This is excellent."

During the entire dinner, Seth and Peggy exchanged glances, although neither one addressed the other in direct conversation. And, although the slight was not obvious to Poag and Clarisa, Ben clearly noticed the tension building between them.

The conversation flowed freely throughout the meal until Poag began clearing the table to prepare for dessert. Almost on cue, he signaled Seth that it was time to reveal the fruits of their conspiracy. Seth set dessert plates in front of everyone, while Poag reached into the tallest shelf of his cupboard and pulled out an envelope, which he placed on Clarisa's empty dish.

"Open it," Poag directed.

Clarisa was overwhelmed. This was not like Poag at all. He never surprised her. He was a man who always discussed things in advance.

After Clarisa tore open the envelope, she remained speechless, but only for a moment.

"Oh. Poag. What a wonderful surprise!" Clarisa beamed as she held a sheet of paper, along with two tickets. "Poag's taking me on a cruise after New Years." Clarisa continued to chatter as she rose from her chair to embrace Poag with a kiss.

"I have another Christmas present for you," Poag joked, "but you'll have to spend the night with me to get it."

"I'm finding your offer very hard to refuse," Clarisa laughed.

"Go for it," Peggy advised. "Poag seems to be full of surprises."

Seth nodded approvingly at Peggy suggestion and smiled. "That's what I call good advice." Peggy responded to his comment by staring down at her dessert plate.

"Who came up with the idea of a cruise?" Ben asked. "I can't believe Poag thought about it on his own."

"Believe it or not, he did," Seth assured him. "I just browsed the computer for Caribbean cruises. Poag couldn't do it without Clarisa finding out. But, Poag made all the arrangements. He chose the cruise, the cabin and the date. That was all his doing."

"I knew you couldn't surprise my nosy sister without someone's help," Burrows said to Poag, who was busy serving apple pie and ice cream to everyone.

"But, it worked," Poag answered, giving Ben no time for a response.

"Oh, this is so good," Peggy broke the silence of those around her busily devouring their dessert. "Who baked the pie?"

"I did," Ben answered, as he swirled the last bit of apple into his ice cream.

"In your dreams," Clarisa smirked. "The King of the Kitchen baked it yesterday. He refused to let me do anything in here this morning. I guess Poag thought I'd hex his meal."

"It's almost eight o'clock and I forgot." Ben jumped up from the table and left the room.

A few minutes later, he returned with an armful of presents.

"It's starting to accumulate out there. We must have three inches already. If something happens, you know I'll be called," he said, "but I wanted to give you the Christmas presents." The detective became more and more impatient as he spoke. It was obvious from his manner he wanted to leave as soon as possible.

"Sit down. We'll open them at the table," Clarisa said calmly. "Then, you can take off."

When Peggy cleared the table, she deliberately kept Ben and Poag occupied in conversation, while Clarisa fingered his Christmas gift and signaled Seth about the two fishermen's presents.

"Oh, Ben, it's beautiful," Clarisa cried, as she opened his gift. "It's cashmere." She held up the beige cardigan sweater. "I've never owned a sweater this soft or expensive."

"I'm glad you like it. The receipt is inside the box if you want to exchange it," he added quickly, anxious to end the gift-giving.

"I love it," she exclaimed. "What a great Christmas present."

"I thought it was very pretty," Ben responded.

Although Ben took the credit, he could not tell his sister the cashmere sweater was not only Megan's idea, but also her selection when he asked for help at Thanksgiving. Paying for the gift was his only real effort in the Christmas exchange. Clarisa would never have understood.

"This scotch isn't bad either," Poag said. "It's above our usual pay grade, and I can't wait to taste it. You must have hit the lottery to buy this kind of hooch."

"I thought we'd try something different," Ben lied.

This was another of Megan's purchases. So far, everything she suggested pleased everyone. The kid was right on target...except when she slobbered all over him at the police station. That was the day he agreed to help her at Thanksgiving. He had a lot of explaining to do that day...to the men who stood around staring at the young, sweet, jumping bean, rocking him to and fro, and drooling all over his face.

"Now, I have a surprise for the two of you." Clarisa parceled out the envelopes.

"I'll be damned. We're spending a weekend in the Finger Lakes." Poag was in shock.

"That's only if you're still living in May," Ben said dryly, referring to his brother-in-law's pretense of sex, room five and the Jacuzzi. "But I like Seneca Lake. We've fished there before."

"That's what you thought." Clarisa caught Seth's stare and nodded.

"He was in on this?" Poag caught her signal. "You've known about all these trips and never said a word."

"And spoil the surprise?" Seth laughed. "Why would I do that?"

Seth reached into his pocket and pulled out two very small packages. He gave one to Poag and the other to Ben.

"I don't believe it." Poag chuckled.

"I got one too," Ben held up a gold money clip.

"I'm tired of you two fumbling around with cash and coins in both pockets. Poag's paper clip doesn't always work too well on dollar bills, so I thought I'd invest in something more practical."

Peggy began to laugh when she pictured Poag pocketing a stack of bills together with a large paper clip. Her laughter was so contagious that everyone around the table began giggling and guffawing.

When the laughter finally ceased, Seth brought in a huge box for Clarisa and set it on the table.

"You shouldn't have done this," Clarisa shook her head. "You're spending too much money on us."

"Pull it out of the box," Seth advised.

"What a beautiful throw," Peggy gasped at the eider down coverlet. She reached across the table to feel the softness of the featherweight gift. "This will keep you warm when you watch television. I have one, but it's not as nice as this."

Still numb by all the expensive gifts, Clarisa finally stood up and kissed her brother and Seth. "I feel like I'm being spoiled." She took a deep breath. "I don't know what to say."

"You might start by telling them what they want to hear," Poag reminded her.

Clarisa's mind went blank. "I appreciate the gifts. I really do," she insisted.

"Tell them you're staying with me tonight. That's what they want to hear."

"Is that what you wanted to hear?" Ben asked Seth who shook his head in response. "It's more than we need to know," he told Poag.

"It's snowing like hell out there. I have to go," Ben reminded them. He kissed his sister goodbye and stood ready to leave the kitchen.

"Wait," Peggy shouted and ran to the living room for her purse. "This is for you, Ben. I don't know if it's right." She gave him a small wrapped package that held six different fishing lures.

Then, Peggy turned to Seth and gave him a small box. "I wasn't sure you'd be here." Inside the very small box lay a brown fuzzy bear cushioned in red velvet. "I saw you examining it when you brought the painting to the shop in October."

Seth eyed her briefly, and then turned his attention to Clarisa. "You're right. She is observant."

Clarisa gave Seth a toothy grin. "Peggy doesn't know about Big Red, does she?"

He ignored her remark and turned his attention back to Peggy. His attitude toward her seemed to soften. "Thank you for the thought, but I have no gift to exchange."

"That makes two of us," Ben added.

"What you've both given me is gift enough," she smiled.

"I'd better go." Ben walked toward the motel office. "I think you should sleep here tonight, Peggy. With this accumulation, driving will be very dangerous. The roads will be cleared by tomorrow. It will be much safer to drive home then."

Ben turned to Poag and Clarisa. "If you're smart, you'll sleep here tonight," he told his sister, while winking at Poag. "When you think about it, I'm the only one going home in this weather. Everybody else is staying here. That's a helleva situation."

Clarisa embraced her brother. "I love you. You know that, don't you? If I don't see you before New Years, come visit us before we leave on the cruise."

"I will," Ben whispered.

Chapter 28
Together

After the four of them watched Ben leave, Peggy raced to the kitchen only to be followed by Poag. Gabriel and Reese stood up with all the unusual commotion and watched the two of them attack the overflow of dishes, pots and pans.

"I'll wash, you dry," Poag said, catching Peggy's nod. "Seth and Clarisa can refrigerate the leftovers and feed the dogs."

With Poag's division of duties set for everyone, the other three proceeded with their assigned tasks and intentionally stayed away from the sink where he stood. With his back to the group, the man had no idea that the topping of kibble in the dogs' food bowls hid scraps of prime rib and apple pie.

A trio of silence began: Peggy eyed Seth, who eyed Clarisa, who eyed Peggy. And, although the three acknowledged the table-scrap meals, they went on with their respective tasks as if nothing untoward had occurred.

"Good job." A tired-looking Poag exclaimed when all the chores were finished. "Anyone want anything to drink?"

"It's nearly ten." Peggy was the first to reply. "I think I'd like to go to bed, if that's okay with you."

"It's been a long day," Clarisa agreed.

"Peggy needs a key," Seth reminded them. "I already have mine."

Seth and Peggy shrugged into their heavy outerwear, bracing themselves for the cold snowy weather before following Clarisa and Poag to the front office.

"Room five," Poag said, dropping the key into Seth's hand.

"He will take you there." Poag addressed Peggy directly. "Thank you for coming. It was a fun Christmas." A wide smile crossed his face.

"Watch where you're walking," Clarisa cautioned. "I guess we should have used the snow blower. Ben said it was starting to accumulate."

"She'll be safe," Seth assured her.

"Breakfast's at nine," Poag said. "Or later," he laughed.

Just as Seth was going to respond, Gabriel leaped out of the open doorway into the accumulating snow and, bounding toward the complex of rooms, stopped short at a nearby tree.

"That settles that." Seth took Peggy's arm and trailed his dog. "I guess we're supposed to follow him. He must think he knows his numbers. We always go to room three."

Suddenly, they heard the sound of the loud deadbolt slide across the office door and turned instinctively to face each other in stony silence, the realization slowly sinking in. For the first time in six months, they were together again...just the two of them...alone. They continued their walk in the snow, arm in arm, when Seth expressed the concern Peggy had alluded to earlier.

"If you were so afraid, why didn't you call me?" The icy edge of his full, rich voice indicated more than concern. He was upset with her – even more than upset, he was annoyed. No. He was angry that she would go for months, alone and afraid...and not tell him.

"What could I say? Come over. I'm frightened." She shook her head, as a way of saying that would not be possible. "What could you do?" she added. "Buy me a gun? Pepper spray? Let me borrow Gabriel? I can't keep running to you for help," she sighed, almost surrendering the argument. "You have a life of your own and I'm out of excuses."

Seth stopped abruptly in the snow and glared at her. What did she not understand?

"Excuses? You need excuses? I thought we were close friends," he said, disturbed that she would think that way when they had shared so many things together.

"We are close friends." Peggy agreed, but she could tell he was clearly irritated with her.

"Friends don't need excuses to call," he groused, entirely frustrated by her demeanor. Their whole relationship was becoming problematic. Was she stubborn or blind?

When Seth started to walk again, still holding her arm, he caught Peggy just as she began to stumble and slip on the snow filled sidewalk. Either her high-heeled shoes were to blame or her toes were numbed by the wet snow. In either case, the woman was in trouble.

Without thinking Seth grabbed her torso and placed her body over his shoulder.

"Does this seem like Déjà vu to you?" Seth laughed.

"I think I was a little tied up at the time," Peggy giggled. "So, what's with Big Red?"

"You picked up on that, huh? It's just some college humor of Clarisa's."

"So, where did you go to school?" Peggy was curious about the man who never talked about himself. Was he just shy or was he hiding something?

"Ithaca, but that was a long time ago." Seth patted her butt. "You haven't changed there since June. Hard as nails," he wanted to change the subject.

Holding on to her purse with one hand, Peggy used the other to give him a resounding slap. "You're no softie either," she replied, but her thoughts were elsewhere.

Her sister would know about Big Red. Megan named two colleges in Ithaca at the shop before Thanksgiving. As Peggy recalled, Amy's new boyfriend was affiliated with one of them. Between the two women, Peggy would get the answer very, very quickly.

From three feet away, Gabriel stood glaring at the ridiculous twosome, acting like giggling children playing in the snow. Seth had his hand on her butt and her hand was on his. They were playing Grab Ass, although Poag pronounced Gra Boss. He and Reese watched that game before and thought it was pretty dumb then. He remembered Poag and Clarisa running around the kitchen, grabbing each other's butt. Why didn't Poag just hop on and get it over with? Dogs had a much better ways of doing things. That's why they were considered man's best friend. Every master needed a helping hand. And, in return, man's best friend gets kibble. How fair was that? Maybe Seth should try eating it. But, he'd only spit it out. His master was a steak and potato man.

He didn't think Seth would go for something this spirited or that stupid, as the game they were continuing to play. Was this the start of something, or was he just losing it altogether? The woman wasn't too swift either. She was the same one, who cried a lot last summer and kept on talking last fall, while his body froze on the sidewalk near her gift shop. Were they in trouble or was this their idea of foreplay? How stupid, if that was the case. They needed his one line manual for lovemaking between dogs. The requirements couldn't be simpler: a female in heat and a sex hungry male. No further instructions needed.

Then, Gabriel wondered if the cold weather had caused their brain cells to freeze. Normal people would realize how cold it was and get inside the motel room. What could they be thinking? The woman looked like an ice sculpture already. Couldn't Seth see that? Gabriel grumbled inwardly. Knowing that leading them to her room was useless, he decided to follow the couple as they continued to weave their way along the new fallen snow.

When they finally reached room five, Seth set Peggy down and framed his body against the doorway, shielding her from the wind. The small overhead fixture offered very little light for the two huddled figures feeling the need for more conversation. He tucked a few stray hairs inside her knit cap, his eyes never leaving hers.

"What do you really want from me, Peggy?" His manner was both direct and insistent.

Seth's question begged for an answer, and he waited silently, his eyes still fixed on hers.

He had been patient long enough. His direct inference left no room for speculation. At last, she had to come to terms with their relationship. His question demanded an answer: one she was afraid to give.

"I don't know." Her voice took on the whisper of confused emotion.

Inwardly, she knew what she wanted, months earlier, but was afraid to disclose her true feelings…to herself and to him. She was afraid of making another tragic mistake with her heart. She was afraid of loving someone unconditionally again, and of being scarred by another betrayal in kind. And, yet, the time had come when she had to be honest with him and true to herself. Their months of separation no longer seemed to matter. He was here now…with her. They were together, just the two of them… like before.

Seth tilted her face upward with both hands and brushed her lips lightly.

"Don't you think it's time we stopped dancing around each other?" He did not wait for an answer. Instead, Seth closed in on her. His arms pressed the lower portion of her body to him, as he ran his tongue along the outline of her lips before completely enveloping her full mouth with his.

As if suddenly awakened from a long dormant sleep, Peggy's heart began racing wildly with his body pressing hers. She could feel his readiness. Her eager hot mouth responded by crushing her lips against his, while holding him in an arm lock from which there was no escape. She was filled with the want of this man and the heat surging through her body longed for an immediate release. No longer could she contain the growing blistering appetite that had to be satisfied. Only he could give her the relief she so desperately sought.

"I want you, Seth," she spoke softly. "Now," Peggy sighed, pleading with him. "Don't make me wait, please."

There was this urgent hunger, this whispered need of fulfillment, flowing from her that caused Seth to quickly pull her with him as he unlocked the motel door. But before his foot could kick the door closed, Gabriel pushed around them and settled in a corner of the room.

Through a slit in the drapes and dim illumination from the motel light, Gabriel watched the two of them scramble into a big bed, after a frenzy of clothing flew in every possible direction.

From his corner, he heard a series of loud gasps and moans coming from the undulating movement of covers.

Knowing that his master was not in serious trouble, Gabriel got bored and went to sleep.

His way was so much easier: no clothes to contend with, no intimate words to exchange, and no loud moans and groans.

In the canine world, sex was no big production. It served its purpose, much like any old tree.

***

A few doors down from room five, in the bedroom of the motel office, Clarisa refused to allow Poag to go to sleep without responding to her thoughts.

"So? Do you think they're together now?"

"We'll know soon enough," Poag turned away from her. He wanted to go to sleep.

"What's that supposed to mean?" Clarisa bristled at his tacit dismissal. She wanted a more cohesive reply.

"When we check room three tomorrow, we'll see if the bed's been slept in. Then, we'll know."

Poag's simple solution only aggravated her further.

"Ben should have been your brother instead of mine," she snapped.

Poag recognized his wife's persistence. She wanted his attention.

"It's not in my genes."

His vague reply really upset her now.

"Meaning what?"

"Meaning, Ben's got big eyes and you have big boobs," Poag lied. His reference to Ben's genes in detective work had escaped his wife completely.

"And you've got a big mouth," Clarisa snapped.

"Come over here." He pulled her to him. "Let me nestle in my favorite pillow."

"This isn't room five, you know," Clarisa reminded him.

"And this isn't a Jacuzzi faucet either."

"Oh, Poag," Clarisa whispered softly.

***

It was Christmas night and everyone at Poag's motel was fast asleep. However, the fifth person who had attended their dinner was not. Ben Burrows was called to the scene of an accident. Alice Beck had fallen down the stairs of her home. She was dead.

\#\#\#

The sequel: **Continued Pursuit** will be published later this year.

45296281R00142

Made in the USA
Charleston, SC
19 August 2015